IN DAYLIGHT

CAROLINE FLARITY

MIKA'S heels clicked through the theater as she walked to the podium at the tip of the stage. Bright lights warmed the top of her head. *You got this.* She'd practiced her presentation a dozen times but assumed the audience would be in front of her, not on all sides of a triangular thrust stage. *No big deal.* Aware of her quickening breath and a new dryness in her mouth, she adjusted the microphone.

"Good afternoon, everyone. Thanks for being here. As Zuri said, our new Impact Funds can be bought a la carte or purchased in portfolios tailored to your client's values." Mika cleared her throat. "Whether it's diverse boards, net zero emissions—" She coughed, feeling eyes on her from every direction. "Excuse me."

She could neither fathom nor explain the threat she felt from the audience, a group of harmless middle-aged money managers. *They're just people. They have no power over you.* Still, her muscles contracted, her body preparing to run or fight. Distracted by the menace she perceived, Mika's well-practiced talking points evaded her.

The hushed Wall Street crowd waited for her to speak. She coughed again, struggling to clear the tightness in her throat, her tongue a slab of cotton stuck to the roof of her mouth. She reached for the water bottle on the podium, desperate for moisture, but her trembling hands spilled the liquid down both sides of her chin,

1

drawing a concerned murmur from the audience. The plastic bottle slipped from Mika's grasp and hit the stage with a wet *splat*. A woman in the audience gasped.

Mika bent down to pick up the bottle. *Don't look at them. Do* not *look at them.* Straightening up, she focused her gaze above the audience on an exit sign at the back of the room. She imagined sucking on a lemon, which brought traces of saliva into her mouth.

It's not too late. You can salvage this. She managed to say a few words. Then a few more. *You're doing it.* Then her gaze flickered down to the audience. The crowd of money managers seemed to surge forward, looming over her like malevolent giants. Pressing forward from every direction, they merged into a grotesque, fleshy mass intent on suffocating her. The floor shifted under Mika's feet, a tectonic plate on a new and wicked world where crushing gravity prevented her from running off the stage. The exit sign at the back of the room receded, becoming a tiny glow at the end of a black tunnel.

I can't get air. I'm dying. Her heart thundered, the room tilted, and Mika was vaguely aware of dropping to her knees before her boss, Zuri, dragged her off the stage.

By the time the hotel's in-house medic cleared Mika to leave the greenroom, Zuri had slipped away to do damage control. Mika took the Marriot's glass elevator up to her room alone. She called Zuri's cell several times but kept getting sent to voicemail.

The public humiliation was embarrassing, for sure,

but the heaviest weight on Mika's shoulders was how badly she'd failed her boss. Zuri had taken a chance hiring Mika, who lacked an Ivy League degree and a roster of well-heeled connections, and now Mika had repaid her by turning the debut of Zuri's hard-won passion project into a sideshow. Mika sent her a long, apologetic text, saying she would do whatever it took to fix things. *You deserve an explanation. I wish I had one.* She spent the next several hours in a cold sweat, clutching her phone and waiting for a response. Zuri did not reply, then or ever.

1

—

Mika Crane's father was covered in blood. It stained his hands, smeared his bare chest and linen pants, and darkened the navy t-shirt he held to his face. A sickening copper tang infused the air.

"Stop hollering!" he said. "They'll hear you."

She'd been calling for him in the woods behind the Crane family compound when he stepped out from behind a thick pine tree.

"What happened? Let me see." She reached for the balled-up t-shirt in his hand.

He turned, evading her grasp. "What are you shaking for? Everything's fine."

"Show me!"

Grumbling, he removed the t-shirt from the left side of his face, revealing an inch-long slash following his jawline. Mika spotted a globule of pale fat glistening from the red depths of the coagulating wound, and her gag reflex twitched. She looked him over, asking if he had any more injuries.

He shook his head and pressed the t-shirt back to his face. "Nah. Got blood on my hands and ended up smearing it everywhere. Figured I'd wait till the bleeding stopped before heading back to the house for breakfast. I don't want your mother to see me like this."

He's confused. "Mom's at the store now. You've been gone a while."

He squinted at Mika then flicked his wrist, dismissing her words as nonsense.

"What happened to your face? Did you fall?"

"Fall? No, *I* did it."

"You did that to *yourself?*" Mika balked. "Why?"

His gaze darted around the trees. "I felt it scurrying around under my skin, and I came out here to cut it out in private, but the damn thing moved when I got close."

"What *thing*, Dad?"

"The chip," he said, his brown eyes shining and indignant in his wrinkled face. "The damn chip—the one the government uses to track me. Had to get rid of it before I go and get your sister. Can't have them following me to her."

Her father's loathing of the government had merit, given the harassment he once suffered. But to cut his own face? The paranoia plaguing his twilight years was getting worse. They'd have to watch him more closely from now on.

"You can see Paige back at the house." She took hold of his free arm, but he didn't budge.

"I'm not talking about Paige. I'm talking about your other sister. I found her. I found Naomi. Hired a private detective. A good one this time. Real smart. He knows all the latest tech. The facial recognition stuff. They got cameras everywhere now, and he can access them and search through the footage. He tracked Naomi down in New York City. She's on staff at a residential building." He held a filthy finger to his lips. "But let's keep this Naomi business between me and you for now. We don't want to upset your mother."

Excitement buzzed inside her. Could it be true? Naomi, after all this time? Her missing sister who left nineteen years ago and never spoke to the family again. She would be thirty-six now, four years older than Mika.

"Thought I'd pop the chip out, but the damn thing moved when I got close." He leaned toward her, whispering. "You know the feds won't let up until I'm dead. Maybe not even then. You gotta make sure I'm cremated so they don't snatch my body for their experiments."

Mika nodded like she was taking him seriously. She texted Paige. *Found dad in woods. Disoriented with facial injury. Heading to the house.* Paige and her husband Bill were driving to Lake Absegami to see if one of Art Crane's buddies from the firehouse had picked him up to go pickerel fishing. Her mom had called them all in a panic that morning, saying Art took the garbage out while she cooked breakfast and never came back.

Mika led Art past a section of rotting and topless trees—snags, they were called—killed by blight or lightning. The snags marked their exit from dense woods into sun-dappled pinelands. It felt surreal to walk her bloody father through this peaceful section of forest. A cushion of sand absorbed their footsteps, the sweet trill of birdsong the only sound, and starbursts of blue-green pine needles turned the harsh sun silken and tender.

A few minutes later, they cleared the tree line and emerged onto the acre of land behind Mika's cottage. Art shouted back toward the woods. "I'm eighty-four and want to see my girl again before I die! You dirty sons of bitches, I know you're listening!" Fresh blood oozed from his exposed wound.

Federal agents had shown up unannounced at the Piney Mart a couple of years after Naomi took off. The agents refused to divulge what illegal activities Naomi had engaged in, then grew hostile when the Cranes insisted they hadn't heard from Naomi since the day she left. For the next several years, Mika's parents endured aggressive inspections from health department reps, as well as state and federal audits. Yet despite it all, the Cranes agreed a silver lining prevailed: if Naomi was out there causing trouble, then she was still alive.

Mika took her father's arm. "Please try and calm down. You're bleeding again."

He pressed the t-shirt to his face and ran his free, blood-stained hand through his sparse silver hair. "We can't just lie down and let the feds ruin us. Don't you want to be free?"

She murmured what she hoped were comforting words, worried by what he might do next, then maneuvered her dad around the side of her cottage and onto the expansive gravel driveway connecting the cottage, main house, and the Piney Mart parking lot.

Paige and Bill pulled up and spilled out of their haphazardly parked minivan. Paige rushed to their father's side, her delicate, symmetrical features pinched with concern. Paige gasped at Art's wound and demanded he hand over the penknife he always kept in the pocket of his linen pants—his so-called "church pants," though he hadn't been to church in years. Seeing the knife, Mika winced. *I should've looked for that.*

With Art situated in the back of the minivan with Bill, whose round face glowed from too much sun, Mika pulled her sister aside and told her about their dad's "tracking chip" paranoia.

Paige snorted. "I've heard all about the imaginary chip. Who do you think spent time with Dad while you were off living the high life?"

Mika let the dig slide. "We need to be prepared. If the hospital staff believes he's a danger to himself or others, they'll have to follow protocols—"

"He was picking his teeth with the penknife and his hand slipped. That's what I'll tell them. He's not going to do it again. You heard him, he's convinced it's a lost cause, that the thing moves when he gets near it."

Mika frowned, hesitant. "You don't think he'd hurt someone do you?"

"Don't be silly. Of course not. He's an eighty-four-year-old insomniac. Things can go sideways from time to time. We'll take care of it within the family."

"Let's talk about this more at the hospital." Mika moved toward Paige's minivan.

"Mika, you should relieve Mom at the store, update her on what's going on."

Mika nodded her agreement, then knocked on the minivan window to say goodbye. Her dad shooed her away through the glass, as if embarrassed by the fuss.

As she crossed the gravel toward the Piney Mart, her father's words echoed through Mika's mind. *I've found Naomi.*

Nineteen years ago on a cool June morning, Mika had awakened to the sound of her seventeen-year-old sister Naomi packing up her dinged-up Honda on the gravel driveway. Mika had plodded outside in her pajamas, and Naomi told her she was going away, refusing to say when she'd return. She warned Mika never to trust anyone. *People are evil. You might think you're safe with someone, but the evil is inside them, waiting to be born. You better learn to protect yourself.* Mika had begged her not to go, grabbing the sleeve of Naomi's hoodie, but her sister wrenched free and drove away, leaving her stunned in a cloud of gravel dust.

Mika shuddered, not only from the memory of Naomi's last words, but at the thought of New York City, where Art claimed Naomi now lived. Mika's last visit there was six months ago when she experienced a severe panic attack while attempting to deliver a presentation. She wondered, and not for the first time, if Naomi was to blame for the inexplicable terror she felt on that stage, if her sister's cruel goodbye had somehow planted that terror inside her.

Although they'd carried on with life, none of the Cranes had ever recovered from Naomi's disappearing act. A sense of righteousness spread through Mika's body. *How could she leave us like that?* She doubted her dad had located her missing sister, given his declining faculties, but if he *had*, she might get the chance to ask Naomi herself.

2

—

Late night customers usually sought to feed a vice or craving. Mika sold pints of ice cream and bags of potato chips while the organic blueberries on the *Local Goodies* shelf collected dust. But a midnight visitor broke the monotony of a typical night shift at the Piney Mart.

A middle-aged trucker, his long, graying hair parted and tucked behind his ears, entered the store and glared at Mika with disappointment. He asked for Paige, and when Mika told him in a dry voice that she was home with her husband, he bought a coffee and left in a sulk. Customers occasionally developed crushes on Paige. All unrequited, of course. Poor Bill had the barrel chest and poor posture of a much-injured high school jock now riddled with early arthritis, but he had Paige's full attention.

At three a.m., two young women came into the store wearing t-shirts and flip flops, discussing in breathless bursts which energy drink gave their Adderall buzz the best bump. Their shrill vibe grated on Mika, but she remained amiable. After getting stitches, her dad had spent the last two nights in the hospital under observation due to his elevated heart rate. She was looking forward to visiting him there after her shift.

As the first fiery glimpse of the sun stirred the birds outside, Mika flitted around the store, taking inventory and singing along with songs she played on her phone. Her positive energy persisted, even after Paige arrived half an hour late to relieve her.

Thanks to a mild sedation, her father had avoided infection and secured some rare sleep. Mika wasn't overly concerned with his heart rate; he'd been in and out of arrhythmia for years, and there was no reason to think he wouldn't bounce back again. And no one at the hospital had questioned Paige's story about his teeth-picking injury. But that didn't explain the airy feeling in her chest, a space for a sweeter breath, at the end of a long shift.

It's Naomi, Mika realized, steering her Volvo down quiet, local roads. She wanted to hear more about Naomi, even if the whole story turned out to be a fantasy. She sat in the hospital parking lot, strumming her fingers on the dashboard and listening to Fiona Apple until visiting hours began. But the moment she walked through the sliding glass doors into Ocean County Medical, any enthusiasm she had fell off a cliff. Thoughts of her dad bleeding and ranting in the woods suddenly dominated her mind. As much as she wanted to see him, anxiety about his state of mind welled within her.

A tall steel elevator took Mika to the third floor where the geriatric ward loomed down a hallway reeking of disinfectant. Thank-you cards and photographs of smiling octogenarians with their gap-toothed grandchildren were pinned to bulletin boards on the walls. Art's room sat directly across from a nurse's station where two seated nurses nodded at her in recognition.

"He quieted down a few minutes ago," the older one said, grim despite her neon pink lip gloss.

"Thanks. I know he's a handful."

Mika knocked before opening the door to Art's windowless room. The weak fluorescent ceiling light cast the room in a murky tint, in sharp contrast to the bright hallway. The number 142 glowed on the heart monitor next to the room's single bed—a bed that was empty. How could the monitor register a heartbeat with no one else in the room? The change in light was oddly disorienting, and she pulled the door shut and leaned back against it.

Was her dad in the bathroom? She pressed the soles of her feet into the floor to root herself, and she felt blood rush from her brain like it did sometimes if she stood up too fast. *I should have gone home and tried to sleep for an hour instead of waiting in the parking lot.* The room blurred, and her legs went rubbery. *I'm fainting!* She slid down the door, but instead of hitting the tiled floor, she felt the stiff embrace of a chair.

Mika took in a new and jolting perspective of the room. Her father slept in the bed, ensconced under a blanket that looked like a giant paper towel, and she sat on the chair beside him, thirsty and perplexed. An IV inserted into the back of his left hand was attached to a bag of fluid hanging from a stainless-steel infusion stand next to the bed. Another wire, protruding from the short sleeve of his hospital gown, connected to the heart monitor against the wall.

Mika didn't remember sitting down, but had at least avoided falling. *What did I eat today?* Nothing but a small bag of Twizzlers from the store. *Dumb.* Eating only candy on little sleep could wreak havoc on brain function. No wonder she almost faceplanted. It must have been a trick of the light, seeing the bed as empty, or a brain glitch. Sometimes her sleep-starved brain put on a show, presenting her with things not actually there: bugs zipping in and out of sight, large spiders scuttling up walls, shadowy movement in her peripheral vision. *No biggie.*

Her father's eyes flew open. "Mika, good to see you." He lifted his unencumbered arm in greeting.

Art smiled, and the stitches in his jaw, black and wiry, stretched away from each other. The metallic smell of blood filled Mika's nasal passages, a sense memory of their last encounter. *Suck it up, buttercup. You found him, didn't you?*

"How are you feeling, Dad?"

"Getting pumped full of elixirs. Be shipshape lickety-split." His grin suggested one of those elixirs was a narcotic.

Mika went to the low sink in the corner of the room and turned the faucet on, drinking four paper cups of water before her thirst softened. She filled two cups for her father and placed them on the plastic tray attached to his bed.

Art looked frail in his patterned hospital gown. "My ticker's not right, though. It bangs around like it's trying to get loose then sputters like a clogged engine. Damn thing's tired."

"Your doctor said you're back in arrhythmia."

"Feels different this time."

"You might need another ablation if they can't get you out of it. But you're otherwise okay." She squeezed his hand. *Besides the nasty scar you're going to have.*

He took a sip of water, and the movement pulled on his stitches. "The pain meds," he said, grimacing. "I can't reach the godforsaken button."

A plastic push-button sat on the bed, attached to the IV piercing the top of his hand. She pushed it twice and watched medication drip into his bloodstream.

Soon after, his face softened. "You're an angel, you know that? My little surprise."

He was fifty-two when Mika was born, his wife forty-eight. They did not think a pregnancy could happen at their age, especially after their difficulty having Naomi. Mika's mom only discovered her pregnancy when Mika began kicking; she'd assumed the halt of her menses signaled her entry into menopause.

Art's expression turned serene, dopey with meds and nostalgia. "You and Naomi were two peas in a pod, you remember? Oh lord, what a pair. And you looked so much alike."

Mika chuckled. "Yeah, eyes too big for our face."

"Your eyes are just right. Stop that." His grin sagged at the edges. "I should have tried to understand that girl instead of coming down on her so hard after the accident." Art glanced at Mika, looking ashamed, as if the words had slipped out unexpectedly and he longed to take them back. He quickly changed the subject. "Remember when I made her sit at the table all night when you two were little?"

As infants, both Mika and Naomi couldn't tolerate animal products, and their mom learned to combine grains and vegetables to make complete proteins. One night when Naomi was nine and Mika five, Art decided the time had come for them to eat like the rest of the family.

New rules. In this house, we eat what's put in front of us, her father announced when they sat down to dinner. *No one leaves this table until they clear their plate.*

Mika had chewed dutifully and even swallowed, but her body rejected the meatloaf. Her puking was not palatable mealtime behavior, so Art caved and sent Mika to her room. But Naomi refused to put a single bite of meatloaf into her mouth, and she remained stubbornly seated at the table until their dad left to work the day shift at dawn. Mika and Naomi never outgrew their aversion to meat and were eventually diagnosed with a rare allergy.

She touched Art's thin arm. "Okay, that night wasn't your finest moment, but it's not what you're feeling remorseful about, is it? We *can* talk about what happened, you know. I have my big girl pants on." She winked at him, working to control her own jumble of emotions.

The Crane family believed Naomi left home because she felt guilty about an accident in the community pool the day before her departure. Naomi and their father got into an ugly fight when she returned home with Mika, both of them waterlogged and shaken. Art, distraught over nearly losing Mika, had yelled at Naomi, demanding answers she couldn't or wouldn't give.

"You were shook up, Dad. We all were. But for Naomi to react like she did, to leave and never return, never even call? Nothing any of us did justified that."

Art blew out a shaky exhale. "I wish I didn't fly off the handle when she clammed up and wouldn't explain how she lost control like that, given the swimmer she was. And then she went and locked herself in her room for the night. I didn't understand how traumatized she was. Laying into her only made it worse."

Mika nodded her understanding. "If I didn't swim over to her when I saw her struggling, if I alerted the lifeguard instead, the situation wouldn't have escalated. If there were a few more clouds in the sky, maybe we wouldn't have gone swimming in the first place. If only we were closer to the pool's edge, or closer to the shallow end, I wouldn't have swallowed so much water. I've gone over that day countless times, and there are infinite ways things might have been different. But they weren't, Dad, and no amount of self-torture can change that."

Art met her gaze, hopeful. "Will you go talk to her for me? Get her to come home? This estrangement has gone on too long. It needs to end."

She saw no trace of doubt or confusion on his face. "It's true then? You found her?"

His grin returned at half-mast. "Sure as shit I did."

Energy poured into her body, a nervous zapping in her core. Confronting Naomi would be like traipsing into a minefield. *What if she treats me like a stranger or a stalker?*

"You could tell her I'm in the hospital," he said. "Lay it on a little thick."

"What if Bill went to the city instead of me?" Mika asked. "I think if you told Paige it was important to let him go—"

"Hell, I could go. I'm old as dirt, but I still feel young inside."

"Bill is a neutral party with no history with Naomi. She might feel blindsided by one of us."

"You got a point there." He gestured for her to come closer and she leaned toward him, somewhat apprehensive about what he might do. "Do you think I'd let the government overtax me all these years without putting something away? I got cash hidden in the shed by your grandfather's old charcoal pit, tucked inside a toolbox. Been saving it for you and your sisters. No way I'd trust a damn bank. The papers from the private investigator are in there, too. Whoever goes and gets Naomi, I'll cover the trip and any expenses."

He yawned. "I feel like I could sleep for hours. Now isn't that something?" Then his mind seemed to drift. "After I'm gone, you could go to one of those islands you got pictures of on your computer. You always wanted to travel and see the world. Don't let your dreams pass you by, now."

His voice trailed off. Mika watched him doze, happy to see him sleep—and also a tad envious.

Mika steered off the main roads and into the pines. Something nagged at her, but it took her a few minutes to put her finger on it. The narrow back road looked naked, overexposed, the trees on either side casting no shadows. That only happened when the sun sat directly overhead.

Mika fumbled for her phone in the console and looked at the time. 12:38 p.m. *Impossible*. She replayed the events of that morning in her mind. Paige had arrived late to her shift, keeping Mika waiting until almost six thirty. She then drove to the hospital and waited in the parking lot until visiting hours opened at eight thirty, then sat with Art for less than an hour. *It can't be noon.* Her chest tightened, a birdlike flutter beneath her sternum. *I had a blackout at the hospital.*

She pulled to the side of the road, too unsettled to drive, and the wheels of her Volvo dug into sugar sand. Her last daytime blackout occurred three years ago when she'd pulled into a parking space outside of Macy's, determined to return a pair of heel-shredding shoes. Mika had closed her eyes for what felt like several seconds then stepped out of her car to find herself outside her old apartment two hours later. That blackout occurred after a string of high-stress days following a nor'easter that knocked out the power at her parent's house.

Stress brings them on. Her father fileting himself, the possibility of confronting Naomi—these were stressful events. Frustrated, Mika gave her steering wheel a good thump with the base of her palm.

The Cranes occasionally experienced blackouts, the worst side effect of genetic insomnia. These thankfully rare episodes resulted in an unpredictable, complete loss of agency while going about waking life. A hyper-extreme version of arriving at a destination with no memory of the long drive there, leaving the driver unsettled because they'd maneuvered heavy machinery on auto-pilot, possibly endangering others or themselves.

Don't catastrophize. Maybe it wasn't a blackout. Maybe she was simply asleep in the chair by Art's bedside the whole time. Her body, always low on sleep, had simply crashed and rebooted itself like an overheated laptop. But how did she get in the chair? *Why don't I remember?* She couldn't blame it all on Twizzlers for breakfast.

Mika thought about her father manic in the woods. *I came out here to cut it out... The damn chip—the one the government uses to track me.* As if operating on their own accord, her fingers poked tentatively around her jawline, a part of her almost *hoping* to feel something other than smooth skin and bone. It was suddenly so tempting to believe her blackout might not be a product of an intractable genetic sleep disorder, that some nefarious external force lay behind it instead—that Art's rants about the government might be true.

She thought about the head rush she experienced in his hospital room, how his bed appeared empty. A clammy sweat oozed from her pores, and the trees on either side of the narrow road hovered menacingly outside the car. She ordered herself to chill, but her thoughts went right on tumbling like sugar-stoned kids in gymnastics class. What if her father *wasn't* in the hospitable bed? What if someone moved him? Paranoia foamed inside her like a sloppy pour of beer. What if someone pumped gas into his hospital room, causing her to pass out?

She peered through her Volvo's window at the woods crowding the road, half-expecting to see feds hiding behind trees. The prickly feeling of being watched gave the sun a sinister glare. Her clothes rubbed harshly against her skin, and she recoiled when a pickup truck drove by. She met her eyes in the rearview mirror, her reflection both frightening and familiar. Pupils small, shoulders tight and hunched—she looked like her father in the woods. A caged animal. Mika massaged her shaking hands and slowed her breath. She should go home, take two sleeping pills, and burrow under the covers. *But then I'll feel woozy working my shift.*

The beach, then. She'd treat herself to Island Beach State Park, try to slow her roll.

———

After paying fifteen bucks to avoid the crowded public beaches, Mika stood in a near-empty parking lot before rising mounds of sand dunes blanketed in seagrass. An ungated path over one of the shifting hills led her to a water world shining in the sun. Warm wind buffeted her with the briny essence of shellfish and seaweed, the intermingling of life and salted decay. She kicked off her sandals and plopped down at the bottom of the dune. The sky was so clear and blue, looking at it she could see the squiggles of white blood cells traveling through the capillaries of her retina.

Seagulls squawked overhead, and the waves lapping the shoreline sparkled like champagne. She dug her toes and fingers into the hot pale sand, watching sandpipers run toward the muddy wake left by receding waves. The birds fed on minuscule creatures, then scampered back up the beach ahead of the returning surf, their twig legs blurring.

The ocean calmed Mika, as it always had. She'd stopped swimming after the accident in the pool, a form of self-punishment after Naomi left. It wasn't safe to swim alone, she'd told herself. After all, she had a sleep disorder and poor coordination.

Screw it. She left her clothes on the sand and moved toward the water in her underwear and bra. The sea rushed to meet her, gushing up her shins and between her legs, thrilling her with its chill, its dirty-clean, life-death scent. She dove under a small wave, gasping after breaking the surface and feeling more awake and like herself than she had in years. She allowed the next wave to propel her toward shore, her legs floating in front of her as the foamy surf deposited her on the wet sand.

Best not to overdo it.

Back at the base of the dune, Mika dressed quickly then reclined on the sand. She watched the sea, awed by its planet-carving power. It glittered today, but she knew the waves could turn harsh in an instant. A riptide could pull a swimmer out to sea, and God help them if they tried to fight it. The water could darken under a sudden squall, kicking up waves that exposed their murky underbellies before slamming a swimmer to the sea floor and keeping them there, spinning in the blackness, only to hit them even harder when they broke the surface desperate for air.

Once, she'd been young and fearless and had charged into the sea, turning her back on rising swells to await the perfect moment to push off on her foam bodyboard. The waves had placed her like a crown above their heads and whisked her to shore. She'd also been "tumbled and humbled" on many occasions, but the only time she felt real fear in the water was the day she drowned in the community pool. Even drowning, though, had felt less terrifying than standing on stage at the Marriot Marquis.

Was it fair to blame Naomi for Mika's bizarre breakdown? *There's no point in second-guessing yourself.* Isn't that what she told her dad at the hospital? She could wear herself out asking questions she didn't have answers for. Why had a panic attack unraveled her life? Why hadn't Naomi called home in all these years?

Naomi was the reason the Cranes were stuck in the pines, the reason none of them ever traveled too far. They were waiting for Naomi to call, to come home.

Mika stood on the warm sand. The breeze hit her face again, firm and balmy. She felt change coming in the wind, had felt the cold shock of it on her skin when she hit the water. She saw it on her father's face as he confessed his regret. Whether that change would be good or bad, she did not know. She figured change was like the sea, not your friend, not your enemy—just inevitable. And for the Cranes, change was long overdue.

3

—

Paige entered the main house through the kitchen door, careful not to jostle the cast-iron skillets hanging above the black steel stove.

"Where's Bill?" Mika asked, drizzling olive oil into a dish of bean salad on the kitchen counter. They'd planned a family dinner to welcome Art home from the hospital, but he felt too weak to come down the stairs. Without her dad backing her up, it was up to Mika alone to convince Bill to go to New York.

"Closing up. He'll be here in a minute. A customer's talking his ear off." Paige's eyes narrowed. "Swear to God, every year their tattoos get larger and their bikini tops shrink." She opened the fridge and took out a flavored seltzer and a bowl of chicken salad.

Tessie Crane, their mother, stood next to Mika, softening mashed sweet potatoes with an electric whisk. At eighty, Tessie still possessed much of the conventional beauty she'd passed down—Mika would say exclusively—to Paige. Wearing curlers and ironed mom jeans, one would never guess she'd once brained a guy with a bat. But the slope of her shoulders spoke of the burdens she bore, as did the purplish puffiness under her eyes. Although she'd married into the Crane lineage, Tessie had acquired her own insomnia over the years, as if by osmosis.

"Your father was fine till he went to his buddy Larry's to play cards. That wiped him out." Tessie's voice dropped to a whisper. "Larry's wife has dementia, you know. She tries to kiss the mailperson on the *lips*." She smiled. "Sit down, the two of you. It's nice to have some girl time."

When the three women settled at the table, Paige said, "Do you buy Dad's story about Naomi?"

"There's only one way to find out for sure," Tessie said, beaming. "I could zip into the city and poke around."

Paige made a face. "You hate the city."

Tessie lifted her chin. "I haven't been there in ages, that's true, but if it means seeing Naomi again…oh, good lord." She breathed into her hands, eyes shining.

Paige snorted. "And who do you think will cover your dayshifts if you make this half-baked odyssey to the city? I need my time off, you know."

Tessie made tentative eye contact with her blustery daughter. "Bill?"

Paige gasped. "My husband should spend *more* of his free time covering our shifts? He has another full-time job, Mom."

"We could close the store," Tessie said.

Paige shook her head. "It's a nice idea, but do you think your social security is paying the second mortgage? And assuming Naomi is even in the city, which is doubtful, she wants nothing to do with us. Never has."

She's not wrong, Mika thought. Naomi had not reached out in the last nineteen years: not a birthday card, not a phone call. She'd never popped up on any of the social media accounts Mika created in high school, desperate to hear from her. Did they have a right to invade her life when she clearly didn't want them to? Mika grew steely in her chair. Did *Naomi* have the right to cut them off without a word of explanation?

"Paige has a point, I'm not sure it's wise to just show up on Naomi's doorstep," Mika said. "It's not fair to put Naomi, or any of us, in that position. But *if* Dad found her, I think we do have the right to reach out in a non-aggressive way. Perhaps if someone went to see if she's actually in New York, someone *adjacent* to the family, but not—"

Their mom clapped her hands together. "What if she does want to come home and thinks *we* wouldn't be open to it? What if she's still in legal trouble? We're still her family, you know. If I did go, we could always hire someone to cover my day shift."

Paige sighed. "The idea of you gallivanting around the city." She wore a grim, pitying smile. "I mean, you haven't really tested yourself, have you, Mom, since your run-in with Chapman?"

Their mother's neck blotched red. "For God's sake, that was years ago."

"I'd worry about you on your own in such a stressful environment," Paige said quietly. "I don't think it's a good idea, given your history."

Tessie turned to Mika. "I forgot to mention I heard the mailperson made a complaint about Larry's wife trying to kiss them. It's a whole big thing in the township now."

Paige would not be ignored. "Seriously, Mom, what if you ran into trouble and had a bad reaction? Ask Mika. She knows all about losing her wits in the Big Apple."

"I can handle myself just fine!" Tessie Crane hit the table with both hands, her plate clanking against her water glass.

"Paige, you are upsetting Mom," Mika said. "Stop it."

Paige patted her mother's hand. "Let's put a pin in this Naomi discussion until Dad's feeling better. We have enough to worry about with his health."

Tessie slumped in her chair, radiating defeat, and turned to Mika. "At the hospital, Art mentioned he wanted you to go to the city."

Mika shook her head. She couldn't put herself through that, showing up on Naomi's doorstep and begging her to come home, only to be rejected. Again. And in New York of all places. She thought of the Pine Barrens, how it had wrapped them all in a thorny embrace with its tick-filled, pitch-pine prison walls. She did want to get away, but not that way, not by chasing down Naomi.

"Someone Naomi has no relationship with should go to New York, see if Dad's story is a fairytale or not," Mika said to Paige. "Mom and Dad's needs should be paramount here. Dad's going to be eighty-five in June. He won't be around forever. If he wants closure with Naomi, we should do whatever we can to get it for him."

"That's right," Tessie said. "And your father hasn't been himself lately. The poor thing."

"Don't be morbid, Mika," Paige said. "And how are you suddenly an expert on what this family needs? Where were *you* when Dad almost got put away for shooting at trees from the roof?"

"Jesus, Paige. I was ten years old."

"But you still went to college, didn't you? You know, I was *this close* to going back to get my degree when Naomi took off. And Mom's incarceration"—she patted their mom's hand again—"might never have happened if Naomi stayed around. Mom wouldn't have been capable of that kind of viciousness if her daughter hadn't abandoned her."

Tessie nodded at the floor.

The Let's Blame Naomi game was obviously familiar to Mika, but watching Paige play it this hard vexed her. Paige never went back to school, Mika suspected, because her sister couldn't bear to let her first husband Miguel out of her sight for any length of time.

Paige pointed her fork at Mika like a weapon. "Who was there when you cried your eyes out every night after Naomi left? Me, Mom, and Dad, that's who. Family looks after each other. That's how it should be, at least, but Naomi tossed us away like trash. The stress of it weakened Dad's heart, I'm sure. And then to be hassled by the FBI? Who knows what kind of criminal Naomi is now, out there shaming our family name."

Mika simmered. *The family name.* As if they were the Rockefellers. She reminded herself that Paige had been deeply hurt by Naomi's absence. Paige used to bake Naomi a birthday cake every year, even after Naomi hit adolescence and wiped her face whenever Paige kissed her cheek. Paige had refused to come out of her room to say goodbye the morning Naomi left, and the fire of her initial, frantic grief had slowly retreated into cold stone.

"We should leave Naomi in the past," Paige said. "It's better to let certain things lie. Don't you agree, Mom? Mika is right about one thing. Naomi's your kid. *Your* voice counts the most."

A light appeared in Tessie's eyes, as if she remembered how to make her shame go away. "It's true," she said. "I love my Naomi, but she was a troubled girl. Could be she's the same kind of woman. The kind who would drag us all down with her."

Don't say it, Mika silently implored.

"Like she did to you in that pool, Mika," their mother whispered.

A wave of sadness crashed over Mika. Few were spared from Tessie's maligning when she felt compelled to distract herself from her violent encounter with Ed Chapman—but to use the tragedy of what happened in the pool? To use Naomi, whose body had betrayed her with its convulsive need for air when Mika swam over to try to help her?

The kitchen door opened, startling the women. Bill entered with his chest out and a smile on his face.

"What's got you in such a good mood?" Paige asked, her eyes slits. "Or should I say, *who?*"

Tessie got Bill a plate of food and brought another upstairs for Art, leaving Mika alone with Paige and Bill. Undeterred, Mika waited for a lull in conversation then struck, addressing Bill. "Dad and I wanted to talk to you tonight. About Naomi."

"Actually, Bill and I wanted to chat with *you* about Callum," Paige said, clearly irked by more talk of Naomi. "He came by the car rental office yesterday to talk to Bill. Isn't that right, hon?"

Bill nodded, eating his mashed potatoes.

Paige pointed her fork again. "He said you'd been ghosting him. Tell me that isn't true. That kind of behavior is so juvenile. He's one of the good ones, you know. You should keep that in mind before you send him packing like the rest."

Mika hadn't seen Callum in the last three days, partly because she'd been preoccupied with her dad's condition, and mostly because she was avoiding him.

Mika kept her focus on Bill. "Did you hear my dad hired a private investigator to find Naomi?"

Bill chuckled, tucking his napkin into the collar of his shirt, bib-style. "Pop also thinks the FBI tapped the land-line."

Mika sat taller in her chair. "My Dad and I were hoping you could confirm whether Naomi's in the city."

Paige snapped her tongue. "Has anyone even seen this supposed picture of Naomi?"

"What do you say, Bill?" Mika asked.

Paige guffawed. "He's never even met Naomi!"

"Exactly," Mika said. "Bill could go as a neutral party representing our family, and if he locates her, we can take it from there. We'll send her a letter, or maybe call, rather than blindside her in person. Now, can Bill please answer me, Paige? Is he allowed to answer?"

Bill wiped his mouth with a napkin. "I guess I could check out Pop's story, then maybe take a trip to Long Island while I'm up there. I have a couple of old work buddies who live along the Sound I can say hello to."

Paige's death glare oscillated between Bill and Mika, as if she were trying to decide who to eviscerate first. Bill took in another mouthful of potatoes, adopting an air of innocence.

"Long Island?" Paige said. "Oh, excuse me, Mr. Gatsby. What friends along the Sound? You never told me about any *friends along the Sound.*"

Paige's possessiveness over her exceedingly average husband had always struck Mika as odd. But if Paige and Bill were making it work, who was she to judge? As Paige loved to point out, Mika was almost thirty-three and had been in exactly one relationship longer than six months—the one with Callum—but even that statistic was suspect, since Mika had been itching to break up with him for a while.

Bill swallowed. "Jesus, Paige. Yes, I have."

"Bill, if you don't want to go, just say so," Mika said. "No need to send Paige into a tizzy."

He cocked an eyebrow at Mika. "This Naomi character, she's the one who put you off meat?"

"I'm allergic," Mika said. "Naomi is too. From a tick bite. The alpha-gal allergy. You know that."

Bill mumbled something about the odds of both Mika and Naomi being bitten by the same tick.

Paige stabbed a glob of chicken salad and gnashed it between her teeth. She turned to Mika. "I'm sorry hanging out with us and working at the store isn't what you wanted out of life. Sorry we're not good enough for you. This is called life. You work, you have a family. At your age, you should be thanking your lucky stars you have a decent man in your life and planning your next steps instead of pushing him away. Maybe if you had a Chloe of your own, you'd stop obsessing over Naomi."

Chloe, Paige's daughter with her first husband, had escaped the Pine Barrens at seventeen for a West Coast college and made two perfunctory visits a year.

"At my age?" Mika said. "Mom was almost fifty when she had me."

"That was a fluke, Mika. Do you think that happens on the regular? Do I really have to tell you this? It's so exasperating."

Mika bristled. "No matter what she's done, Naomi is a part of this family, and if she's one state over, working and doing well, then we deserve to know. We deserve some answers." Bill clearly had no intention of seeking out Naomi as a Crane family ambassador, so Mika let the ire in her throat come up for air. "Stop trying to control everyone, Paige. It is possible to find another way to manage your emotions."

"Are you diagnosing me? Are you a doctor now?" Paige rolled her eyes dramatically.

"Naomi was a kid when she left," Mika said. "She's thirty-six now. Don't you think it's time you grew up and forgave her?"

"Ha! Did you hear that, babe? I should grow up. *Me.*"

Bill nodded. "Not too smart, getting all snarky when you want a favor."

Mika stood and picked up her plate, more than ready to retreat to her cottage. "There's plenty of things to be proud of besides having a man, Paige. Plenty of things more meaningful in life."

"Oh yeah, like what? What have you done that's so meaningful?"

I've survived, Mika thought. But what had she survived? A tornado of understanding swirled just out of reach, Naomi at the center of it. A decision came from somewhere deep inside her, as deep as the iron-rich, underground lake fueling the tea-colored streams outside.

"I'll go to the city, and if Naomi's there, I'll bring her home."

Old wood creaked. Art stood beneath the arched entranceway to the kitchen, his hand gripping the molding for balance. "That's my girl."

His dentured smile trembled, then fell, and he crumpled to the floor.

4

―

The Piney Mart glowed like a lighthouse in a sea of trees. Jersey folk tended to cram themselves close to the cities of New York and Philadelphia, but here they lived inside a million acres of protected woodlands upon the sands of an ancient seafloor. There had been Cranes in the Pine Barrens for generations. As Mika's mother would say, they were Pineys "from their heads to their hineys." The store stayed open 24 hours and was one of the few back-road convenience stores customers could always rely on to be open. A fitting livelihood for a family riddled with genetic insomnia.

Intending to mop the floor, Mika wheeled out a bucket from the storage room and tried not to picture her dad's heart shaking like jello on a dish. The upper chambers of his heart weren't beating as much as *quivering*, his doctor had told Paige and Mika after they re-admitted Art to the hospital seven hours ago. Art's doctor, jovial and relaxed during his previous hospitalization, now used the word *concerning* to describe his arterial fibrilization. Dr. Reinfeldt wanted to try a cardioversion in the morning: an electric shock to Art's heart that would hopefully reboot it back to a normal rhythm.

The door emitted an electronic bleat when two young men entered the Piney Mart. The taller one, a tough guy with a baby-hair mustache, swaggered up to the register counter. Mika went behind the register, and he slapped a wrinkled twenty on the counter and asked for a pack of Marlboros.

Mika asked for I.D. He didn't look twenty-one.

His eyes bulged. "You serious?"

She shrugged politely. "Write your congressperson. I don't make the rules."

The shorter, stocky one by the door sent a display stand of canoe and hiking brochures crashing to the floor with a well-placed elbow jab. "Oh no? Was that against the rules?" His smirk expanded the two scabs on his upper lip.

Mika gestured to a security camera on the wall behind her. "Get out and don't come back. You two are banned for the mess you made." She stuck her foot underneath the register cabinet. Her sandaled toes made comforting contact with a wooden bat.

She waited until the sound of their car engine faded into the silence of the Barrens before returning to the mop bucket. She imagined the clickbait headlines if the teens had been killers instead of garden-variety delinquents: YOU WON'T BELIEVE WHAT HAPPENED TO THIS WOMAN WORKING ALONE AT NIGHT. Yet, even with tonight's unpleasantness, Mika preferred night shifts. They were mostly quiet, and nothing that unnerving had occurred at the Piney Mart, besides the occasional shoplifting tweaker, since Ed Chapman tried to rob the place two years ago and left in a stretcher.

Mika slapped the wet mop back into the bucket and crouched on the linoleum floor, her right knee producing an audible *pop*. Rearranging some misplaced candy on a shelf, she nudged a bag of Skittles to the floor when her clumsy fingers failed to follow orders. Thanks to her insomnia, sections of her brain dozed when she was awake. Parts of her were always missing.

A car whipped into a parking space in front of the store's large front window with its brights on. Sure that the teens had returned with ill intent, she dashed behind the register to wrestle the bat from its hiding place, then hesitated after glancing at the security camera. After what happened to her mom, she knew better than to look aggressive. The glaring lights winked out, and she recognized the cop car and the tall man emerging from it.

Her shoulders dropped, but along with relief came a flash of irritation. *Why didn't he tell me he was coming?*

The door bleated as Callum entered the store in uniform. "Thought I'd pop by and kiss you good day." Night shift humor. Behind him, the pre-dawn sky had yet to lighten. Callum frowned at the toppled brochure stand and rubbed his stubbly cheeks, making a sound like sandpaper on wood. "What happened here?"

"Dumb kids. They won't come in again." She downplayed the incident so he wouldn't insist she make a police report. Doing so might attract attention from the local press, and the Cranes had made enough headlines.

Callum pinched his nose with his thumb and index finger. "What is that stench?"

"I just mopped the floor."

"Jesus, you didn't dilute the cleaning solution first?"

Before Mika could answer, Paige walked in, two hours early for her shift. Her face pinched. "It reeks of ammonia!"

Mika relished the sharp, clean smell. It cleared her sinuses like eucalyptus oil in the shower, or a dab of wasabi on a vegetable roll. "Why are you here?" she asked her sister.

Paige—apparently still annoyed with Mika, but not enough to have any qualms about butting into her love life—ignored her and addressed Callum. "Saw your patrol car, and I was up anyway. I figured, why not allow you two some together time? Go ahead. Get out of here, the both of you." She pretended not to see the frosty look Mika gave her.

Mika's cottage sat behind the main house, unseen from the road and with its back to the barrens. The main house, where Mika's sister and brother-in-law lived with her parents, stood a hundred yards behind the Piney Mart. Both homes were at least a century old, their pitched slate roofs and pale stucco exteriors designed with post-Victorian simplicity, the addition of skylights the only modern flair.

Mika and Callum made the short walk to the cottage, both droopy with fatigue and shrouded in the miasma of their failing relationship, the crunch of gravel beneath them the only sound. *Yep, this is awkward*, Mika thought.

Paige and her first husband had lived in the cottage when they were newlyweds, then outgrew it after having their daughter Chloe. After that, the cottage served as an extension of the Piney Mart's storage room until Mika moved in after losing her job at Solstice Funds, breaking the lease on her apartment and no doubt plummeting her credit score.

Once inside, Callum plopped face-down on Mika's bed, his arms and legs splayed out like a starfish, and conked out in five minutes. Mika took a sleeping pill and tried not to resent him, which became difficult when he started snoring: a series of cascading growls that diminished to near silence before roaring back to life. She fidgeted on her small sliver of bed, confined and resentful, waiting for the pill to kick in.

Don't you want to be free? Art had asked her that in the woods. She didn't answer him then, but yes, she did want to be free. Free to find her missing pieces and shake them awake before she ended up like Paige and their parents, stuck in the pines forever.

"I'm scared," she said out loud. *But that's okay. I'll just keep moving.* She swung her legs over the side of the bed.

Mika headed for the tree line behind her cottage under a cobalt sky. Her canvas slip-ons stayed dry, despite earlier rain. In the barrens, rainwater passed through loose, sandy soil to an underground reservoir spanning hundreds of miles. This water, filtered and refined, turned orange from the iron-rich earth and emerged again in streams and lakes.

In the woods, Mika turned left on the trail she found her wounded father on and skirted the perimeter of a defunct cranberry bog, now a marsh full of croaking frogs. A rustling in the surrounding trees unnerved her, and she stopped to turn her phone light on. The light illuminated a four-foot radius directly in front of her but caused the spaces between the trees to blacken.

A dark blur fell from a nearby pine, and she tapped her phone light off and squinted into the near-darkness, straining to discern its form. A growing number of small black shapes swooped out of the trees and into the air above the dried bog. A needle-like stab pierced her forearm, followed by the buzzing of a mosquito hovering in front of her nose. The buzzing ceased when something quick and dark flitted past Mika, creating a whoosh of air that tingled the tip of her nose.

Ladies and gentleman, the theme of the day is Bats.

They dropped from their perches, emerging from inside dead pines and behind the loose bark of decaying cedars. They fell, catching the wind with their membrane wings and soaring over the bog before circling back in a rising cyclone of furry bodies. The bats didn't scare her. Her heart actually swelled as the colony ballooned into the sky above the tallest pines, pulling apart then rejoining each other in a rhythmic flow.

The swarm moved like a single organism across the early dawn sky. A shape-shifter swimming through the air, unfurling a tail here, a wing there, it absorbed a few strays before propelling toward a destination unknown. Mika watched the bats with awe, envious at their ties to one another, to the earth and its seasons. Had she ever been so at ease in the world, so sure of purpose? Maybe a long time ago. *I was Naomi's little sister, and that was good enough.*

She left the bog behind and continued on an overgrown, sandy trail. She reached her late grandfather's shed and cracked open the spindly wooden door, surprised it didn't break off its rusted hinges, then used her phone light to illuminate a plywood shelf cluttered with bits of charcoal, crushed oyster shells, and the metal toolbox she was looking for.

Her heart began to pound. Mika stepped toward the shelf, and the rotted floor groaned under her weight. A musty staleness entered her airways, and she sneezed several times before unlatching the toolbox and illuminating its contents.

Inside lay a gallon-sized, clear Ziploc bag filled with cash. Her father really had been hoarding money. She felt somewhat appalled thinking of the second mortgage on the main house that hung over her parents' heads like a cartoon anvil. Her focus shifted to a worn vanilla folder wedged alongside the money bag. She picked it up and inspected it with her phone light. Art had written Naomi's full name on the folder in his still-neat handwriting.

Adrenaline set Mika aflame.

Just keep breathing. She opened the folder and found a letter and several photographs. In the first photo, a woman with a striking resemblance to her long-lost sister travelled up a subway escalator. The next photo was a shot of the same woman entering a residential building in a navy jumper and tan work boots. The pictures were grainy, leaving Mika uncertain the woman captured was Naomi.

But the last photograph appeared sharper than the other two. Mika could see the lines etched across the woman's forehead and around her mouth, her face perhaps a little broader than the Naomi Mika remembered. The woman wore her hair short and swept off her forehead, while Naomi had worn hers long and hanging in her face, creating a barrier between her and the rest of the world.

The woman's eyes, however, large and hooded, resembled Naomi's to an uncanny degree, even if they sat a smidge deeper in her head. She stood outside in this picture, washing down a sidewalk with a hose and directing her sideways grin at a shorter man, probably in his fifties, who had a shock of well-coiffed white hair. Cars lined both sides of the street and blurred bodies occupied the sidewalk.

New York.

It was the sideways grin that stopped Mika's heart. What were the chances a look-alike also had Naomi's slanted smile? Mika couldn't be sure the woman was Naomi, but a dangerous hope sped her investigation.

She moved her gaze to the single piece of paper. Below the letterhead of Samuel Greenwald Investigative Services, Inc. was a double-spaced list of stats.

> *Subject (unconfirmed): Naomi Crane - high-probability facial match*
> *Work address: Property of Gateway Realty Holdings, LLC*
> *510 62th Street, NY, NY 10045*
> *Lobby Ph: (212) 555-7229*

Naomi was possibly only two hours away, with a job and friends. Despite the hurt her sister had caused, Mika wouldn't wish her suffering, so why did it sting to see her looking happy? She blinked back the wetness in her eyes.

Naomi may have altered her in terrible ways the day she left, filling Mika's mind with dread, perhaps costing her the ability to connect with people. But Mika had always felt connected to her missing sister. She'd envision this connection as a thick, sinewy cord between them. When especially sad or angry over Naomi's absence, she'd try and chop the cord apart with an ax in her mind, but no matter how much she swung, the cord only frayed.

Before leaving the shed with the toolbox in hand, Mika looked to the sky, hoping to see the bats again, the only mammals that could truly fly. But they were gone, riding southward on their naked wings.

Returning home, Mika lay on the edge of her bed and listened to the birds wake up before finally dozing off. She woke an hour later with the morning sun blazing beneath the curtains above her bed, directly into her eyes. She pulled the sheet over her face and groaned. This woke Callum, who immediately rolled toward Mika and spooned her, allowing her even less space on the bed. He cupped one of her breasts and began kneading it in a way that reminded her of a breast exam.

She removed his hand and dropped it on the mattress. "Can you move, please? I'm falling off the bed."

He raised his upper body enough to slump his head against the headboard and rubbed his eyes. "Wish you didn't wake me."

She escaped to the bathroom. When she returned, Callum was scrolling through his phone. The curtains were wide open, illuminating the thin layer of dust on the floorboards. The view from her bedroom window revealed a plot of shrub-filled, sandy soil stretching toward a wall of trees. A lone deer grazed at the tree line. The animal lifted its gaze as if sensing hers, and the feeling of being exposed to something malevolent spread over Mika like hives. The deer bounded away, but the wall of pitch pines glared back at her. Sweat warmed the back of her neck.

"You have the weirdest look on your face," Callum said.

"I was thinking about hiring someone to cover my shifts when I'm gone." She still had a little left in her 401K, the last remnants of her old life, to pay her way. She didn't need the cash in the shed, but she would leave some for Paige to cover odds and ends while she was away.

"That's right, you're off to New York! This is the first time you've been back, right, since the Marriot?"

Is he smirking? A retort came to mind, but she squashed it with the back of her tongue.

The first time she met Callum, he'd snapped handcuffs around her mom's wrists the night Chapman tried to rob the Piney Mart. That night, and in the months that followed, Callum had expressed only sympathy for Mika's mom, even urging the prosecutor (a friend of his from high school) to offer Tessie a plea for aggravated assault instead of the attempted murder charge Chapman's family lobbied for.

Given his public support of her mother, Mika's initial crush on him came easy. And when they first started seeing each other, she had brimmed with gratitude and post-trauma lust. She fell quickly into a relationship with him even though he took selfies at the gym and his phone chirped with "spam" messages from various dating sites. Looking at him now, it was beyond clear those new-relationship endorphins had long dissipated.

He fluffed his pillow, making a show of not being able to get comfortable. "How old is this thing?" He moved on from the pillow and fingered a sheet corner with disdain. "You know, these sheets and the ratty towels in the bathroom. Those old t-shirts you sleep in. They're not expensive items. They can be *freshened up* every so often."

Mika swallowed. "We should talk, Callum."

He chuckled and sat up. "Here we go with the *we need to talk* schtick. You want to end things, is that it?"

"This isn't about you. It's me. My issues." She cringed inwardly at the slight screech in her voice and her spontaneous use of the ultimate break-up clichés. "The truth is, I'm half-dead most of the time, and trying to manage your needs on top of that is just too much. I sleep so little as it is, and when you're over here, I have to be hypervigilant about not waking you. You need to be alert on the job, and I get that, but it feels like I'm trapped in bed with you. I hate that it feels like a burden, but it does. You wake up irritated, and then you want to be intimate or vent about work—which is normal. Totally normal! But it's too hard, as exhausted as I am, to prioritize your needs, and then I feel like I'm failing you. You're unhappy, too. I know you are."

"There are plenty of women who want all they can get from me. Trust me."

"Have at it."

"Been doing so. Not to worry." There was no mistaking his smirk this time.

His words stung her face like a slap. Blood rushed to her cheeks. "You know, you're right about that pillow. I've lived with it for too long. Thank you for enlightening me. I won't make the same mistake with you."

He stood from the bed and reached for his clothes. "I guess I felt sorry for you. But you know, I think you're right. Someone with your issues should probably be alone. I'll stop by the store when you're back in town and get the bat. I never should've trusted you with it in the first place."

Callum had snuck the bat her mother used on Chapman out of his station house after Mika mentioned it might help her feel safer at work. Her family had no clue she kept it hidden under the register cabinet.

"Oh, I'm the untrustworthy one?" Her attempt at a scornful laugh yielded a wet sound that hurt her throat.

A satisfied gleam appeared in Callum's eyes. "Good luck, Mika." He took his gun belt from her bureau top and let the front door slam on his way out. She heard him whistling on his way to his cruiser in the Piney Mart parking lot.

After stewing for several minutes, she took everything he ever gave her—a velvet baseball hat, a *Thelma & Louise* t-shirt, an unused South Pacific travel guidebook—and his boxers, razor, protein powder, and Dunkin' Donuts k-cups to the dumpster on the side of the Piney Mart.

Back inside, she deleted every photo of the two of them from her laptop and phone. Callum's admission of cheating, though searing, had at least freed her from guilt over ending things. Then she remembered what lay ahead of her in a few short hours, and lethargy oozed back into her bones.

She still had to pack and count the cash in the toolbox. *I could pop a pill, maybe sleep for an hour.* But what if she slept through her alarm and missed the bus to the city?

Mika lay on her mattress and rubbed her sore eyes, fighting off a growing suspicion that the voyage ahead of her was too much to face all alone. *But I'm not alone. I'm never alone, remember?*

The day Naomi accidentally drowned Mika was a terrible day, with an even worse aftermath. But it also contained moments of unmistakable bliss. No one would believe what Mika had experienced, she knew, so she'd kept it to herself. She never told anyone that she'd separated from her body in that pool and existed briefly as a discarnate soul staring down at her lifeless form. A celestial presence, somehow familiar, had spoken gently to her. Mika had trusted it completely and felt a profound sense of peace.

Seeking comfort, Mika now retreated to that day in her mind—the day she saw her drowned body at the bottom of a pool yet continued to exist, consciousness intact. She remembered the joy of connecting with a majestic, familiar presence who greeted her with love and not judgment. A muted version of the same presence had carried her through the loss of Naomi, her mother's incarceration, and other less-significant but still trying times. But on the day Mika died, it spoke to her for the first and last time, and she heard the voice of God.

You are not alone
I am always with you

45

Mika's body relaxed, and she fell into a series of fitful dozes, never quite dreaming of anything until her alarm went off ninety minutes later.

5

—

Mika marveled at the stack of bills atop her freshly made bed. $38,580. *Not a bad haul.* She tucked two thousand dollars into an envelope for Paige—a bribe of sorts—and placed the paper containing Naomi's address in the outside pocket of her American Tourister roller bag, a bag she once hoped would accompany her when she travelled the world. The rest of the money was going back to the shed, for now.

In a late-morning haze, she headed to the Piney Mart to face Paige. The larger journey ahead evoked less trepidation than saying goodbye to her sister. The gravel sucked at Mika's sandals, and a buzzing horsefly took a bite out of her shoulder. It didn't feel like the start of a great adventure.

Entering the storage room, she saw Bill, not Paige, cleaning coffee pots in the sink.

"She's been holed up in our room since finding out you're leaving today," he said. "I had to take off work to cover the rest of her shift." He raised his hands, exasperated. "No clue who's covering your shift tonight.

Won't be me, that's for sure. And I would stay clear of your sister if I were you."

"Did you see the leak around the base of the toilet?" Mika asked. Bill grumbled that she should have called a plumber on his way into the cramped storage-room bathroom.

"What leak?" he called out. "It's dry as a witch's hoo-ha in here."

Charming. "Run the water for a full minute. You'll see it." Of course, there was no leak.

Mika hurried out front and crouched behind the cash register, retrieving the softball bat from its hiding place and slipping out the Piney Mart's front door. She didn't want anyone to discover the bat while she was gone. Back at her cottage, she stashed the bat under the living room couch, then brought the envelope of cash over to the main house.

Mika stood on the threadbare Persian rug on the second floor of her parent's house, breathing in the familiar smells of old drapery and savory kitchen aromas wafting up from the first floor. She had the unsettling sense this might be the last time she smelled them. *Don't be a drama queen. Everything's fine.*

Paige wouldn't open her bedroom door. "Get out of this house!" she yelled after Mika knocked.

"Listen, I'm leaving you some money, a couple grand in case there's an emergency."

"If you're going, then *get out!*"

"Try to keep it together, okay? Especially now with Dad back in the hospital."

There were loud footfalls from inside the bedroom. "I know exactly what you'll do if you find her," Paige hissed through the door. "You'll disappear just like she did. Dump it all on me. Mom, Dad, the goddamn store. Mika Crane, if you get on that bus, you're dead to me. Do you understand?"

"Where would I disappear to? I'm coming back with or without Naomi. Look, I don't want to hurt you." Mika bent down and slid the envelope under her sister's door, feeling the chill from Paige's air-conditioner on the tips of her fingers. "Take this cash. Close the store early, if you want, until I get back. I'll see you—"

Something hard hit Paige's door from the inside. From her bedroom down the hall, Tessie Crane gasped in surprise. Mika slunk down the stairs and out of the house, feeling guilty over her sister's unhappiness yet eager to increase the distance between them.

An hour later, Mika sat next to a texting, perfumed woman on a stuffy NJ Transit bus. She never drove her car into the city and saw no reason to do so today while exhausted. The bus held a spattering of zombie-like commuters in corporate wear, perspiring in a morning heat that conquered their deodorant.

Mika took a sleeping pill before locking up her cottage, and when the bus pulled onto the Turnpike, the engine's purr lulled her into a brief slumber. She dreamed about standing naked on stage at the Marriot Marquis, and woke herself up making a weak, wailing sound: a sleep scream transformed into something ridiculous.

The texter no longer sat next to Mika, though the scent of her flowery perfume remained in the fabric of her empty seat. The texter had moved to a seat across the aisle and regarded Mika cautiously, perhaps wondering if she would be a problem.

Outside, the landscape had morphed from thick walls of conifers and oaks to a dozen lanes of asphalt rolling past factories and refineries spewing smoke and gases. The bus lurched off the turnpike and stuttered in traffic around a declining curve leading to the yawning orifice of the Lincoln Tunnel.

Mika couldn't shake a sense of impending doom. It felt like a mountain of rock was falling through the sky and about to flatten the bus like roadkill. She concentrated on slowing her breath and massaged each palm with the thumb of her opposite hand, telling herself there was nothing to be afraid of. What was the worst that could happen? *Naomi wanting nothing to do with me. Having a blackout on the street and waking up in a bathtub with a kidney missing.*

The bus inched ever-slower toward the tunnel drilled through silt and stone. *See, look. You're about to cut through a mountain of rock, not the other way around.* She took a deep breath.

If she did find her sister, Naomi might be offended by the intrusion. But, if nothing else, Mika *would* demand answers from her. She'd find out how Naomi justified turning her back on their family. Their parents deserved those answers. *And so do I.* Mika was an unfinished puzzle, and if Naomi was the largest missing piece, did it matter if she didn't easily snap into place? If she curled at the edges and refused to connect? Mika could still achieve some closure for herself and the rest of the Cranes.

She thought about Callum and how their bond had proved weak once the butterflies wore off, the same as in all her past relationships. She went through life like an old sock, full of holes and wedged between drawers, disconnected and trapped. If she could just pull this off, this trip could be the first step to finding a relationship that worked, maybe even to regaining her career. All she had to do was confront the city she'd crumbled in and the specter of her missing sister.

The air pressure changed as Mika left New Jersey and entered the rounded walls of the tunnel. An almost reverential silence filled the bus. She reached into her purse, her fingers seeking comfort from the smooth plastic of her pill bottle. Searching but not finding. She'd forgotten to pack her insomnia meds.

6

—

Mika emerged from the bowels of Port Authority into a packed subway station, where a group of robed Hare Krishnas played drums that hung around their necks. Reverberating off the tiled walls, the lively beat turned foreboding, and she climbed the steps to 40th Street feeling like an offering to a god she'd mistakenly offended. Crowds blurred past her on a sidewalk cluttered with smoky food carts, and no one looked twice at her. She forgot this pleasure of the city: anonymity. *As long as you're not on a stage.*

Thirty minutes later, she sat in the back of an Uber weaving through five lanes of bridge traffic on Second Avenue. Her phone pinged: a text from Callum. *I never cheated on you. I said that to hurt you. Hurt people hurt people.* She deleted it, preoccupied with her imminent arrival at Naomi's purported workplace.

"You have big eyes," her driver Ari said, surveying her in the rear-view mirror. He had a smooth voice, a shiny, black man-bun, and the sharp-nosed profile of a roman statue. She could smell him, the pleasant musk of a salty peach.

She found his bluntness refreshing. "All the better to see you with."

Am I flirting? It had been a while. Some part of her was strolling out, hips swinging, now that she'd called it off with Callum.

Ari swerved to avoid a bespectacled woman on an electric scooter. "Oh, I get it," he said. "Good one. Where you from? Not here, right?"

His smile felt like an air-conditioned room, and it was nice to focus on something besides Naomi. "How can you tell? My luggage?"

"Yeah, and the white shoes."

He probably flirted with ten women a day and maybe just as many men. She tried to do the math in her head. *Probably works a ten-hour shift and picks up at least two people an hour, unless he's doing an airport run.* He wore a slew of friendship bracelets in natural tones that could've been made by a child. No wedding ring though.

He caught her looking. "My niece made these for me. This is my cousin's car. I drive it for him sometimes, but I have my own business, a party bus. You got a bachelorette party, birthday party, something like that? Text me at 1-800-NYC-RIDE."

"How did you get that number?"

"You can get any number you want online. Almost there. It's coming up on the left." He pointed up the block to a pale brick, six-story building on the corner of 62nd Street, right next to the sprawling base of a bridge depositing six lanes of traffic onto the avenue.

Even from a hundred feet away, Mika recognized her sister immediately, and every nerve in her body began to vibrate. Naomi stood under an awning on the building's front stoop, talking to a UPS driver. Mika wanted to flee in the opposite direction. *This is happening too fast. It's too easy.* There was no second-guessing it, though. The shape of Naomi's head, her long torso, the charisma she exuded even from a distance—it was unmistakably her.

Mika pulled her black baseball cap over her eyes, her breaths quick and shallow, her chest full of rocks. She'd planned to scope out the address and get a feel for the neighborhood, then later, from the safety of her hotel room, call the number the private investigator provided. If she did get Naomi on the phone, they could discuss if she felt comfortable meeting in person. But now, Mika feared if she didn't take this chance to confront her, she might lack the cajones to do it later.

"Don't pull up right in front."

"Where do you wanna go? Other side of the street?"

She met Ari's gaze and nodded, no longer trusting her voice. He veered the car into the far-right lane, cutting off a Con Edison van.

When Mika didn't move, Ari said, "I can't block the bus lane." Horns caterwauled behind them. "You getting out?"

She stepped out of the car and into the path of a Fresh Direct truck. The driver screeched to a stop, yelling out his window that Mika was an asshole. By the time she made it to the curb, the streetlight turned red, prompting a renewal of bitter honking from the cars she'd blocked.

Mika spotted Naomi and the UPS driver watching the commotion from across the street. She pulled her hat even lower and hustled down the sidewalk away from them. More honking came from her right, which she ignored until the gentle taps grew more insistent.

"Lady! Lady! Your bag!" Ari rolled to a stop ahead of her. The trunk of his car popped open, revealing the roller bag she'd forgotten. "Remember me, okay, if you need a party bus?"

She thanked him, retrieved her bag, and pulled it behind her on the uneven sidewalk, praying Naomi had not recognized her. *She couldn't have*, Mika assured herself. *I was a kid the last time she saw me.*

Finding a restroom became her new priority. She passed a liquor store, a cabinet maker, and a store for fireplace accessories. She passed two smoke shops, a laundromat, a doggy daycare, and a florist before being shooed out of a nail salon. Finally, a gracious China Fun server let Mika use their facilities.

In the bathroom, Mika finger-brushed her hair and changed into a sleeveless blouse. She washed her hands and cupped water into her mouth, tasting notes of chlorine and rust.

"It's not about you," she said to the mirror, recalling the sickening *thud* of her father's body when he collapsed outside the kitchen. *Do it for Dad.* She dabbed her forehead with a wet paper towel. Naomi stood a few blocks away, delivered to her by fate or perhaps a higher power. Hadn't she prayed for exactly that? Surely now, as an adult, she could handle a face-to-face, however pained, with her missing sister. Why should she be a sweaty mess when it was Naomi who had ghosted her entire family? Mika may be invading her privacy, but how horrible was that, really, in the face of Naomi's cruelty?

She crossed the street and dragged her bag and indignation to the stoop of Naomi's building. Naomi no longer stood outside, but a young doorman with protruding ears emerged from the glass doors wearing a uniform much too roomy in the shoulders.

"Need help with that?"

"No thanks, I got it." She climbed the steps. "I'm here to see Naomi."

"The super? She's in the basement checking the compactor. You want to wait?" He ushered Mika into the air-conditioned faux-marble lobby and invited her to sit on a loveseat against the wall. "You two are related, right? I can tell."

She sat for several minutes, ready to crawl out of her skin with anticipation. Finally, the elevator rose from the basement with a pleasant *ding,* and her insides vibrated like a plucked guitar string.

"That's probably her," the doorman said. Mika stood, and her stomach floated up inside her, unencumbered by gravity, as if every mile she'd traveled to get there had been a click of a roller coaster climbing a cliff of metal railing, and the freefall had just begun.

The elevator door opened and Naomi walked out, a ring of keys jangling from the beltloop of her navy work pants. She moved with less grace than Mika expected. She was thicker now, her hair swept off her forehead, opening up her face. Mika met her sister's gaze for the first time in nineteen years, and the lobby seemed to recede and blur while Naomi's achingly familiar features stayed in crystalline focus.

"Meeks." Naomi's voice had deepened with age.

"No one calls me that anymore." Mika was falling through space, and it was too late to test her seatbelt.

Naomi smiled without showing any teeth, one side of her mouth higher than the other. A scar marred a corner of her lower lip, age-faded but new to Mika. Naomi stood with a hip cocked, tapping her foot like she used to while on the phone with a love interest or playing chess with their dad.

"What should I call you?" Naomi asked.

"My name. Do you remember it?"

Naomi didn't respond, and they grew still, taking each other in, their connection a raw and tangible thing that smelled of pine and quarry water and tasted like the salt of too many bitter tears. Mika glanced at the doorman; his seated form pointed out to the street, but one of his ears was tilted back toward them.

"It was you," Naomi said. "In traffic. I thought so. But I thought I'd spotted you so many times over the years. In grocery stores, the subway, but each time it was someone else."

"I was right where you left us. I'm surprised you could even recognize me. You haven't seen me in—"

"I have. On social media."

She did look for us. A heat prickled the back of Mika's eyes, which she quashed with a couple of hard blinks. "I didn't come here to confront you." Not exactly true, but there was another, more important reason. "It's Dad. He's in the hospital and wants to see you. It would mean a lot to him."

Naomi's smile faltered. "I'm happy you came, Mika. But I can't go back home. I'm sorry."

The finality in her voice surprised Mika. "No one blames you for the accident, Naomi."

"I'll never forgive myself for that, but it's not why I left."

Blood rushed to Mika's cheeks. Why would she leave if not for the accident? "Am I supposed to stand here and guess?"

Naomi stopped her foot tapping and gestured to Mika's roller bag. "You just got here. Can I get you a drink? Are you hungry?"

So that was it? *She's not coming home, but did I want a snack?* "What about Mom? Do you have any idea what she's been through?"

"I saw the video on the news."

"And you didn't think to check on her after seeing it? She went to jail!"

Naomi's eyes darted briefly to the doorman. "I thought it was best not to. I knew she'd want to see me, and I couldn't do that for her."

"You mean you could, but you chose not to."

Her sideways smile returned but didn't reach her eyes. "I don't expect you to understand. It's complicated."

"Try me."

"Leaving was the right thing to do."

Her confidence infuriated Mika. "The right thing to do, to never speak to us again? Are you serious?" Mika's rising voice bounced around the lobby walls.

The doorman swiveled around in his chair and openly gaped at them, as did an elderly couple checking their lobby mailbox.

"Forget it." Mika fumbled for the handle on her roller bag. "This was a mistake."

"Wait," Naomi said. "Slow down. You're here now, and I don't want you to go." She eyed her bag again. "Need a place to crash?"

"I booked a room in Long Island City."

"Screw that. I have extra space," Naomi said. "Perk of the job."

Naomi wanted to take Mika for a meal, but those plans changed when several residents congregated in the lobby, upset over a temporary halt of the building's hot water supply.

While Naomi sorted the mess, Mika treated herself to a glass of wine and a long lunch at a chic restaurant on the opposite corner. *Cheers to me.* She'd survived the initial encounter with her sister. Even though Naomi had flat out refused to visit their family, their confrontation in the lobby had released some of Mika's anxiety and, embarrassingly, left her almost giddy. *Naomi asked me to stay.*

She dawdled at her quaint table for one, enjoying her pinot noir and the luxurious look of the pale yellow tablecloth. Wall-to-wall French windows revealed the people in Naomi's neighborhood going about their lives. She watched them keenly, eager to absorb her sister's world, then sent a text to Paige and her mom. *I saw Naomi. It's really her.*

Tessie sent back a string of crying-face and heart emojis and asked Mika to call as soon as she could. Mika didn't mention Naomi's cryptic refusal to return home. She planned to change her sister's mind. Paige never texted back.

When Mika returned to Naomi's building, the hot-water situation had yet to be resolved. Naomi slipped away to show Mika her sixth-floor apartment, a two-bedroom decorated with expensive-looking but mismatched furniture, discarded by her residents. Naomi presented her with two keys on a Gateway Realty lanyard.

Mika settled into the compact guestroom hoping to nap. That turned out to be a pipe dream. She was too keyed up to do anything but unpack then scroll mindlessly on her phone. Mika heard Naomi come home after 11 p.m., and she snapped off the gold-leafed floor lamp next to her bed, feigning sleep. She wanted to talk to Naomi when her sister was fresh and open-minded, not burned out after a long day at work. Minutes later, she saw the thin bar of light under Naomi's door wink out. Her sister's ability to fall asleep so quickly shocked Mika. After all, Naomi was a Crane and bore the family curse.

Lying on the twin bed beneath a dramatically tall and tufted headboard, Mika began to mourn the loss of her insomnia meds. For most of her life, beds were a place of looming failure, wolves in fitted sheets. And a strange bed was a particularly savage beast. Sleeping somewhere new was always a long shot, even with pills.

For several hours, she played word games on her phone, trying to exhaust her brain. The melody of muted horns and sirens outside didn't help. Naomi told her earlier that many tenants in the building wore earplugs to bed because of the bridge traffic.

At four in the morning, Mika's fingers felt especially thick and clumsy on the small screen of her phone. Still far from sleep, she put on a pair of flip flops and took the elevator to the lobby with the hopes a brisk walk might relax her. Outside, the city grumbled and shook at a weaker volume, but the heat sizzled unabated. Along with the hot, oily air, came an unexpected homesickness. She wondered how her dad was doing, and if his thoughts were preoccupied with Naomi and their possible reunion. *I'll make it happen.* An air-conditioner dripped on her head as she passed a darkened restaurant, refreshing despite the obvious ick factor.

Realizing she wouldn't get far in the heat and therefore had little chance of tiring herself through exercise, Mika decided to pull an all-nighter. *That means caffeine.* Coffee served as the first, second, and third winds moving her through the doldrums of her fatigued existence. It allowed her to function, if not as a whole person—her sleeping parts were always missing—then at least a reasonable facsimile of one.

She paused on the sidewalk and looked around for an open business, flinching when something flew past her and landed on the gating of a hardware store to her right. The ancient insect dropped to the sidewalk and scuttled on its six legs between two trash bags under a broken streetlight. Her shoulders rose, quivering with disgust. Bats were one thing—they could be cute, depending on the circumstances—but she drew the line at cockroach appreciation.

"Flying roaches." A petite woman with a buzzcut and giant hoop earrings stood ahead of her, walking her Spaniel and vaping. "Happens when it gets hot like this. The heat gets their wings going; the creepy little shits love it." Her robust voice defied her small stature. "Tonight on the news, this so-called expert, some kid, acted like it was breaking news. Every year, they discover things we already know, like Brooklyn and how good the tap water is."

Mika shook her head in commiseration. "Newbies. What are you gonna do?" She spied an open bodega across the street on the next block and headed for it, wary of flying cockroaches.

Once inside, she immediately smelled hummus going bad on a refrigerated shelf and coffee too stale for human consumption—and that was saying something, because she'd choked down some gnarly coffee in her time. She considered buying instant coffee and making a cup back at Naomi's—she didn't have a coffeemaker, the *blasphemy*—but a tall white can with spidery red lettering and a cartoon rocket ship caught Mika's eye. It was one of those energy drinks with a dumb name. *Master Blaster* promised to propel her into orbit for only $3.99 a pop. She could try something new. Why not?

The euphoria kicked in a few minutes after gulping half the can. It chased off her lethargy and held her hand. *Everything's gonna be alright.* She'd figure it out. Mika decided to loop around the block and take the long way back to Naomi's building. She passed a stretch of tenements with black-iron fire escapes that doubled as low-rent balconies. She hadn't noticed a single person on a balcony since she'd gotten there. Even the spacious balconies on the ritzy buildings were barren. *Isn't that bizarre?* Her heart started to pound. *Isn't that hysterical?*

The city kept up its incessant chatter, and she kept watch for airborne attacks. Garbage trucks rumbled by and the subway screeched through street grates. Mika reveled in the newness of her gritty surroundings, but her vague homesickness persisted. Back in the barrens, when the crickets and frogs grew still, the silence was so complete nothing could ever sneak up on her. Except, she remembered, for a herd of white-tailed deer.

Mika slowed her pace, wondering why a long-ago encounter in the woods had suddenly come to mind: the day she and Naomi shared an unusual close encounter with a herd of deer. Maybe because it occurred the same week Naomi made her exit from their lives? Or maybe it was the flying cockroaches. *They're not supposed to be here either, like the deer.* Still, it was strange something creepy had triggered her recollection of a brush with graceful wildlife. She blamed her misfiring neurons, or perhaps the mysteries of memory.

7

—

Mika emerged from her room later that morning after hearing Naomi moving around her kitchenette, an extension of the living room outfitted with high-end appliances with clashing finishes. Naomi beamed at her while gulping down the last of her orange juice. Her cell phone rang and she silenced it. "Sorry, I know my phone's been blowing up all morning. I still can't believe you're here."

Mika returned her sister's warmth. "Feels like a dream, doesn't it? But unfortunately, I can't stay much longer with Dad in the hospital and Paige and Mom covering my shifts."

Naomi's expression turned grim before rebounding. "What did you want to do today? Check out the Chelsea galleries or a museum? It's on me."

"I'm leaving tomorrow morning, so I'd hoped we could talk."

Her sister apologized and rattled something off about the boiler and her porter taking a sick day. "I won't have a moment to sit down with you until this evening. Can you meet me at the diner on sixty-first and Lex at 6 p.m.?"

Dejected, Mika reluctantly agreed. Naomi handed her fifty bucks, gave her a quick kiss on the forehead, and left. Mika felt like a dumb kid instead of the confident woman who hours ago felt ready to bend her sister to her will.

Back on the busy street outside, her spirits rebounded after another half can of Master Blaster, so she decided to enjoy the day by going on an app-guided architecture tour of midtown.

The city's stoplights glowed brighter, and music blasted from car windows in a vibrant soundtrack matching her gait. On 42nd Street, she admired the statue of Hermes atop Grand Central, his arm stretched out in both offering and demand. By then, Mika felt downright euphoric despite not sleeping a wink. The kick she got from the energy drink far surpassed what she was used to from coffee. She'd discovered the caffeine big leagues.

She thundered west as if a Greek god herself, her powerful strides capable of launching her atop Mount Olympus. She approached the steps of the New York Public Library and beheld the two marble lions, Patience and Fortitude, guarding the entrance. *Excellent attributes*, she thought. After waiting nineteen years, she'd get Naomi home through sheer will.

Her optimism faded after arriving at the diner to find Naomi had invited along one of her residents, Marcus Kitterman. Mika had taken note of Marcus yesterday in the lobby. He'd emerged from the elevator, indignant about a dust bunny in the laundry room, and interrupted Naomi, who was placating a group of residents frustrated over the lack of hot water. Mika had caught a glimpse of Marcus before her New York arrival, as well. He was the white-haired, fifty-something man standing next to Naomi in the photograph her father kept tucked in his toolbox.

After they were seated in the bustling eatery, Marcus held his fork up to the window and demanded the waitress acknowledge a microscopic water spot. He didn't order off the menu but instead swiveled his head around to see what other patrons were eating, loudly disrupting their meals to ask for the names of dishes he found appealing. Mika slid a few inches down in her chair, but Naomi didn't raise an eyebrow. *Marcus must do this all the time.*

Mika tried to engage with Marcus while they waited for their food, but he seemed intent on ignoring her as much as possible without being overtly rude. When he excused himself to use the restroom, Mika asked Naomi if she'd somehow offended the man. Naomi assured her Marcus was just socially awkward and not to take it personally.

Mika sensed Marcus had become, in a way, like family to Naomi, and juvenile envy constricted her like a corset. When Marcus returned to the table, he eyed Mika's curry dish, repeating how *yummy* it smelled. He gaped at her, hyena-like, and she subtly curled around her plate like an animal protecting its food. *You can't have what's mine.* As Marcus and Naomi discussed the latest misguided maneuverings of the building's co-op board, Mika wondered if part of her ill will toward Marcus could be explained by sleep deprivation. She considered transferring her insomnia prescription to a local CVS, then decided not to bother since she'd be home tomorrow with Naomi. *God willing.*

After their meal, the long summer day left plenty of light, and Mika asked Naomi to show her the East River. Marcus muttered there was not much to see and, to Mika's relief, returned to his building. She and Naomi stopped at a bodega so Mika could buy another Master Blaster. Heading east through the heat, she tipped her head back to drink the last drops from the tall can. Her sunglasses slipped off her head and, reflexes sharp, she whipped a hand back to catch them. Naomi chuckled and said she moved like a ninja.

Seagulls squawked above when they reached a pedestrian overpass and crossed the congested FDR Drive to a concrete overlook of the river. Beneath them, joggers and bicyclists sped by on the esplanade between the freeway and the water. Although the current moved swiftly below, the windless air, sullen with humidity, offered no relief.

"It's not usually this crowded," Naomi said.

Throngs of people congregated on the overlook, peering down at the water. Their dogs wheezed as they strained against leashes, desperate to investigate one another. Mika asked a blonde woman holding binoculars what had drawn the crowd.

"A humpback is heading this way," the blonde said. "We're all tracking it on a coast guard app. There's been a resurgence in the baitfish population, and humpbacks can't get enough of them."

A whale in Manhattan? She and Naomi exchanged delighted glances. Reverting to childhood exuberance, they quickly squeezed into a spot against the railing with a view down to the water. A family of Canadian geese swam by, and Mika was surprised to see their webbed feet paddling under the clearer-than-expected water. They watched a barge pass, then a ferry. Both ships left rolling wakes that battled the current to strike the sea wall.

"You're a hard woman to get alone," Mika said.

"You got me now."

"I'm taking the 10:42 bus out of Port Authority in the morning."

"Any chance you can stay until the afternoon? Tomorrow's my day off. I'm on call for emergencies, but the porter's handling my day to day. I thought we could go downtown, maybe walk the High Line. Do something fun before you leave."

"Come to Jersey with me."

"I can't."

"Just for the day?"

"Mika, let's not ruin our time together."

"For one meal. I have a car and will drive you back tomorrow night."

"I'm sorry, but the answer is no." And like the day she left, Naomi brooded into the distance.

I won't beg her again. Mika exhaled through her nose. "Tell me why."

Naomi faced her. "People are watching me. They could be watching me right now. And if they are, I don't want to lead them back to the house."

"The FBI? Oh, they know exactly where we live. We saw plenty of them over a decade ago. They thought we knew where you were and put pressure on Dad for years before crawling back under their rock."

Naomi's face revealed surprise, then comprehension. "They probably backed off after we were arrested, but that doesn't mean they stopped trailing me."

"We?"

"A man I traveled with."

"I see." *Always her weakness.*

"It wasn't like that. When I left home, I got involved with a group of animal rights activists who operated under the name Free Species."

A strange twist. "Like PETA?"

"Sort of but willing to engage in illegal practices to accomplish their goals."

This dumbfounded Mika, but she kept her expression neutral while Naomi gave her an overview of Free Species. The group's members gained access to factory farms and live-cargo shipping containers. They recorded video of systemic cruelty then posted it online to raise awareness. To Mika, her monologue sounded like a prepared speech.

"Only videos of farm animals?" Mika asked. "Not wild animals?"

"Ninety-six percent of mammals are farmed for human purposes, and over seventy percent of birds. Free Species focuses on where the suffering is greatest."

"And you went to prison?" The thought of Naomi in a cell sickened her.

"To jail. Free Species had their lawyers get me out. I was never convicted."

"Of recording video?"

"Trespassing and illegal recording, yes. That kind of work takes a toll. There's a lot of burnout."

"I'm sorry. It must have been horrible."

Naomi shrugged. "It's a cruel world, Mika. And what have you been doing in it, working at the store?"

"For the last six months, yes." Mika gave Naomi a quick description of exchange-traded funds and explained that the company she used to work for offered these ETFs, tailored to certain causes, to socially conscious investors.

"Ethical investing, that's interesting," Naomi said. To her credit, she belied no trace of cynicism.

Mika found herself scrambling to impress this new, activist version of Naomi she didn't know existed. "They have a fund for plant-based stocks like Beyond Meat. It's somewhat limited now, but Impossible Foods is going public, and there's a ton of capital going into a European startup making fungi-based meat."

"I'm proud of you," Naomi said. "Why don't you relax your death grip on that can and drink some of this?" She offered her bottled water, which Mika declined.

Mika took a moment to digest everything her sister had said, but she couldn't make sense of it. Naomi cut off their family for nineteen years because of Free Species? "Why didn't you ever reach out to us?" she asked. "Let us know you were alive, at least."

Naomi stared at the water. "I had to go completely off grid to join Free Species," she said somberly. "I couldn't share my plans or location with anyone. I was committing crimes, and if you guys knew, you'd be considered accessories under the law.

"I also had to look out for your safety and the safety of my team. Free Species activists have been assaulted and worse. Sometimes their families are targeted. That's why they live off the grid. And it's not just the FBI I'm worried about. There are other factions. Even human life is cheap when there's billions in profits at stake." She looked at Mika. "I knew leaving home would hurt all of you, but I thought…I thought I could change the world."

Mika scrutinized her sister. She believed Naomi joined Free Species and went to jail for it. But something felt off. "Does every member of Free Species write off their family?"

Naomi frowned. "It's not a cult, if that's what you're suggesting."

Mika didn't press further, remembering her mission. *Get her on the bus.* "I don't fully understand your motivations, but I'm thankful you shared them with me. One thing about us Cranes, though: we're not scared of the FBI or anyone else." She touched Naomi's forearm. "Come home, just for a short visit, to see Mom and Dad."

"I won't put our family in danger, even if you hate me for it."

"C'mon, Naomi. Why would anyone still be watching you? And even if they were, you're not active in Free Species anymore, so who cares? Let them watch. Take the bus with me tomorrow. Tell our family about this cause that meant so much to you. Let them know it's not their fault you never came back."

Naomi's large eyes implored her. "Can you please trust me?"

Mika's frustration broke through its gates. "Naomi, we have the alpha-gal allergy and don't eat meat, but you never once mentioned anything about wanting to be an animal rights activist or the plight of livestock. I would've *known* if you cared that deeply about something. You're not telling me the whole story. I can feel it."

"There it is!" someone yelled, pointing to a spout of river water spraying into the air.

Sweaty bodies pressed around them to get a better look at the river. The dark barnacled head of a humpback whale emerged from the water, shockingly close to the sea wall, followed by its charcoal-blue body. The whale twisted in midair with lumbering grace before splashing down on its back and exposing its pale, lined underbelly. Cool water spritzed Mika, and the whale dove back under the water, its serrated tail the last to dip beneath the sea. Seconds later, its huge knobby head reappeared, now turned sideways, revealing one of its elephant-like eyes inside a pouch of wrinkly skin.

"It wants to get a look at us, too!" shouted the blonde with binoculars.

The crowd whooped and gasped. An army of cell phones waved. Mika turned to Naomi, grateful to share this moment with her long-lost sister. But Naomi's forehead folded in distress. Mika followed her sister's gaze back to the whale, and what she saw chilled her marrow. The whale's intelligent gaze locked onto Mika in sharp rebuke, as if the animal regarded her, specifically, with judgment and scrutiny. *What have you done?* its round eye asked. *What will you do?* Mika felt a pang of deep, inexplicable guilt.

Naomi touched her shoulder. "You okay?"

She swallowed. "Yep."

"You're pale."

Mika's mouth felt greasy and acidic. "I hardly slept last night. An hour tops."

The gravity increased tenfold over Naomi's face. "But you went to bed before midnight."

The whale submerged again, moving north toward the Bronx. The crowd eased as people hurried down the ramp and onto the esplanade to follow it.

"You got me," Mika said shyly. "The lights were out, but I was up all night surfing the web on my phone. Unlike you, I still have insomnia."

A vein bulged in Naomi's neck. "Your insomnia's improved though, hasn't it, since I left?"

Mika squirmed under the intensity of Naomi's gaze. She tapped her can on the railing, flustered by the thoughtless question. "Do you think we were miraculously cured because you vanished?"

"Over the years, I mean, it's gotten better, right?"

She almost said yes because she could see how desperately Naomi wanted to hear it. "What's wrong?"

"Answer the question," Naomi said.

"No. If anything my insomnia's progressed, which isn't unusual. Why, is that how you beat it, you improved gradually?"

"All of you? You all still have insomnia?"

"Of course. It's genetic. What's interesting is you *not* having it."

Naomi struck her fists against the top of the railing, scaring off a lingering spectator and errant pigeon. "I thought they'd leave the rest of you alone. I left because I wanted to *protect* you."

"From the FBI?"

Naomi locked eyes with her. "I never wanted you to know any of this. But maybe it's time. That day in the pool, you might wonder how I could forgive myself—"

"Never. There's nothing to forgive. It wasn't your fault."

"I know, Mika. It was *them*. It was their fault!" Her wild expression reminded Mika of their father.

"Who is them? I have no idea what you're talking about." Mika's mind reeled. Surely Naomi couldn't blame the FBI for what happened in the pool.

Naomi pushed off the railing and strode away from her, the remaining crowd quickly parting to let her pass. Mika scrambled to catch up, and they crossed the pedestrian walkway and moved off the river's edge and into the city toward the dying sun.

Mika jogged to keep pace with her. "Where are you going? Slow down."

"I need to think. Let me walk."

Naomi didn't stop until they reached the wall of a red-bricked armory that occupied an entire block, a fortress home to massive art installations. She leaned against the wall of the armory and thumped the back of her head against the brick. "I thought they'd follow me, that I was their focus, that your lives would normalize after I left." She worked to compose herself. "I couldn't tell you this, Mika. You were a kid, and the truth was too evil."

"Go on," Mika said. "I want to understand."

"Are you still having blackouts?"

Mika nodded. "Occasionally. Why?"

She thumped her head again. "Goddamnit, I thought you'd all be safe."

Safe? Mika thought about the landline at the main house, the pale green, push-button phone on the side table next to the living room couch. How hyperaware of it the Cranes always were, hoping Naomi would call, even after moving on to mostly using cell phones. For years, the only calls that came into the landline were scammers pretending to be jailed grandchildren or the IRS, and every one of those calls had hollowed them out for days.

"What if I told you," Naomi said, "that I was taken."

"By who? The FBI? Free Species?"

Naomi shook her head, her nostrils flared. "Aliens."

A car passed, a thumping bass pounding out of its open windows. A gust of wind blew a large plastic bag down the street.

"What do you mean? Immigrants?"

"No, the other kind."

"From outer space?"

Naomi nodded.

A laugh tried to force its way up Mika's throat. She closed her eyes and said a quick prayer that Naomi was playing an elaborate joke, that she would chuckle and say *Got ya, sucker!* But when she opened them, Naomi said other things, about a ship, about experiments. Mika struggled to follow Naomi's words, shocked by their absurdity.

Naomi continued, her voice cracking. "The things that took me? They tortured me, Mika. Made me look at ghastly things. It was like they tried to justify doing whatever they wanted to me by revealing the heinous things *we* do, mostly to animals and the planet, but also to each other. They did something to me so I couldn't close my eyes, then made me witness a series of hyper-virtual realities. I could smell the blood, feel the terror. And they *knew* me, those monsters. I felt them prying into my mind. I can't express how obscene it was, the violation. How evil they are.

"I remembered it all that day in the pool, everything they did to me. That's why I panicked. I didn't know you were next to me. I didn't even know I was in the water. All I could see, all I experienced, was the memory of my abduction and what they put me through. I was trying to get away from them, and the water—" She wiped her palms over her face. "I must've choked on the water. But I didn't know what I was doing. *I didn't know I was hurting you.*"

Mika's tongue felt thick in her mouth, but she pushed the words out. "I know you didn't. I never doubted that for a second. None of us did. But what you experienced in the pool sounds like a waking nightmare."

"No." Naomi shook her head rapidly. "It really happened. My abduction was as real as you and me standing here. Don't ask me how, but toward the end I got my hands on one of them, around its long, skinny neck. It started mewling and then it sounded like hundreds of them, maybe thousands, were making the same awful sound. I didn't let go, though. I bent its neck almost all the way back, but it wouldn't snap." She throttled the air in front of Mika to demonstrate, then hooked her thumbs, clear mucus forming a bubble in one of her nostrils. "I tried to gouge out its bug-eyes, but I couldn't do that either. Its eyes looked soft but they were solid, like the thing had goggles on." Her fingers flexed and curled. "They got control over me again, long enough to release me." She wiped her nose with the back of her hand.

"I didn't lie about joining Free Species. After remembering my abduction, I knew I had to hide, had to leave all of you behind. But I also had to *act*. I couldn't live with myself if I didn't, not after everything I witnessed. After camping out in my car for a while, with the violence on a never-ending loop in my head, I realized humanity was too tribal, too bloodthirsty. I wrote off most of humanity as hopeless, started seeing them as the enemy. I discovered Free Species and contacted them, told them I was willing to work the front lines to expose animal cruelty. I traveled the country with a small team for a few years. We were nomads, no address, no obligations other than the work we did. We used burner phones and lived off donations."

Mika shifted on her feet, trying to find solid ground on the pitted sidewalk. She no longer saw Naomi as the star she merely orbited around, but she still felt the strength of their bond: that thick cord time and an imaginary ax had barely frayed. Naomi was obviously in a disturbed state and needed help—a part of Mika cackled at that observation. *You don't say? What gave it away, the bit about strangling a goggle-eyed alien?*

Mika adopted a conversational tone. *Just two sisters shootin' the shit!* "All I'm saying is, it's not unheard of for people with sleep disorders to experience strange phenomena. Sleep paralysis, for example, the feeling there's something in the room with you, that you're trapped in the presence of something malevolent and can't move. It used to happen to me all the time in high school, scared the hell—"

"They took me, Mika, and they tortured me. And processing that truth, however awful, is the sole reason *I don't* have a sleep disorder anymore."

Cars passed. People strolled by. The world continued to spin on its axis, and Mika had finally learned why

Naomi left nineteen years ago. Her sister had lived, clearly still lived, with a mental health issue that had gone untreated for far too long. Instead of receiving the treatment she needed as a teenager, Naomi ran away and joined a possible cult. She went to jail, then ended up in a stressful job in a stressful city.

Mika saw the garbage bags piled on the corner through a new lens. The city no longer appeared as a dusty yet majestic place. It was a trash heap brimming with danger, stuccoed with grease and pigeon shit. Naomi needed to come home and be evaluated by a highly-trained professional. She needed her family. *It might take some time, but she'll get through this.* Naomi had overcome a genetic sleep disorder. She would conquer her delusions, too.

"You almost drowned," Mika said. "You were traumatized, physically and mentally. It's no wonder you became sensitive to the horror in the world, that your mind tried to make sense of the accident by finding a boogeyman to blame."

A wry expression slid over Naomi's face. "Stubborn as ever, aren't you? I didn't *create* what happened to me. And I'm not alone. There are others like me. People with similar experiences. We have a support group, and there's a meeting tomorrow. If you came with me, you'd see I'm not delusional."

Mika followed Naomi everywhere when they were kids, even tagged along on some of her dates. She couldn't remember a single time her older sister had not patiently tolerated her presence. Now it was Mika's turn to be patient.

Mika switched gears, using the same measured cadence she employed to placate Art during his rants about the government. "I'll do it. I'll go to your meeting. But you have to promise you'll come home with me for a visit after I do. We can take a later bus tomorrow afternoon. A few hours to see your family again, that's all I ask. Will you promise me?"

Naomi nodded, but her eyes were shadowed by a street light.

8

—

Mika retreated to the guestroom, where her bag lay open on the floor, her scuffed white flats shoved inside a mesh panel. She knew she should call her mother, who no doubt felt anxious to hear from her, but what would Mika say? *Naomi thinks alien abductions justify her self-exile?*

She sent Paige a text asking about their father's health. The text, like the last one she sent to her sister, floated unacknowledged in cyberspace. *She blocked me. Real mature.* After midnight, Mika relented and called the Piney Mart. A part of her hoped no one would answer, that her older sister had taken her advice and closed the store early, but Tessie Crane answered after the first ring.

"I just can't get over it. You and Naomi together." Her mom's voice cracked with emotion. "Is she there with you now? Is she listening?"

"She's asleep. She actually sleeps now, can you believe it?"

Mika heard rustling on the line, then her mom blew her nose. "Isn't that something? You two coming home together?"

"I hope we'll both be back tomorrow. I'll call again with the time."

"Oh, good lord. I'm so excited I can hardly stand it. What's she like now? Is she real different?"

Mika wanted to prepare her mother for the possibility Naomi might not come home. She didn't know if she could trust Naomi to stick to their agreement, given her mental state. "She's a busy woman, Mom. She oversees every inch of this building and manages a revolving door of staff, plumbers, deliveries, and contractors on top of the residents. If an emergency comes up, she might need to stay here and deal with it."

Tessie sniffled. "But what's she *like*?"

"She still smiles on the side of her face and gives that thousand-yard-stare when she's sorting out her feelings."

"I remember that stare."

"How's Dad doing?"

"They discharged him this afternoon, but his arrhythmia hadn't gone anywhere, sorry to say. Paige is fussing over him and worried about what Medicare's paying."

"Tell her not to worry about the medical bills. Dad has it covered."

"He does?"

"I'll tell you about it when I see you. I should go. I have plans in the morning. Will you do me a favor? Tell Dad I'm working on things with Naomi, and I'll call him soon. I don't want to get his hopes up quite yet, in case something goes wrong."

Tessie's voice dropped to a whisper. "Does Naomi know about…what happened to me?"

"Of course not," Mika fibbed. "That video is ancient history. I wish you'd stop dwelling on it."

"Oh, that reminds me of what I wanted to tell you! Gary's losing his business."

"Gary?"

"Your dad's mechanic on Beach Drive. You know him, he wears shorts all year long, even in the winter? He lives above his shop with his boyfriend? Well, turns out Gary and the boyfriend are getting *evicted*. Gary lost all their savings playing poker on the internet and hasn't paid the rent in two years. But you didn't hear that from me."

Tessie then launched into a story about a Piney Mart customer in the midst of divorcing his wife after discovering her affair with their son's soccer coach. "Get this. The customer's wife sends her kid's coach a text full of sex stuff. The coach's wife intercepts it and blasts it all over Facebook. That's how he found out his wife was cheating—he saw it on freaking Facebook! Two marriages right down the shitter!"

Mika squirmed, imagining her mother leaning into the phone, her face as bright as a department store Christmas tree. Such chatter was a compulsion, Mika believed—her mother's way of distracting herself from the shame of the beating she gave Chapman in the store two years ago. When the security footage of the attempted robbery went viral, the resulting media spotlight drove Tessie indoors the weeks before her sentencing, depressed and humiliated. She'd emerged from prison a different woman, quick to latch onto the scandals of others.

After saying goodbye, Mika drank a warm Master Blaster hoping for a rush of clarity. No question about it,

Naomi needed the support of her family and a good therapist. But how could she convince Naomi to accept help while her sister was so deeply entrenched in fantastical beliefs? Beliefs apparently validated by a group of people Mika would have to face tomorrow.

The caffeine released a surge of serotonin, and chemical optimism percolated in her gray matter. She would walk with Naomi through her recovery. Her parents would too, she felt sure. *We'll be okay. All of us.* Paige would come around, and their mom, especially, could offer Naomi empathy and advice, having survived her own struggles.

Tessie had worked the late shift the night Ed Chapman tried to rob the Piney Mart. Earlier that same evening, he'd emptied his bank account and maxed out his credit card feeding a *Wheel of Fortune* slot machine in Atlantic City for six consecutive hours. Chapman's later lawsuit against the casino revealed two waitresses had served him a total of eleven mojitos before he made the drive home to Tuckerton. He'd spent the drive devising a clumsy, rum-soaked plan to pick up a ski mask from his off-campus apartment and rob the convenience store he sometimes stopped at for laxatives while trying to "make weight" for a wrestling match. But that plan, like his gambling spree, went disturbingly awry.

Back then, the softball bat Mika kept under the register cabinet had sat on a shelf next to the storeroom door for over two decades, displayed not as a crime deterrent but as something for Tessie to show off. Her daughter Naomi had been presented with the green-and-gold-painted bat after her All-Star team won a middle school softball tournament.

The security footage told the story. Mika had watched it online like the web surfing masses, but instead of finding it darkly hilarious, her heart almost detonated in her chest.

In the video, Ed Chapman demanded money from the register. Clad in his ski mask, he screamed at Tessie to hurry up, or he'd take the gun out of his sweatshirt pocket and blow her head off. Turned out there wasn't a gun, but Tessie didn't know that.

Chapman thrust a plastic ShopRite bag at her and demanded she fill it with cash. When she didn't move fast enough, he punched her in the face. Tessie's head whipped back then snapped forward, a trail of blood leaking from her nose. She stood for a moment, frozen with shock, then turned and picked up the softball bat from the shelf behind her.

Chapman dropped the bag—and his gun-wielding pretense—and caught the bat before it crashed down onto his skull. He was five foot six, wiry and wasted, whereas Tessie was a taller, solid woman. They were locked in a tug of war before Chapman shifted his grip from the barrel of the bat to Tessie's hair. In a clumsy attempt to draw Tessie into his signature chokehold, he pulled her over the counter and on top of him, underestimating her heft. Tessie delivered the first blow to the pinned college student, ramming the barrel of the bat into his nose, which exploded in a splash of blood as he lost consciousness. Tessie got to her feet, her eyes wild and bulging, the tip of her tongue pressed to her upper lip as it always did when she concentrated. For thirteen seconds after Chapman stopped moving, the bat rose and fell.

Those thirteen seconds went viral on the internet after the security footage leaked. Slowed down and auto-tuned, accompanied by an array of music from rap to thrash metal, the whacks of the bat were accentuated with bone-crushing sound effects. Chapman survived with a shattered nose, fractured skull, and a splintered femur that would never fully heal.

Thirty-six minutes later, a teacher's aide came to the store for coffee, saw Chapman bloodied and unconscious, and called the police. The cops found Tessie curled up on the storage room floor, hiding in the dark, her muscles so sore she couldn't lift her arms for a week.

The comments started after the security footage was released online. *Sure, the guy was in the wrong, but did she have to swing the bat so many times? Wasn't that kind of excessive?* Outraged that anyone would feel sorry for a man who'd assaulted her elderly mother, Mika had spent hours typing scathing rebuttals to Twitter randos before deleting her account, distraught and disgusted with the world. Her mom was a protective mama bear who had no way of knowing what Chapman would do next if he'd successfully robbed the store. He could have easily gone to the main house to commit more criminal acts against the Cranes.

Despite Tessie's torn rotator cuff, bleeding scalp, and bruising, the jury had only convicted Chapman on one charge of simple assault, and few were particularly outraged about it. He was *troubled*, they said. Then maybe a little softer in the same breath: *Kid was a good athlete.*

Had a bright future. Tessie served fourteen months of her two-year sentence in prison while Chapman got off with three years probation.

9

—

The next morning, sheets of water pounded the street, and the sky hung sodden and gray. Mika and Naomi ducked into a bodega to buy cheap umbrellas that quickly proved useless, jerking violently in the wind and flipping inside out. They ran the rest of the way to the church on Third Avenue. Mika felt lightheaded and short of breath, shaky from a night of minimal sleep and much worry.

A standout among its boxy neighbors, the church's brick base supported a towering steeple layered with rows of arched windows. Both of them disheveled and dripping, Mika followed Naomi inside, then up dimly lit stairs to a sparsely decorated room on the second floor. A long table stood against the back wall, next to a stack of folding chairs, and Mika immediately spotted Marcus pouring himself a cup of coffee. Everything inside Mika sagged.

"What's he doing here?" she whispered to Naomi. Marcus approached them before her sister could respond, and he and Naomi fell into the same banter they had at the diner, rife with shorthand and inside jokes about the hapless co-op board.

"And what is it that you do again?" Marcus asked Mika, acknowledging her presence after Naomi excused herself to take a work call in the hallway.

Now he's curious? Yesterday at the diner, he failed to ask her a single question. "I work at a convenience store in Jersey. And you?"

He peered down his long nose at her. "Like a 7-Eleven? I suppose you'll need to get back to it soon, hmm? I'm retired now but had a long career as an investigator for the public administrator's office, managing the estates of those who sadly die with no next of kin."

Mika nodded politely, but Marcus continued as if feeling the need to explain himself.

"Some might find it a morbid profession, but it was quite lucrative, and I built up a healthy retirement fund over the years."

"Good for you."

"I fancy myself a bit of a day trader these days. Probably missed my calling as a Wall Street shark." He barked a laugh.

Mika had no interest in sharing her career history with Marcus. She noted the strangeness of engaging in small talk while waiting to hear from a group of people who believed in space aliens. A banner over the door read "All Souls Welcome Here." *They're not kidding.*

"Something funny?" Marcus asked.

"I was thinking about something else."

"Where is this convenience store? New Jersey, you say?"

"Naomi never mentioned it? Our family's run it for over fifty years."

Marcus's nose wrinkled as if he'd caught a whiff of something unpleasant. "You and Naomi are sisters, correct? And when did you see last each other? Twenty years, isn't it? It's nice you can reconnect after so much time. I imagine it must feel odd, though, not having a relationship since childhood. You two are practically strangers at this point."

Mika considered this an attempt to provoke her and refused to get riled. "Where's the bathroom?"

She found Naomi in the hallway and waited for her to wrap up her call. "Why would you tell Marcus about these meetings?"

"I didn't. He followed me here a few months ago."

"Followed?" The concrete walls amplified Mika's voice.

"Shhh. He was curious. The man's bored, Mika, and probably lonely." Naomi lifted her shoulders. "And if he says he's had some experiences himself, who am I to deny his truth?"

A thin, graceful man with an impressive head of tightly-curled dark hair descended the stairs and stepped into the hallway. Large freckles sprinkled his nose and cheeks. Naomi moved toward him, and the two spoke quietly before she introduced him to Mika as Adrian. Mika sensed more than friendship between them; Adrian had the androgynous look Naomi always went for. This was their first time meeting in person, Naomi explained, but they'd been chatting in abductee forums for the last six months.

Oh sure, totally normal. Mika followed Naomi and Adrian into the meeting room.

"Looks like the rain is keeping people away." Naomi gestured bashfully to the mostly empty room. She introduced Marcus to Adrian.

Marcus graced Adrian with his trademark curt nod, then handed Naomi a wad of paper towels and pointed at the water accumulating on the tiled floor. "Someone could fall to their death in this place."

Grace arrived next, pallid but strong shouldered, her fine hair dyed a silvery shade. Dewey with rain and youth, she unloaded the waterproof backpack from her shoulders, placed it on a folding chair, then plopped down on the chair next to it. She introduced herself to Adrian and Mika as a Columbia grad student and bike messenger.

Mika and Adrian chose seats on either side of Naomi. Marcus sat next to Adrian and squinted at his freckles. "Where are you from?"

"Connecticut."

"But…where are your parents from?"

"Connecticut."

"I mean *originally*."

"My father's parents are from Ecuador and my mother's family is Scottish. Is that what you're looking for?"

Marcus grimaced. "Forgive me for being nosy."

"I won't hold it against you," Adrian said in a way that conveyed Marcus was wholly insignificant to him. Mika decided she liked Adrian.

"It's a pleasure to meet you." Marcus extended his hand.

"I don't shake hands. It's nothing personal. I'm a nurse, so I tend to be extra cautious about germs." Adrian dipped his chin. "Actually, that's not entirely true, and I promised myself I'd be honest today. I find it hard to touch people, I'm not sure why. It's not an issue at work when I'm wearing gloves."

"I won't hold it against you." Marcus guffawed, delighted by his cleverness.

A hulking sixtyish man with box-died brunette hair arrived wearing a beige trench coat with shoulder pads straight out of the eighties, not that he needed any. He boomed a hello and removed his coat, revealing an expensive-looking suit, then sat in one of the folding chairs with his bent knees comically high. Naomi presented him to the group as Ron, a long-time member, then announced it was time for the meeting to start. Once the door was closed and chairs were shuffled closer, the clammy air smelled like breath, coffee, and perspiration.

"As always, no one has to share," Naomi said, her eyes lingering more on Marcus than anyone else. "If you have a question or want to share, please raise your hand. If you wish, you can identify yourself as an experiencer, a contactee, or an abductee, then talk about anything you want. This is a safe space."

Adrian raised his hand. "What's the difference between a contactee and an abductee?"

"Contactees choose to view their experiences as positive on some level while abductees do not." Naomi failed to hide her disdain when uttering the word *positive*. "Experiencers have witnessed what they believe to be an alien craft or lifeform but have not interacted with it, as far as they know."

Marcus indicated he wanted to share then went on about a strange dream he had about his late grandfather. He suggested the dream was an abduction attempt: aliens pretending to be the spirit of his grandfather, trying to trick him into following them onto their ship. "I'm no fool," he said. "I didn't fall for it."

Mika gazed longingly at the door as the group said, "Thanks, Marcus," with little enthusiasm.

Ron raised his hand, his knuckles the size of golf balls. "Hi, I'm Ron. I'm an experiencer. Maybe an abductee too, I'm not sure. After seeing a UFO, I woke up with my pajamas on backward and had a weird taste in my mouth, like sulfur and citrus, every time I burped."

Mika thought about nuclear war to keep a straight face.

Ron shifted in his seat. "It's been a crappy week. My wife and I had another fight. She caught me taking the recycling to Food Emporium to get cash back and blew her top, asking what a client would think if they saw their lawyer cashing in cans of Diet Coke. She's always worried about what people think. I'm glad I can come here and vent."

Ron looked directly at Mika, and she felt herself shrivel from his attention. His dark eyes slyly studied her as if she was his opponent in a high-stakes poker game. She wondered what kind of law he practiced and pitied anyone who had to face him from a witness stand.

"I mean, I have money now, sure," Ron went on, "but that doesn't change who I am. Janice, that's my wife, she never had to stand in the school lunch line with a ticket for a free meal. Giving away money? Throwing it in a bin? My mother would roll over in her grave and cross herself." He shook his head and tinkered with his shiny cufflinks.

"When I was young, the kids in our neighborhood used to have their own corners, a place to hang out at night with your buddies. Your corner was your turf, and it was all we had. Janice wouldn't understand, so I keep stuff like that to myself. I never told her about what we saw one night, the bunch of us on our corner. I kept in touch with a few of them. One got killed in an accident, one died of an embolism. But none of us ever talked much about what happened. Weird, right? To witness something mind-blowing and barely talk about it?"

"Can you elaborate a little for the newcomers?" Naomi asked.

Ron nodded gamely. "The dogs stopped barking. That's the first thing we noticed. In our neighborhood, at least two dogs barked their heads off at any given moment. Usually more than two, because once a couple got going, the others had to chime in. But right before it came, the barking stopped. Not a peep.

"The ship was the same color as the night sky. We only noticed it because it blotted out the stars. We stood there with our mouths open watching it come. It was smooth, no windows, and shaped like a fifty-foot cigar. It passed over our heads in complete silence, so quiet we could hear each other breathe.

"Once we were directly under it, we saw the ship had a shine to it, like moonlight on lake water. It sailed down the block for another couple minutes. It was about a hundred yards away, we all had eyes on it, and the thing just—*pop*—either vanished or flew off faster than a human eye could track it. Or maybe it didn't go anywhere. Who knows, maybe it cloaked itself like in *Star Trek*. That's the last I ever saw of it, as far as I'm aware."

Ron rubbed his clean-shaven chin and shrugged his wide shoulders. "Like I said, the guys and I didn't talk about it. I mean, maybe once or twice one of them said something like, *What a head fuck that night was, huh Ronny?* And we'd shake our heads and move on to the next subject. But you see something like that in the sky and it stays with you. It changes you. I wish I could tell Janice about it, but she tends to overreact to things. There's always this gap between us, even bigger than the school lunch stuff and the bottle collecting." Ron took a breath. "That's all I have today."

"Thanks, Ron," the group said.

Mika looked away, embarrassed for Ron and even pitying his wife, who sounded kind of unlikeable. Her gaze landed on Adrian and narrowed in on a small scar on his jawline. It looked as though someone had put the tip of a knife there and twisted it, digging around. Gaping at the scar, the skin on the back of Mika's neck puckered into gooseflesh.

"What happened to your face?" Mika immediately wanted to crawl out of her body to flee her shame over asking such a thing. Her racing heart kicked into hyperdrive. She should have skipped her morning Master Blaster and had breakfast instead.

Naomi chastised her with a sharp look, then turned to Adrian. "You don't have to answer that."

"I'm so sorry," Mika sputtered. "It's none of my business, and it's hardly noticeable anyway."

"Hey, it's a good opener," Adrian said. "I'd like to share." He exuded the same brave determination Naomi had yesterday, outside the armory. "I'm Adrian, an experiencer and, I believe, an abductee, too. They put something in my jaw, I think. It tingles sometimes when I have strong emotions, like if I'm frustrated at work or happy to see my cat." He exhaled a wobbly stream of air. "This is harder than I expected. I'm going to stop now."

"Thanks, Adrian," everyone said, with Mika joining in this time. Adrian winked at her. She figured Adrian's kindness toward her hinged on her connection to Naomi, but she was immensely grateful for it nonetheless.

"It's not uncommon," Naomi said. "Many abductees report implants in the head or neck."

Adrian nodded. "I tried to remove it once, but it squiggled away when I got close to it with my tweezers and moved deeper into my jaw. It didn't hurt, and it never has, but it tingles from a new spot now. I don't mess with it anymore."

Mika withdrew from the conversation, thinking of her father bleeding in the woods.

The damn chip—the one the government uses to track me.

It was scurrying around under my skin, and I came out here to cut it out in private, but the damn thing moved when I got close.

"Mika," Naomi said. "Do you have something you'd like to share?"

Mika gave her the side-eye. Was there anything more annoying to an introvert than being volunteered to speak? But after she'd blurted out that rude question to Adrian, she couldn't exactly play coy. "I'm Mika, Naomi's sister. I'm here to support her. I'm not an experiencer or contactee or abductee, but thanks for letting me be here today."

Marcus scowled, but the rest of the group appeared unbothered by Mika's statement. Grace raised her hand and said she had big news. The hypnotist she'd previously mentioned to the group, a doctor in the city, had agreed to meet with them that very evening.

Ron groaned. "Ah, geez. Another quack?"

Grace sniffed. "A hypnotist that worked with John Mack, thank you. Hardly a *quack*."

Ron opened his palms. "Don't get mad at me, kid. I'm just looking out for you."

"You'd like her, Ron. Dr. Patel is brilliant and beautiful and—" Grace blushed. "A beautiful person, I mean."

"Hey, if you like her, she can't be that bad. I just think you're better off falling for ladies your own age."

Grace made a face. "I'm not a child, and this is not about a crush. Dr. Patel's work helps abductees live their best lives. I'm telling you, the woman is a genius."

Ron made a noise in his throat. "Not for nothing, but you said the same thing about the professor you had a fling with."

"Who? Oh, she was my advisor." Grace flicked her wrist. "Ancient history."

"Well, she advised you into a broken heart."

Grace clucked her tongue. "Hardly. I do feel a vibe with Dr. Patel, but nothing's going on between us. She's my mentor. Our relationship is strictly professional."

Ron appeared dubious.

"This Dr. Patel, you're saying she worked with *the* John Mack?" Naomi asked, and Grace nodded, smugly.

"Who's John Mack?" Mika asked.

"An abduction researcher, a Harvard Professor who won a Pulitzer," Naomi said. "He died in 2004."

When the meeting wrapped, Ron and Grace said their goodbyes while Naomi and Adrian huddled near the coffee pot, chatting. Marcus hung around after Adrian left, watching Naomi and Mika stack the folding chairs in a corner.

"Mika, are you accompanying us to the diner for coffee?" Marcus asked. "It's our ritual. Or maybe you'd rather take a nap? You do look tired."

"Sorry, I gotta break protocol today and take my sister here out for a drink," Naomi said. "She deserves one."

Marcus's features pinched, and he muttered that it was barely noon. The glance he gave Mika before leaving simmered with barely disguised contempt.

Outside, the rain had dwindled to a heavy mist, and streams of water washed debris into storm drains on the street. Mika could smell the heady scent of wet earth whenever she passed a tree planted in the sidewalk. The air felt fresh and full of promise, and so did Mika. The gathering at the church was over, and now she and Naomi could return to the barrens. The two of them avoided puddles and ducked into a narrow but surprisingly deep karaoke bar. They sat on wooden stools and ordered pints from the model-gorgeous bartender.

"Marcus obviously ad-libbed his whole dream story," Mika said, once the two of them clinked pint glasses, toasting their reunion. *At least the others sounded like they believed their fantasies.*

"Yeah, he makes stuff up sometimes, exaggerates," Naomi said. "Probably for attention. I let it slide. He's a quirky guy. Sheltered, you know? I doubt he's left a twenty-block radius in the last ten years."

So much for worldly New Yorkers. Mika sipped her beer, gearing up for the most crucial stage of her mission. "So, our bus leaves a little after two this afternoon. You should probably pack a few things, just in case you want to spend the night after dinner. We'll order in something that we can all eat."

Naomi tapped on the side of her pint glass, reducing the foamy head. "How about we head to Jersey tomorrow after meeting up with that hypnotist Grace mentioned?"

The absolute temerity of this woman. Mika took another swig of beer, swallowing a sudden fury. "I did what you wanted. I went to your meeting. One meeting. That was the agreement."

Don't lose your temper. She's not well.

Naomi asked the bartender for a pen. "Remember that day by the creek? We had a picnic and those deer came into the clearing?"

Mika nodded. "Funny you should mention it, because I thought of that day recently."

Naomi peered at her. "What do you remember?"

"Everything." Mika recalled the day with vivid clarity: the tea-colored stream they'd followed into an expanse of orchids and leafy ferns, where dandelions swayed in a gentle wind and the shrubs were pale with pollen.

She and Naomi had picnicked in the clearing after swimming in the creek. They were munching on peanut butter and jelly sandwiches when, out of nowhere, a herd of deer emerged from the deep woods. The sisters had exchanged thrilled glances and an understanding they should not move or utter a sound lest they scare the elegant creatures away. Acting wholly out of character, the deer hadn't fled in the presence of humans. Instead, the animals kept their dark, liquid eyes on Naomi and Mika while drinking from the creek and nibbling on the leaves of young trees.

Mika had felt sure a shift in the wind would bring the herd back to their senses, send their white tails up in alarm before they bounded back into the forest. But the deer remained in the clearing, drinking and feeding for some time before getting spooked and bolting into the pines.

Despite her anger over Naomi trying to weasel out of their deal, Mika grinned at the memory. "We got chastised for missing dinner."

When Mika and Naomi arrived home, their mom had clutched her chest, saying *Thank God* over and over. Annoyed the iron-rich creek had stained their clothes, Tessie said they could eat their dinner cold, and if they didn't like it, then tough tootsies. The sisters were surprised they'd been gone for so long. Mesmerized by the rare beauty of the herd, their time in the clearing had flown by.

Naomi removed the white paper napkin from beneath her pint of beer. She wrote something on the napkin with the bartender's pen and then folded the napkin on the bar.

"We didn't regret a thing, did we? Witnessing those deer was worth getting into trouble, wasn't it?"

"Sure, we just thought, you know—"

Naomi leaned toward her. "What, Mika? What did we think?"

"That it was a magical day and we experienced something special. Why do you want to go to this hypnosis thing anyway? You said you remember your abduction, that it all came back to you in the pool."

"One of the abductions, yes. The last one. Did you ever wonder, Mika? If insomnia was passed down to us through the Crane gene pool, why does Mom have it too?"

"Seems obvious, doesn't it? She caught it like the flu after years of living with Dad. Not literally, but you know what I mean."

"What if there's another reason?"

"Wait. Don't tell me. The aliens again?"

Naomi opened the napkin and laid it flat on the bar, on it a single sentence. *It was a magical day and we experienced something special.*

"What the hell, Naomi? You're doing parlor tricks now?" A spinning sensation occupied the top of Mika's head. She regretted the beer she'd poured into her empty stomach.

Naomi dropped her fist on the napkin. "We both have this exact same thought, Mika. Even after all these years, we remember it word for word. We never really dissected what happened that day, did we? How surreal it was. How *unreal*. Why would deer get so close to people? They wouldn't. And why did what felt like half an hour, take three? You don't remember, but they took me from the clearing that day. There were no deer, Mika. It was them who came out of the forest. The aliens."

"I remember that day. That's not what happened."

"What do you remember, Mika? That we sat and watched a herd of deer for almost three hours? Does that sound plausible to you?"

"Not for three hours. Come on."

Mika leaned closer. "Then why were we so late? Why did we miss dinner? They took me, Mika. And they did something to you so you couldn't move, couldn't run. I saw you on the ground after they released me. You were terrified. Your mouth was open and your throat convulsed like you were screaming, but instead of screams this awful clicking sound came out of you."

"Stop this. Please." Mika's head was a whirling blur, helicopter blades revving up for lift-off.

"It's true. All of it. They chose me to torture, to perform their sick experiments on. The rest of you were collateral damage, witnesses to be restrained. If you can remember what they did to you that day in the meadow, and probably other days before it, there's a chance you can sleep again. I know that for a fact because it happened to me. You can change your life for the better. If I could give that to you after everything—"

"They were starving animals, Naomi, acting out of character. Don't you remember the deer population had exploded? No one *took* you." Mika paused. She didn't want to argue with Naomi and blow her chance at getting her sister home, getting her sister *help*. But Naomi had lied to and manipulated her, and it made her feel sullied, like the soot of the city filled her pores and oiled her scalp.

"This thought." Naomi jabbed the napkin with her finger. "It didn't come from us. They put it in our minds."

This is too much. Mika downed the last gulp of her pint and headed for the door. Naomi did not call out to stop her.

10

—

Mika went back to Naomi's apartment and paced the floorspace in the guestroom, frustrated by her sister's duplicity and her own inability to control the situation. What choice did she have but to do Naomi's bidding and attend another creepy meet-up? *Naomi has me by the scruff of my neck, and she knows it.*

And what about the people in her sister's alien-abduction group, or whatever the hell they called themselves? Was Naomi the group's official leader? Her sister could be quite convincing. Mika thought about Ron, who felt disconnected from his wife, and Adrian, who couldn't touch anyone unless he wore gloves. Were they vulnerable people sucked in by Naomi's charisma and conviction? The word *cult* popped into Mika's mind again, like it had when Naomi told her about Free Species. Her sister was an impressionable teen when she joined Free Species. Did she learn to deceive people from them?

Mika used her cell phone to call the landline at the main house. "I'm coming home tonight," she blurted when Paige picked up, afraid her sister would hang up.

"Is *she* coming back with you?"

"Maybe not."

"I knew it. What a waste of time and money. Where did you get the cash from anyway?"

"I'll show you when I get home."

"What do you mean, *show* me?"

"How's Dad?"

"Stopped sleeping—I knew that was too good to last—and still refusing to eat. He got out of bed, at least, and made it to his recliner last night. He chatted with Mom about the old days. Then things took a turn and he started peering through the blinds and shining a flashlight around the driveway looking for feds. That kept him busy till the sun came up."

"Where is he now?"

"In the kitchen."

"Can you put him on?"

"Christ, hold on."

Mika waited for several minutes, during which a wretchedness encompassed her, one beyond the usual misery of her brain-rotting sleeplessness. A painful zapping bombarded her limbs, causing her muscles to twitch as if stung by snapping rubber bands.

Her scalp itched, and her fidgety fingers moved to her head, but she couldn't find the source, couldn't scratch the itch. An image of Adrian's scarred jaw popped into her mind, and she prodded her own jawline with her fingers, feeling only smooth bone.

"Mika?"

Her shrill, fake cheer filled the guest room. "Hi Dad, how are you feeling?"

"Can't say I'm tip-top, but I got some mojo back."

"I heard you're not eating?"

"Not hungry. Gotta listen to the body. It's too old to be breaking stuff down with my heart flapping around like a flounder in a crab cage." Art Crane coughed, wet and deep.

"Maybe you should get checked out. Have Paige drive you back to the hospital."

"I've had it up the wazoo with hospitals. Those doctors can't do nothing for me. I got high blood pressure and a bad ticker, that's all. I'll be eighty-five in a couple of weeks. What do you expect?"

"What about that cough? You could have pneumonia. Can't mess around with pneumonia at your age."

"I've had enough poking and prodding from squirrelly looking halfwits. I'm not going back to the hospital, and that's that. Go on now and tell me about Naomi."

Mika took a breath. "She asked all about you, of course, and the rest of the family. She's doing well. She works hard running a residential building and seems to enjoy it."

"A whole building? Isn't that something? She's coming home, right? I knew you could do it."

"What if I can't?" Mika asked, her voice a scratchy alto.

Art cleared his throat. Emotional women made him uneasy. "Then I'd know you tried your best. Hope I didn't put too much pressure on you with this Naomi business. When you get old, the unresolved stuff weighs on you. You want your conscience light before it's your time to go. That way the spirit can fly where it needs to."

Mika hoped he would say more, grateful for the chance to talk about their shared belief in a spiritual world. A smoother current joined the river of cortisol in her bloodstream. But her father's voice soon rose to a higher pitch, and she both sensed and related to his utter exhaustion, the teetering of his mind.

"Now you remember to light me up when the time comes. Don't let the feds get hold of me. When Naomi gets here, we can all sit down and strategize."

A lump swelled in her throat. "Dad, I don't want to let you down, but it's also not fair to get your hopes up too much. Naomi has dozens of people depending on her for every little thing now. I'll do my best to bring her home tonight, but if I can't, maybe you two can have a nice chat on the phone."

Her father cleared his throat again. "Your best is all I can ask for, honey."

Paige yelled in the background that lunch was getting cold.

"I'll see you later, Dad."

She continued to scratch at her scalp, searching for the elusive epicenter of the maddening itch. One of her fingernails landed on a small, hard bump, and she picked at it until she felt it loosen on one side.

Dandruff?

Then, it moved.

Her fingers dug in. *Get it out. Get it out.* It twitched again, more forcefully this time. The peanuts Mika ate at the bar rose to the back of her mouth, hot and acidic, and for a moment the rug beneath her feet transformed into a patch of sphagnum moss in the barrens, rough like the fur of a wild animal. There was sun on her face, and something metallic slid down her throat.

She sucked in air, the vision passed, and she clasped the thing on her scalp between her nails, feeling it squirm as she bolted into the bathroom.

She flicked the wriggling thing into the sink, recognizing its circular brown form against the white porcelain: a tick, bloated with blood, its eight legs searching for traction. She could leave the barrens behind, but they remained burrowed into her skin. She rinsed out the sink, glaring at the tick as it circled the drain, hating it for making her think it could be—no, she wouldn't think the words. But they came anyway. *An alien implant.*

Naomi appeared in the bathroom doorway. "The meeting with the hypnotist is set for this evening at six-thirty."

Mika glared at her sister, wanting to argue but realizing resistance was futile. Naomi knew she had the upper hand, but her eyes were soft and haunted, as if she took no pleasure in her advantage. Mika tried to temper her frustration. Naomi did not act out of malice, but from a long held and twisted belief she was protecting their family from harm. To let go of this belief would mean accepting the sad reality that she'd instead devastated them for no reason. Her deceit was born of desperation.

"Where's the meeting, back at that church?" Mika asked.

"Central Park. We couldn't get the church room. The hypnotist said outside is better, anyway. You and I can leave in the morning. I already told my management company I needed another day off."

"No, Naomi. We're leaving tonight after this meeting wraps."

Although Naomi quickly agreed, Mika couldn't fully trust her sister. She dreaded another attempt to indoctrinate her into a likely cult.

"Are you okay meeting up with Adrian and the three of us going together?"

Mika shrugged. "Whatever you want."

Naomi's expression chilled. "I wouldn't ask you to do this if I didn't think it would be good for you. This isn't easy for me either. It's never been easy. At least you had our family around."

As a kid, Mika rarely fought with Naomi. She'd idolized her too much. But Mika had nineteen years' worth of grief and bitterness frothing inside her now, and despite her efforts it suddenly bubbled over. "The family *you* left. And you did it in such spectacular fashion. Do you remember filling my head with all that garbage when you said goodbye? Do you remember the gruesome things you said to me? I was a kid!"

Naomi looked at her feet. "After witnessing so much horror, I wanted to scare you so you'd be careful."

"You terrified me and then you vanished." Mika imitated her sister, her voice shaking. "People are evil. The evil's inside them just waiting to be born! You better learn to protect yourself, cause I sure as shit ain't doing it!" She flailed her arms during the mockery, banging one into the medicine cabinet. A part of Mika was thirteen-years-old again, had always been thirteen, stuck in time inside a cloud of gravel dust.

"I've thought about those words every day," Mika continued. "Do you know I've never been in love? Not once. I had a meltdown on stage because too many people were looking at me, and I lost my career because of it. Do you know how ashamed I am all the time?"

Naomi's eyes narrowed. "How long have you had that fear?"

"I don't know." She tried to backtrack, already regretting the way she'd lashed out. "I'm sorry. I'm overtired and overstressed and shouldn't be blaming you for my problems. Everybody has them, right? Maybe it's just the card I drew." It was Mika's turn to look at her feet.

"Did you ever think it could be something else?" Naomi searched Mika's face, her gaze piercing. "I was an asshole for saying those things, a dumb kid who wanted to frighten you so you kept out of trouble. But what if it wasn't me who put that terror inside of you? What if something happened to you, something terrible you can't remember?"

"Enough of this." She shouldn't have confronted Naomi. Her sister wasn't well. "I need to brush my teeth and pack." Mika gestured for Naomi to give her some room.

Naomi backed out of the bathroom doorway. "You don't want to drag your luggage through the park. Leave it here, and we'll pick it up on the way to Port Authority."

Instead of feeling encouraged that Naomi verbalized her intention to go to the bus terminal later, Mika wondered if it was another manipulation. She shut the bathroom door and picked up her toothbrush. Her phone vibrated in her pocket. It was Callum. She let the call go to voicemail, then considered deleting his message without listening to it. She played it instead.

"Hi Mika, it's me. I just heard from Paige. Sorry to hear Art's not doing well. Paige says you're still in New York and you found your sister. That's wild, girl. Wish I could be there to show you around a bit. I could drive up there if you wanted. Take you to Times Square and 9-11 and all that. If you need help, need anything at all, let me know. I still care about you, Mika. Okay. Miss you."

Callum's voice provided her momentary comfort, a familiar sound from a previous life devoid of goggle-wearing aliens. But then a looming weight, another mountain of rock, bore down on her. She gripped the edges of the sink, her mind frantic and churning.

You're an idiot, she thought, waiting for the worst of the panic attack to pass. She could've avoided it altogether by switching her insomnia prescription to a local pharmacy instead of relying on the frenetic energy Master Blasters provided. After consuming the energy drink for breakfast, then a beer and a few peanuts, how did she expect to feel? She ran cold water over her wrists and prayed for strength. She hadn't felt this scattered since losing her wits at the Marriot Marquis.

Prior to that fateful day six months ago, her future looked bright—and not by accident. Mika had carefully followed her chosen career path for ten years. A few years out of college, she'd secured an analyst position with a hedge fund outside Philadelphia and put in two years of grueling fifty-five-hour workweeks before leaving to join Solstice Funds as an associate. The healthy bump in salary afforded her an apartment with a view of the Delaware River, and she stopped combing through the clearance racks at Burlington and TJ Maxx when she needed new clothes. She contributed to her 401k and started a travel savings account. She picked up the tab on the occasional night out with friends and started to feel like a success for the first time.

Mika had enjoyed her work too. The stock market was a great and fickle beast that reacted in real-time to rumors, earnings reports, and world news, sending cash flowing from one sector to another in a flurry of buying and selling. She'd studied these moving parts and how to capitalize on their symbiotic relationships. For seven years, she'd kept her head down and worked at Solstice, staying on track to make vice president and reach her goal of living a life without the financial struggles plaguing her parents and sister. Then came the Marriot Marquis fiasco.

After leaving the Marriot that awful day, Mika had walked to Penn Station and taken the train back to New Jersey alone. That same night, she'd received a cold and legally-worded email from human resources instructing her to obtain a physical and mental health evaluation before returning to the office. In Mika's reply email, she apologized for derailing the presentation and offered her immediate resignation. There was no further contact with HR. Just a packet in the mail with details of her expiring medical coverage.

You experienced a severe panic attack, her local doctor had told her the next day. *An extreme manifestation of perhaps the most common fear: public speaking. Your insomnia and the unfamiliar surroundings likely contributed to the outsized reaction.*

There were things she could do next time, the doctor assured her. Talk therapy. Toastmasters. There were beta blockers and benzos. Mika had nodded, understanding what the doctor did not. Finance professionals did not recover from alarming public spectacles. No one would trust her with their client's money again. There wouldn't be a next time.

Whenever anyone asked Mika for advice about investing in the stock market—not that it had happened much since her return to the Piney Mart—she would say get in and stay in, because the market usually rose to new heights over time. One only had to view its long-term performance to see most market crashes appear as blips on a chart reaching ever skyward.

Whenever her Marriot humiliation burned through her like brushfire, she brought herself out of it by believing everything happened for a reason. God had a plan. It was this hope she held onto in Naomi's bathroom. A hope that allowed her to compose herself, finish brushing her teeth, and wash her face. Despite feeling overwhelmed by her sister's subterfuge and delusions, Mika prayed that, with time, they would become mere blips in lives that turned out well for both of them.

11

—

"I could drive you back to Jersey in the morning," Adrian said when they reached the 72nd Street entrance to Central Park. Inside the park, bicyclists and pedestrians roamed freely on a roadway closed to car traffic. The returning sun warmed the surrounding grass, still muddy from the rain.

"That's so generous." Naomi said and turned to Mika.

"It is and thank you, but we have family expecting us tonight." Mika's smile felt tight.

They maneuvered around an expansive man-made pond. People stood around its borders operating miniature sailboats with handheld devices. A gangly heron perched on one leg atop a rock in the center of the water, blasé about the tourists taking its picture.

Mika spotted Ron waving his long arms at them across the pond, a giant in a cream-colored linen suit. He waited for them in front of a bronze sculpture of Alice sitting atop a giant mushroom, the Mad Hatter and White Rabbit at her feet.

"Where's Gracie?" Ron asked Naomi when they reached him.

"At the regression site with the hypnotist. I figured it was best for us to meet here and walk there together. I know the park pretty well, but it's easy to lose your bearings."

"Good idea," Ron said. "I'm not much of a park guy. Janice is always getting on me to start jogging. I got one strike against me already, she says, being so tall, because the big ones die sooner, like with dogs."

Mika cringed. *With a wife like that, who needs enemies?*

Naomi led them deeper into the park through a short tunnel inhabited by a young woman playing the violin, the elegant notes reverberating off the rounded stone walls. They passed a sprawl of ballfields and veered onto a path that bisected a playground and tennis courts, then led them to a greenspace populated with pine trees. The pine needles distilled the afternoon sun and bathed the area in a soft glow, reminding Mika of the barrens.

"There they are." Ron pointed to two women sitting on a colorful quilt, which was laid atop a blue tarp. Grace and her backpack were settled next to a woman with auburn hair styled in a corporate bob. *The hypnotist.* Mika had no expectations for this latest gathering, only a desire to get it behind her.

Mika and Adrian trailed Naomi and Ron to the garishly out-of-season red and green Christmas quilt. *At least it doesn't have UFOs on it. Be grateful for the small things.* Grace waved a friendly hello at them.

"Naomi!" Marcus appeared from behind a tightly bundled copse of trees, wearing seersucker shorts and a safari hat.

"You gotta be kidding," Ron said.

Mika nudged Naomi. "I thought you didn't tell him."

"I didn't." Naomi's forehead crinkled. "What are you doing here?"

Marcus gestured to the quilt, a wounded expression on his face. "You didn't invite me?"

Naomi didn't take the bait. "How did you find us?"

"I was out for my walk and saw Ronald across the pond," Marcus said. "It's hard to miss Ronald."

"Guys, hurry up! You're keeping the doctor waiting." Grace's gaze silently implored them to not embarrass her.

"Yes, please everyone," the hypnotist said, patting the ugly quilt. "This may not be seasonably appropriate, but it's comfortable and dry. Do take a seat and we can get started."

Ron took the longest to get settled. His bones creaked as he maneuvered himself onto the quilt, in the process revealing the top of his head, where his hair thinned to a galaxy-like spiral. Grumbling, he took off his linen jacket and loosened his tie, exposing the sweat stains on his white button-down.

"Now that we're all here," the hypnotist said, "let me introduce myself. I'm Dr. Laila Patel. As a certified hypnotist, I specialize in retrieving hidden memories and work mainly with individuals who suspect they are abductees. On a personal note, I consider my work with abductees to be my life's calling and am truly honored to be here with you today. I know Grace well. She's attended many of my seminars, is familiar with my book and case studies, and has spoken with me at length about her contactee experiences. Today, I'd like to hear from the rest of you. Let's go around, if that's all right, and say why you're here and what you hope to accomplish with your regression." Dr. Patel looked at Mika expectantly.

"I'm Mika. I've never seen a UFO, and I'm only here to support my sister." Vexed by once again having to address the group, she'd blurted it out somewhat defensively.

The hypnotist's face conveyed polite confusion.

"Mika's had missing time episodes since she was a kid," Naomi said.

"Denial ain't just a river," Ron loud-whispered to Grace, who giggled.

"I'm not in denial." Mika shot Naomi a dark look. "I have insomnia-induced blackouts on occasion. It's a genetic condition. Please move on. Thank you."

Dr. Patel shifted to Naomi.

"I'm Naomi. I can recall one abduction. While it was happening, I broke free of their control and hurt one of them. I want to understand exactly how I did that. I don't think they're taking me anymore, but if they ever do, I want to inflict as much damage as possible."

Grace tut-tutted her disapproval. Dr. Patel moved on to the lawyer.

"I'm Ron. I'm not sure if an E.T. ever got hold of me, but if so, I want to remember everything it did, get it out in the open, and stare it down. Tell my wife about it too, and close the distance between us. After listening to Naomi, I'll add taking a swing at one of them to my bucket list. That good enough?"

It was Marcus's turn to introduce himself, but he addressed Mika instead. "You're not an abductee. You've stressed that twice now. So, what are you doing here when I didn't get an invite?"

Mika regarded him coolly. "I just said why I'm here."

Marcus's mouth twisted. His eyebrows were two white caterpillars charging each other. "We're not circus animals, you know."

"Ease up," Naomi said. "She never said we were."

"Thank you, Naomi," Mika said. She smirked, hoping to further irritate Marcus and getting some much-needed pleasure out of doing so. His clinginess with Naomi reminded Mika of her own, which strengthened her disdain for him.

"Mika's just being honest," Ron said to Marcus. "I respect people that aren't full of shit."

Grace ducked her head, suppressing laughter. The hulking sixty-something lawyer and grad student made odd allies. Marcus crossed his arms like a sullen toddler.

Dr. Patel ignored the exchange and directed her inquisitive gaze to Adrian.

"I'm Adrian. Hi again, everyone. Like the rest of you, I also want to know if something I can't remember might be limiting me. I couldn't talk about it at the church earlier, but I think I'm ready to now."

The group made encouraging noises and Dr. Patel invited Adrian to say as much as he felt comfortable about his experiences.

Adrian cleared his throat. "When I was in high school my family lived in a cul-de-sac in a Connecticut suburb. One September night, not long after dusk, a bright-green light appeared outside our house. My brother saw it first through the living room window then called me over. I remember he sounded excited, but also scared. The green light hovered about fifteen feet over the street. It was big, but not huge, about the size of one of those smart cars people drive in the city because they're easy to park.

"Our next door neighbors went outside to get a closer look, and my little brother and I did too. Our parents weren't home. We all stood on our lawns staring at it for several minutes, trying to figure out what it was, then it simply blinked out of existence. And that's all that happened, I think. I'm not sure though, because after that night I changed."

Adrian shifted on the quilt. He spoke confidently, but Mika noticed a slight tremble in his chin.

"It happened the summer before my senior year," Adrian said. "I'd recently moved into the basement of our house and finally had my own room, which I loved. But for reasons I never understood and can't explain, I spent almost *all* my free time in the basement after seeing that green light. I didn't want to be around people anymore. Even my close friends made me uncomfortable. A twitch developed under my left eye, flaring up whenever someone got too close.

"My brother never had any social issues as far as I know. He played sports and went to parties, but I stayed in the basement as much as possible during my senior year and then through nursing school. Even now, when my shifts end and I take my gloves off, if someone brushes by me on the street or subway, my heart starts pounding, my eye starts twitching, and I want to jump out of my skin. Before the green light, I hugged my friends and family. I dated. I went to the movies and basketball games. I want to know what changed. Was there something about the green light? Did it give off radiation that affected my brain? Or did something else happen to me I can't remember?"

Adrian looked shyly at Naomi, who beamed encourage-ment at him. Their gazes locked in a way that caused Mika, feeling like an intruder, to look away.

The fine lines on Adrian's forehead deepened as he searched for the right words. "I have this unsettled feeling all the time, like I'm forgetting something crucial. You know those dreams about high school where the teacher hands out a test you're not prepared for? When your heart sinks? That's how I feel. Like I'm missing something vital, something I should know but forgot about."

Mika's clothes suddenly felt too tight. *Missing pieces. He has them too.*

Marcus giggled. "Maybe you are missing something. Your sperm."

Adrian looked irritated. "My...sperm?"

Marcus swiveled his head, looking for support. "I'm just *saying*, isn't that what they supposedly want, the aliens?"

Naomi leaned toward him. "Cut it out."

Marcus flushed. "For God's sake, we've all heard it before."

Dr. Patel piped in. "It's best not to interpret the experiences of other group members. Also, I don't believe there's a *singular* agenda when it comes to E.T.s. In all likelihood, there are multitudes. Nor do I believe there's only one species of extraterrestrials visiting us." She addressed Adrian. "Thank you for telling your story. And Grace, did you want to add something quickly?"

Grace, who'd been twirling a lock of her hair while listening to the doctor, placed both hands in her lap. "Thank you, Dr. Patel. Like everybody else, I want to retrieve as many memories as possible, but I don't believe there's malicious intent behind most abductions." Grace made eye contact with each member of the group, her gaze lingering on Naomi. "Please everyone, try to consider my words with an open mind. After studying hundreds of abductee reports, I believe E.T.s are trying to help us. They want to save humanity from destroying itself and the planet. I don't want to hurt them! I want to *know* them."

Naomi's jaw flexed, but she allowed Grace to have her say without comment.

Grace eyed the hypnotist. "I hope to one day publish my own research, like Dr. Patel, and help abductees live their best lives."

"If anyone can do it, you can, Gracie," Ron said and turned to Dr. Patel. "So, what can we expect during the hypnotic regressions? You doing everyone at once?"

"Oh, no. The actual regressions will take place one at a time under that cherry tree over there. It's far enough away to afford everyone privacy. After the last regression, we can discuss your experiences as a group if everyone agrees. You may want to support one another. Regressions are sometimes upsetting, but retrieving hidden memories is the *only* way to begin processing abduction trauma."

"I find it hard to fathom," Adrian said, "how something I don't remember can have power over me."

"It's important to understand," said Dr. Patel, "unremembered trauma is always present in the mind of an abductee. It subconsciously informs their choices, their sense of safety. It's why they continue to make self-destructive choices despite the best therapies. Abductees can unknowingly recreate their abduction trauma by placing themselves in relationships or situations where they experience helplessness, rage, or fear. Abduction trauma also manifests as chronic pain, difficulty sleeping, paranoia, and mood disorders. And again, without at least some abduction recall, it's unlikely any of these unfortunate side effects resolve on their own."

Naomi peered at Mika. She pretended she didn't notice and kept her focus on Dr. Patel, despite feeling frustrated with the hypnotist for backing up Naomi's delusions.

Naomi raised her hand. "Is chronic insomnia common among abductees with repressed memories?"

Dr. Patel nodded vigorously. "Oh, yes. Insomnia runs rampant in the abduction community. A strong fear of abandonment is also quite common. Any person, especially a child, taken against their will is deeply violated. Imagine how unprotected, how vulnerable one might feel on a subconscious level when their parental figures are unable to shield them from such an event.

"And then there's the abject terror of simply encounter-ing an extraterrestrial, even if no abduction takes place. During an encounter, one is confronted with an experience so outside their known reality that the paradigms they hold about the world don't just shift, they shatter. How do you trust a world that can disintegrate under your feet?

"Many abductees and witnesses struggle daily with severe anxiety, and they deal with it by maintaining a constant vigilance against perceived threats. They may exhibit abusive behavior or hyper fixate on people they rely on for a sense of safety, which can lead to extreme jealousy or even violence. Or they may create falsehoods about themselves that help them feel secure, such as believing they are invincible, immortal, have special powers, or are simply superior to others."

Naomi continued to direct solemn glances at Mika, as if some great truth had been revealed. Mika stewed with indignation. Naomi wanted her to believe their family had all been unknowingly traumatized by space boogeymen, wanted her to believe that's why their mom ended up in jail, why Paige monitored Bill's every move, and why Mika lost control during her presentation. *Why every one of us has insomnia.* Her sister wanted to manipulate her, to put bad thoughts in her head like she had when Mika was thirteen. *It's ludicrous*, Mika thought. *Laughably so.* How many people had difficult personalities or odd quirks? Were they *all* encountering extra-terrestrials? Is that seriously what this doctor, what Naomi, wanted her to believe? She kept her disdain to herself, remembering her mission: get Naomi home.

"Wait a second," Ron said. "I'm not violent or any of that crap. Those are the kinds of labels the outside world puts on people like us. I didn't think we'd hear them from you."

"I hate to say it," Marcus said, "but I agree with Ronald."

Unruffled, Dr. Patel lifted a manicured finger. "I only want to express the wide-ranging damage abductions inflict on the psyche. I'm not suggesting any of you are struggling with the more serious issues I mentioned. But if you are, it's certainly not anything to feel ashamed of. Quite the opposite. I think of abductees as warriors. They're some of the bravest people I've had the pleasure of knowing. And, again, it's my honor to be here with all of you. My sincere hope is that the regressions we do today will begin the process of allowing you to experience, and thus *integrate*, any hidden memories, and your lives radically improve as a result. Nothing would make me happier."

"Why wouldn't these aliens make their intentions known?" Mika asked as respectfully as she could.

Naomi turned to her. "Do research scientists explain themselves to mice before experimenting on them?"

"They wouldn't know how," Mika said. "No offense, but I'm asking the doctor."

"I would argue that we barely consider the mice," Dr. Patel said. "I'm speaking generally, of course, but we as humans are interested in our own purposes, and I believe E.T.s are too. But, as I mentioned, we shouldn't speak about E.T.s as a monolith. There's no reason to think there's only one alien agenda. Our universe is unfathomably vast and ancient. But given that abductees usually are not physically harmed, one could argue the protocols extraterrestrials appear to follow for their experiments—not inflicting serious tissue damage, blocking abduction memories, etcetera—are for lack of a better word, more humane than our own."

Everyone balked at this, except for Grace, whose head bounced in agreement like a dancing cockatoo.

"Sometimes language fails us," Dr. Patel said. "Now, I want all of you to trust I can safely lead you in and out of a vulnerable state, so before we begin the regressions, I'd like to conduct a short demonstration of group hypnosis, so you can get a taste of what I do."

Everyone looked to Naomi, who nodded.

"Excellent. Let's begin."

Dr. Patel had them close their eyes and take a series of deep breaths, relaxing each part of their bodies from the heels of their feet to the top of their heads. This took a while and Mika grew bored, and then uncomfortable, trying to control muscles she wasn't usually aware of. But soon enough, the constrictions inside her softened.

"You may have heard the term *third eye*," the doctor continued. "It's a spot in the middle of your forehead, close to where the pineal gland lies. Everyone, please, with your eyelids shut, look up at your third eye, up to the space in the middle of your forehead. While keeping your focus on this third eye, notice it's difficult to open your eyelids. You may be able to open them a little, but they quickly fall shut again. Now you can't open them at all, as if a weight is sitting on each of your eyelids holding them down."

This isn't so bad. Mika's eyelids did feel heavy, and they weren't popping open like they usually did when she tried to keep them closed.

"Now your third eye is beginning to open in the center of your forehead, and you see with it that you're standing next to a bench in a garden full of colorful flowers. The gentle fragrance of these flowers enters your nose. You breathe this fragrance in with each slow inhale, and you feel any remaining tension in your body drain away with every exhale. You're becoming so relaxed you want to sit down. Go ahead and take a seat on the bench. Notice how comfortable it feels, the wood carved to perfectly cradle you. You want to give thanks to your imagination, or any deity or higher power you believe in, for providing you with this garden, and so you clasp your hands together in prayer. Don't just imagine it. Go ahead and bring your hands together."

Mika brought her hands together blindly.

"Now you realize the palms of your hands and undersides of your fingers are made of a fast-drying concrete. This doesn't concern you, and you still feel completely at ease. Press your hands together a little tighter. At first, the concrete feels warm and mushy, but now you notice it's hardening, and your clasped hands are growing heavier—so heavy it's difficult to hold them up. You let them glide down to your lap, not like two hands pressed together anymore but rather one solid mass.

"Notice your third eye is beginning to close. The tiny muscles in your mind that hold it open are tired. As your third eye shuts, the garden around you fades to a peaceful darkness. Existing in this comfortable darkness, you notice your eyelids, your two physical eyelids, are starting to flutter open. Now they open all the way, and you're back with the group in Central Park."

Mika opened her eyes feeling refreshed, as if her lungs had expanded, allowing for more oxygen.

Ron strained to pull his hands apart but they remained together. "What the heck?"

Grace, too, gaped at her clasped hands.

Marcus tried and failed to free his palms. His face reddened. "This is outrageous!"

Naomi and Mika were the only ones able to unclasp their hands.

"Relax everyone," Dr. Patel said. "This hypnosis session will end in five seconds, and any concrete you feel on your hands will completely evaporate before we finish counting down from *five, four, three, two* and *one*."

Ron, Marcus, Adrian, and Grace all separated their hands.

Naomi frowned. "Why didn't it work for me and Mika?"

Because we're not that gullible? Mika thought. *Well, I'm not, at least.*

"Not everyone is easily hypnotized," Dr. Patel said. "It depends on one's ability to concentrate. An actual regression will bring you much deeper into a hypnotic state. The point of that exercise was to get you accustomed to being led into hypnosis and then safely taken out. For those who could not open their hands, do you believe your hands were actually cemented together with concrete?"

"Of course not," Marcus said. Grace, Ron, and Adrian conceded the same sentiment.

"Very good. As you've seen, a hypnotist can make a hypnotic suggestion, but when a subject is brought out of the session, the subject can identify the suggestion as separate from reality. The purpose of your regressions today is for you to retrieve memories, yes, but also to assist you in distinguishing your uncovered memories from any implanted, false memories."

Naomi looked agitated, furiously tapping one foot on the quilt. "What if Mika and I can't be hypnotized? Is there anything we can do?"

Too bad, Mika thought. *You're getting on the bus.*

Dr. Patel exchanged a glance with Grace. "Absolutely, there's something we can all do together."

12

—

"Drugs?" Marcus said. "You cannot be serious."

Dr. Patel's pleasant expression didn't waver. "Yes, drugs. The substances that save us from countless ailments and extend our life span by decades. But I believe your concern, Marcus, is with consciousness-altering drugs. This may surprise you, but several prominent people, CEOs, heads of tech companies, and the like, publicly endorse the use of nootropics to increase focus and creativity for themselves and their employees. Nootropics is an umbrella term for new drugs designed to target the brain, and I'd like your permission to administer a minute dose of such a drug to all of us today. This is something I've done before in group settings, as Grace can attest."

Grace's arm shot into the air. "I can and I do."

Dr. Patel addressed Naomi and Mika. "The nootropic may reduce your resistance to hypnosis by enhancing your ability to focus."

Mika wanted off the hideous quilt and out of the city as quickly as possible, but her sister listened carefully, her interest piqued.

"And it can enhance everyone's recall, which I believe is the goal here. My research shows ingesting nootropics disrupts certain brain processes—your regularly-scheduled programming, if you will—which enables abduction memories to surface. Many mind-altering substances create a shift in baseline consciousness, but nootropics do so in a more profound way, especially in therapeutic environments."

Ron elbowed Grace. "Maybe we should all head to a bar and have a few Appletinis."

Grace shushed him.

"Oh, but alcohol is a crude and dangerous suppressant leading to the deaths of almost three million people a year," Dr. Patel said, "unlike certain nootropics that have been used throughout the world for centuries with minimal harm. Practically no harm compared to alcohol."

"For centuries? I thought you just said they were new?" Marcus said.

The doctor hesitated, her smooth veneer slipping for the first time. "New in the form of nootropics."

Speaking of drugs, I wish I had a cold Master Blaster to get me through this. Mika wished Dr. Patel would get on with it.

"What exact drug do you want us to take?" Ron asked.

Dr. Patel cleared her throat. "The best nootropic for our purposes today is a microdose of lysergic acid diethylamide."

"LSD?" Ron said. "You shitting me?"

"I'm quite serious." Dr. Patel spoke quickly as if she was trying to get it all out before Ron staged a mutiny.

"Everyone will take the same conservative microdose of no more than ten micrograms of LSD, which is roughly ten percent of a recreational dose. You can expect to feel your mental faculties sharpen. The effect is subtle yet very useful during regressions. After you take the microdose, we'll all relax for about forty-five minutes to allow the medication to take effect, then I'll proceed with the regressions. The goal of this first regression is not to have all your abduction memories return in a big rush, but to simply begin the process."

Marcus scowled. "I don't like this. Using *acid* is not something that's ever appealed to me. I don't associate with people who do hard drugs."

"It's entirely your decision," Naomi said. "But you should probably leave if you're not participating."

Marcus gaped at Naomi. "Are you doing it?"

Naomi turned to the doctor. "We're not talking about hallucinating and all that, right?"

"Correct. The dose you'll receive is not even close to the amount needed to cause hallucinations."

"I'm down to give it a go," Naomi said. "What does the lawyer think?"

Ron rubbed his chin thoughtfully. "I did read something about Silicon Valley bigwigs doing that microdosing stuff. It's been in the papers."

"The papers." Grace giggled. She mimed holding out a cumbersome newspaper and turning the giant pages like it was the most ridiculous thing in the world.

"What do you think, Adrian?" Naomi asked.

Adrian addressed Dr. Patel. "Are there peer reviewed studies confirming the dosage is safe?"

"Yes, several."

"Then I don't see why not, if it can help us remember."

With Naomi and Adrian on board, the tension around Dr. Patel's mouth eased.

"I'd rather not be excluded again, so I'll participate, albeit reluctantly," Marcus said.

All eyes turned to Mika. She'd taken mushrooms a time or two in college and enjoyed herself. *No biggie.* A minuscule dose of LSD didn't scare her. And she could use it for leverage.

"Promise me," she said to Naomi, "in front of everyone, that you'll come home with me tonight if I do this."

"I already promised, but I'll do it again."

"Then I'm in."

"Excellent." Dr. Patel said. "Grace here is going to assist me by distributing water bottles to all of you. Each bottle is infused with a microdose of LSD. We'll finish our bottles then begin the regressions in forty-five minutes."

Ron accepted one of the mini bottles of Aquafina Grace took out of her backpack. When they each had a bottle, he counted down from three and they all drank. The water felt good going down Mika's throat, though not as good as her new favorite energy drink, and she didn't taste anything strange. Grace handed a glass vial to Dr. Patel.

Dr. Patel held the vial up and scrutinized it. "Oh dear, you spilled some."

Grace shook her head empathically. "No, I was careful not to."

"Then where did the excess go?"

"That is the excess, in the vial."

"Impossible. How much did you give them?"

"Ten drops, like you said."

"I said put one microgram in each water bottle."

Grace tilted her head. "Ten ughs is one microgram. So, ten ughs each. Ten drops per person."

"What are you talking about? An ugh, as you call it, is the symbol for microgram. *One* microgram."

"You said there are ten micrograms in each ugh."

"I said no such thing! There is one microgram in each ugh. They are the same exact measurement!" Dr. Patel thrust the vial in front of Grace, her painted fingernail tapping on the glass.

"Oh," Grace said quietly.

"You gave them ten micrograms." The doctor's voice shook with fury.

"What's going on, Doc?" Ron asked.

Mika let her head fall onto her folded knees, rethinking all the decisions that brought her to this point. She couldn't look at Naomi. *What's she gotten me into now?*

Dr. Patel spoke in a strange singsong voice. "I'm afraid Grace has administered the wrong dose." Beads of sweat formed on her upper lip. "A recreational dose as opposed to the microdose she was *supposed* to administer. The effects will build for about two and half hours before decreasing, but you'll be affected for five or six hours. We won't be doing the regressions today."

Grace withered like a cat in water, her face draining of color. "I'm sorry. I got mixed up."

Mika couldn't help but pity Grace, but she wanted to shake her too.

"Don't blame Grace," Ron said. "What kind of doctor leaves a kid in charge of making LSD water bottles, for shit's sake?"

"To be fair, I'm twenty-four," Grace said.

"Is there anything we can do to stop it from taking effect?" Naomi asked. "What if we ate something that absorbs liquid, like bread?"

"Can't we drink orange juice?" Grace said, desperate to redeem herself. "Doesn't vitamin C counteract the hallucin-ogenic effects?"

"I don't know," Dr. Patel said. "Google it."

Ron flicked a bug off his linen pants. "You *don't know*? I thought you were a doctor."

Dr. Patel's eyes shifted in her skull. "I have a doctorate."

Ron's mouth dropped open. "You're not an MD? No medical license? What's your Ph.D. in?"

"Comparative Literature."

Ron chuckled, nodding slowly like he had Dr. Patel pegged the whole time. "You have no medical background yet present yourself as a licensed hypnotist?"

"I never said I was a medical doctor." She narrowed her eyes at him. "Perhaps you were making assumptions. I presented myself quite clearly as a *certified* hypnotist. I have one hundred and fifty hours of training from an accredited online course of study," she said, clipping her consonants. "I won't be bullied by—"

"And you worked with John Mack?" Ron pressed on in full lawyer mode.

"Well, I was mentored by a disciple of his."

"A disciple? Who do you think Mack was, some kind of messiah? Let me get this straight, you know some joker who read about Mack on the internet and you got a hypnotist *certificate* watching YouTube videos? Lady, if anything happens to us, I'm going to sue you out of the stratosphere."

Grace sobbed. "Stop it, Ronny. This is *my* fault."

Mika nudged Naomi. "We're still taking that bus tonight. No matter what." She turned to the doctor. "The LSD will wear off by the time we get to South Jersey, right?"

"If you depart in around four hours, assuming it takes at least an hour to reach your destination, the effects of the LSD will be minimal. You'll still see light trails, but you won't be driving so that shouldn't be an issue. Don't drive at all until tomorrow."

"I say we make ourselves vomit," Marcus said.

Adrian sighed. "That won't work. A liquid dose metabolizes almost instantly."

Marcus grunted. "So says you."

"Yes, so says me. A nurse who actually works in the medical field."

Dr. Patel pursed her lips.

Grace, blotchy and pained, fumbled through her backpack and removed her phone. "I'll look up the vitamin C thing."

"Let's head to Port Authority," Mika said to Naomi, "and get situated closer to our bus before the LSD kicks in."

Naomi cautiously met her gaze. "If this gets freaky, the last place on earth we want to be is Port Authority."

We're way past freaky. Mika opened her mouth to protest, and Dr. Patel cut her off.

"It's better you both stay here. We should ride out the peak together so I can keep an eye on all of you, lead you through calming exercises if anyone gets...excitable. My tolerance for LSD is somewhat high from experimenting with microdosing, so I'll remain in control of my faculties. I should warn you, the dose we took is strong enough to cause hallucinations, yes, but it can also prompt abduction memories to spontaneously unleash even after the LSD wears off. Your brain will remain somewhat plasticized for a few days. Memories may return if you're somehow triggered or over-stressed. It could be...an overwhelming experience."

Marcus chuffed. "So taking LSD brings on abduction memories? What did we need you for then?"

"What I'm cautioning you about is a very different experience than a controlled regression on a microdose."

"Why are we still listening to this woman?" Ron asked. "She has no credibility."

Grace sniffled. "Stop it, Ronny. Leave her alone."

"You can stop kissing up to her, Grace. She's not going to *mentor* you after this," Marcus said, scowling.

Dr. Patel straightened her spine. "I understand you're all upset, but if we don't remain peaceful and unified, this situation will be far harder than it needs to be."

13

—

Ron felt the effects of LCD before anyone else—odd, given his size. With the sun sagging in the orange sky behind him, he talked about his wife, audibly grinding his teeth between sentences. "I have to call her, tell her I got dosed. I can't keep this from her, too. Communication and honesty are the keys to intimacy, that's what our couple's counselor says."

Ron's eyes flitted around, drawn to the slightest movement. Mika suspected he wanted to call Janice to come save him rather than out of some truth-telling duty. *Not that I blame him.*

"She's gonna be pissed." His jaw flexed and gnashed. "But we rise together and fall together, Janice and I. When one of us is in trouble, the other takes a dive, too. Like eagles. You guys ever see that? You ever see two eagles on the ground?"

"Ron, chill," Grace said. "You're starting to freak out."

"Let him speak." Dr. Patel said. "Ron, tell us about the eagles."

Gnash. Gnash. "It was the damndest thing. I was in Yosemite with Janice on our honeymoon, and we almost

136

tripped over these two beautiful bald eagles. A male and female, both knocked out on the ground with their claws locked together. Janice believes in signs; she's superstitious like that. When the eagles came to and flew off, she said seeing them meant we're a team. That if life sucker punches one of us, the other helps shoulder the blow, whether it brings us both down or not. No bailing out ever. Ride or die.

"Eagles mate for life. They test each other's moxie by grasping their claws together in the air then tumbling toward the earth. They usually let each other go before they hit the ground, but sometimes they don't and get injured, or worse. It's called a death spiral." Ron's eyes ping-ponged around the group. Although he'd rolled up his sleeves and unbuttoned the top buttons of his shirt, sweat oozed out of him, gluing the fabric to his skin. "I gotta call Janice. I need to talk to my wife."

Grace tried joking with him to get him to relax, and Mika thought she might succeed until Ron asked, his gruff voice wavering, why the trees were breathing. Then Mika noticed the quilt they sat on was also breathing.

They were only forty minutes in.

Nothing any of them said, even Grace's pleading, could dissuade Ron from calling Janice. After speaking to her, Ron announced she was coming to pick him up. He implored the group to go along with the ruse they were in a running club together and had taken the nootropics to enhance their endurance for an afternoon run.

Marcus snickered. "Lying to Janice, Ron? I thought communication was the key to intimacy."

Ron was too shaken to clap back at him. "I can't dump the UFO stuff on her, too. How much can a woman take?"

"No one says UFO anymore," Grace murmured. "They're called UAPs now."

"We're not dressed to run," Dr. Patel said. "How about a walking club?" The hypnotist still emanated a trace of authority. "Let's all focus on something else until Janice gets here, perhaps get to know each other a bit better."

The group was situated in a haphazard semicircle facing Dr. Patel. Naomi sat between Mika and Adrian, and when she leaned back on her elbows, Adrian asked Mika how she was holding up.

"I'm feeling kind of groovy. You?"

Adrian laughed. "You could pick some flowers, put them in your hair? Do people still believe in peace and love, or did that die out with the sixties?"

"I think the Manson Family put the nail in that coffin."

"Speaking of family, do you have any other siblings?"

"Another sister."

"What's she like?"

"She's married, has a child in college. We don't have much in common besides the store and our parents, which is to be expected, I guess, since she's twenty-three years older than me."

"Really?" Dr. Patel interjected. "What an interesting dynamic."

Everyone trained their eyes on Mika. "We love each other, but I'm not sure we like each other that much."

"Does she still get worked up over those summer girls shopping at the store?" Naomi asked.

"You remember that?" An electric optimism flowed inside Mika, almost like a shot of Master Blaster, turning her into a more light-hearted, social version of herself. Naomi and Adrian looked good together, she thought. More than good, gorgeous, as if enhanced by the most flattering of Instagram filters.

Naomi grinned. "Who could forget?"

"Yep, she's still at it," Mika said. "Her second husband doesn't seem to mind. I'm pretty sure he likes it. His name's Bill. You'll meet him later."

Adrian leaned toward Mika, intrigued, his dilated pupils beginning to overpower his brunette irises. "What does she do to husband number two?"

Mika felt a little icky talking about Paige behind her back. "Nothing too serious. She spends a lot of time and energy patrolling his interactions with women."

Adrian's brows arched comically high. "Is he known to stray?"

"No." Mika wondered how to explain her sister's possessiveness when she didn't understand it herself.

"I'd say Paige's jealousy issues were pretty darn serious." Naomi had a strange look on her face. "Can I speak freely in front of everyone?"

"Go ahead," Mika said. *What now?*

"Mika's four years younger than me, and there are things she doesn't know about our older sister. Things our family didn't think she should know. Paige got into some trouble when Mika was just a few years out of diapers. She racked up a series of restraining orders and harassment charges from men she dated, most of which I learned about eavesdropping on her fights with our parents."

Mika laughed. "I don't know what you think you heard, but I assure you Paige's behavior never escalated to the point of retraining orders."

"It did, Mika. And that wasn't the worst of it."

"You haven't seen Paige in nineteen years. Why are you making her sound like some kind of obsessive criminal?"

"Do you remember her first husband, Miguel?" Naomi asked.

"Vaguely."

"So, you don't know why he left."

"I do know. Paige put a tracking device on his car." Mika's cheeks burned. Saying it out loud did make it seem pretty outrageous. She addressed the group. "Miguel had a friend, a woman, who emailed him an invite to a party, and my sister, assuming the worst, replied and accused her of being a homewrecker. She was convinced Miguel was cheating on her."

"She did more than make accusations," Naomi said. "Paige threatened her life. And the following night, someone set that woman's car on fire. The cops suspected Paige, but they couldn't prove she did it."

Mika gaped at her. "There is no way I wouldn't have known—"

"There's more you probably don't know. Mom also had episodes over the years. One time, I went to ShopRite with Mom, and she tried to snag one of the last remaining Thanksgiving turkeys. This elderly man, real ornery, hip-checked her and grabbed the turkey she wanted. When we finished our shopping and got in the expedited checkout line, the same man was in front of us unloading way too many items on the counter. Mom told him he was in the wrong line, and he asked her what she was going to do about it.

"She reached over and threw his items back into his cart. Whipped them in there hard enough to break a jar. A piece of glass shot out and grazed the cashier's hand. The cashier knew Mom from the Piney Mart, so they didn't call the cops, but we were escorted out by the manager after paying for the man's groceries."

"Okay, so it was an accident," Mika said. "Mom didn't mean—"

"And another time, I was in the car with Mom waiting for a parking space to open up in front of Ocean Shade Cinema. A carload of teenagers swooped in and stole the spot, and she started screaming at them out her car window while they walked to the theater, calling them all kinds of names, until one threw an empty Slurpee Cup at her windshield. It bounced off the car, no damage done, but she stomped the gas pedal and headed straight at them. They had to dive out of the way on the pavement. They probably got scraped up pretty bad, but Mom didn't stick around to find out. We went home, and she didn't stop shaking for hours. If something like that happened nowadays, with cameras everywhere, she would have done time."

Mika was dubious, and more than a little annoyed at the picture Naomi was painting of their mother. "Mom's not some volatile outlaw. Are you sure you're not retro-labeling her as such, perhaps exaggerating, after seeing her in the Bat Lady video?"

Adrian's lips parted in surprise. "Your mother's the Bat Lady?" He caught himself. "She shouldn't have spent a day in jail. That she was charged at all is a travesty."

Naomi powered on. "Remember that guy I dated, you said he looked like a thumb?"

"Ricky the Thumb," Mika said. "I wasn't that young when you two dated."

"You were young enough that we wanted to shield you."

"From what?"

Do I really want to know?

"From the worst of mom's rage episodes, the one that dwarfed them all, until the Bat Lady stuff, I guess. Ricky had an older ex-girlfriend, a hardass type named Sunny who once bit a guy's finger half-off on the boardwalk. Sunny banged on the door of the main house one night, fresh out of juvie. She swung at me the moment I opened the door.

"You were doing homework in your bedroom at the main house. I don't think you heard Sunny and me fighting, but Mom did. She tore down the steps holding Dad's shotgun. She saw my bloody lip and the place a mess and let loose a string of profanities so blue I remember blushing. Then she aimed the gun at Sunny and pulled the trigger. No hesitation. The blast obliterated the tip of Sunny's right ear and blew holes through the living room wall into the kitchen. You shouted down the stairs—"

Mika gasped. "And Mom said Dad's truck backfired and to get back in my room and finish my homework or she'd come upstairs and whoop my ass. It was the only time she ever threatened me like that. Scared the hell out of me."

"Yep," Naomi said. "Sunny knew she was outmatched and left, gripping her leaking ear. She sprinted down the road with Mom bellowing after her. Sunny picked up her truck outside the Piney Mart in the middle of the night, and none of us heard from her again. Dad hung a watercolor of Barnegat Lighthouse over the blast holes in the living room and a skillet over the holes in the kitchen."

The painting, the skillet, they're both still hanging there. Yet Mika still doubted her sister's claims. There might be *some* truth to them, but Naomi had twisted things in her mind. *After all, Naomi says a lot of dubious things.*

"I hope that wasn't too much at once." Naomi released a shaky laugh, eyeing Mika nervously.

"Good thing you got yourself out of there," Marcus said, "and away from those people."

"You should see your eyes," Mika said to Naomi. "You're tripping hard." They settled into a tense staring contest which Naomi won.

The group dropped the subject of Crane family dysfunction and circled back to Janice's impending visit. Ron grew quiet, examining his hands, and Grace and Dr. Patel tried gently to engage him. Naomi and Adrian, reclining on their elbows, appeared content to watch the sunset and simply be close to one another.

The LSD wasn't so bad. Aside from the quilt breathing, Mika had yet to see or feel anything outrageous, only the glowy filter over her eyes, increasingly, around her heart. But something nagged at her as she took in the vibrancy of the park. She didn't think Paige would ever physically hurt someone, but the more she thought about it, the more it seemed plausible her sister had lit that poor woman's car on fire. A strange simmering occupied her head as the LSD took stronger hold. *Think positively or you're in for a bumpy ride.* She swept thoughts of Paige aside.

Mika's phone vibrated. Callum texted her a picture of his shirtless and pouty reflection from what looked like the bathroom at his precinct. Mika showed the picture to Adrian and Naomi.

"Thought you two were done," Naomi said.

Adrian chuckled. "A bathroom mirror photo. Not lazy at all."

"He probably sent it to me by mistake," Mika said. "I'm sure there's a rotation he goes through."

Adrian grinned mischievously. "Even more reason to send him back a super shitty one. No head though."

Mika smirked. "I am feeling kinda loose."

"Do it up like one of them summer girls," Adrian said.

"Or don't," Naomi suggested.

"Here I go!" Mika bent over and used her cell phone to snap a picture inside the V-neck of her t-shirt. Blood rushed to her head, and she let the dizziness pass before viewing her self-portrait: an unflattering, veiny picture of her cleavage, harshly lit by the camera flash. "One for the ages." She showed the picture to Adrian, who proclaimed it a work of high art.

Naomi waved Mika's phone away, scandalized.

"Send it," Adrian said to Mika.

"He does have it coming."

"Do it!"

"Done."

They giggled like tweens in sex education class. *LSD is kind of fun.*

Mika's phone vibrated almost immediately, tickling her palm. "I can't look." She handed it to Adrian.

"He said SO HOT, all caps, with three exclamation points and three tongue emojis." Adrian's wheezing laughter sounded like a car motor trying to start, which struck Mika as hilarious. The two of them laughed so hard they could barely breathe.

Marcus's face twisted in annoyance. "Are you two laughing at me?"

Adrian looked at Marcus as if seeing him in a new, less objectional light. "No! Of course not. Scoot over, come join in the fun."

What a buzzkill.

Marcus scooted. "And what is it you do, again? Forgive me, I don't recall your name." He pinched and released the flesh on the back of his hand, as if studying the elasticity of his skin.

Adrian's smile dimmed. "I'm a nurse."

Marcus grimaced. "Dealing with all those bodily fluids and such. Seems awful."

Grace popped her head up from her wilted position next to Dr. Patel. "Have you ever seen a dead body?"

"Grace, that's not appropriate," Dr. Patel said, and Grace's head floated back down.

Ron emerged from his malaise to stick up for Grace. "Lots of things are not appropriate about the mess we're in, lady."

Marcus shuddered. "I'm sure he sees dead bodies all the time."

"Patients do die in the hospital," Adrian said, "and yes, I see them, but I also see people fight and survive. I see them live."

Marcus's mouth drooped further. "Many of them die alone, don't they?"

From Mika's perspective, both Marcus and the sound of his voice were growing incrementally smaller. *Either he's shrinking or I'm getting larger,* she thought. *I must be rolling.* The theme song to an ancient TV western came to mind. *Rolling, rolling, rolling, rawhide!*

Adrian lifted his chin, considering Marcus's words. "I wouldn't say they're alone. There are medical staff and volunteers nearby. Ideally, their loved ones are there too, but that's not always possible."

Grace raised her head again. "It's hard to imagine a person close to me dying. I've never lost anyone. I wouldn't know what to say to them."

"Which is normal," Adrian said. "That's why we have counselors at the hospital who offer advice if needed. One suggestion they give to patients and their loved ones is to say to one another, 'I forgive you. Do you forgive me?'"

"What a lovely and touching anecdote," Dr. Patel said, glancing at Grace. "Thank you for sharing, Adrian."

"I died once, in a pool." Mika instantly regretted her words. Her warm fuzzies evaporated. She'd never told anyone what she experienced the day of the accident, and now she'd blurted it out in front of the group. In front of *Naomi.*

14

—

Naomi squinted at her, baffled. "Mika, you didn't die. Why would you say that?"

Mika wanted to dig a hole in the damp soil beside the tarp and throw herself into it. "Never mind. It's not a big deal."

Marcus scoffed at that. "*Dying* isn't a big deal?" Grace and Dr. Patel shushed him.

"I'm babbling. Forget I said anything." Mika wanted to shield her sister from the knowledge of her brief, accidental death.

"Go on, Mika. It's okay," Naomi said. "You can talk about that day. Say whatever you want. I won't interrupt again."

Mika stared back at her, a wide-eyed mute, and the silence between them became a tangible, porous thing. *The silence is breathing.*

Naomi kickstarted the conversation by addressing the group. "When Mika and I were young, we went swimming and I had my one and only abduction memory. I panicked and started swallowing water." Her voice took on the slightest quiver. "I wasn't aware of doing it at the time, but I pushed her under the water."

Adrian touched Naomi's back, and she gave him a grateful smile before he pulled his hand away.

"We don't have to talk about this," Mika said. "Not here and now."

Marcus rolled his eyes. "Then why did you bring it up?"

"Gee, I don't know, maybe because I'm on LSD?" She couldn't wait to never see him again.

"It might be helpful to discuss this event, Mika, but only if you're comfortable doing so," Dr. Patel said.

Although Naomi bobbed her head encouragingly, Mika could almost see the pain and guilt rippling out of her sister in waves, distorting the air around her. She felt it too, shrieking and hollow. *LSD is wild.* Surely, Naomi would feel better knowing Mika had encountered something beautiful in that pool. It might even be healing. She opened her mouth then closed it again, unsure how to describe a mystical experience that transcended mere language.

"Where were the two of you swimming?" Grace prompted.

"Our local pool," Mika said. "Naomi and I spent the whole summer in either the pool, ocean, or quarry. We practically lived in the water."

Mika could recall their visits to the quarry with perfect clarity: the two of them floating contently atop the cold, dark abyss; their faces warmed by the summer sun, a heat and light that couldn't penetrate the fifty-foot-deep water beneath them. The pool was warmer and easily accessible, though not as awe-inspiring.

When the accident happened, the Ocean Shade community pool had doubled as a training center for an NCAA swimming championship. A few salty locals resented their reduced pool hours and referred to the interlopers as the National Collection of Aquatic Assholes. In the mornings, kids gathered outside the Olympic-size mecca to watch college swimmers pull their triangular torsos out of the pool. Then the coach's assistant would unhook the lane ropes and wind them into large wheels.

"Don't public pools have lifeguards?" Marcus said the word *public* with disdain.

"Yes, and she pulled us both out," Mika said.

The day she drowned, the water felt warmer than the cool June air. The pool wasn't as crowded as other, hotter mornings, but it stayed busy enough for the lifeguard to blow her whistle every few minutes. The whistles, though loud, had blended into the background clamor of kids roughhousing in the water and parents yelling at their children to stop running and put sunblock on.

"The lifeguard stepped away to get a first-aid kit," Naomi said quietly. "Some kid skinned his knee. That's why it took her so long to get to us."

Ron blew a low whistle. "Shitty timing."

Enamored with the idea of becoming a swim coach herself, Mika had busied herself that morning in the pool teaching one of the younger kids to use a kickboard. When she noticed Naomi thrashing in the deep end, she swam over to her, sure her sister was faking it and up to something. But after getting close enough to see the manic yet absent look in Naomi's large, red eyes, Mika reached out to grab one of her sister's thrashing arms, and Naomi latched on to her with a bruising grip.

"Mika tried to help me, but I was so out of it I didn't know she was there."

"It wasn't your fault," Mika said.

Naomi's frantic limbs had only Mika to use for leverage, pushing Mika under before she could suck in any air. Chlorine burned Mika's eyes by the time she registered the urgent need to breathe. Mika fought her way to the surface, clawing at Naomi with water-softened nails, gasping hoarsely when she managed to break the surface. Naomi's eyes were rolled back, the whites reddened by broken vessels—blood eyes that looked right through her. Naomi pushed her under again, her fingers tangling in Mika's hair, her legs kicking the last traces of air out of her lungs. The pressure in Mika's chest grew excruciating. Her heart roared in her ears. And then, quite suddenly, her lungs no longer felt like hot lung-shaped coals, and her perspective changed.

"After I went under," Mika told the group on the quilt. "I couldn't breathe. Couldn't get to the surface. It was scary, yes, but then something shifted inside me, like a *click* at the bottom of my throat. The pain in my chest vanished, and so did my fear. And something was there with me, a presence that felt familiar and loving."

"Like an angel?" Grace asked.

"Maybe." Mika was hesitant to use the word God. She didn't want to sound unstable. *The irony.* "I saw my body lying face-up at the bottom of the pool, my hair floating around my head. I remember thinking I needed a haircut. No bubbles escaped my nose or mouth, so I knew I was dead. Or that my body had died, I should say. I remember thinking my body must be heavy with water to anchor itself like it did. I wasn't afraid, though. I felt at peace."

Dr. Patel leaned toward her with keen interest. "You said the presence felt familiar. How so?"

Again, Mika struggled. How could she describe such an intimate connection? "I'd felt it before, many times, but in a subdued form, more like a peaceful feeling that came over me when I needed it most, a reassurance that I'd get through whatever was happening in my life. But in the pool, the feeling was…tangible, intense. I knew it was a presence and not just a feeling. I didn't see a tunnel or anything like that. I only saw my body, and I felt this presence offer me a choice. I could join it, if I wished, or go back to my normal life.

"I don't recall making a decision, but somehow I reentered my body, and the next thing I knew the lifeguard yanked me out of the water. I immediately threw up on the side of the pool. But even while puking, a big part of me wanted to be back in the water with that presence." She turned to Naomi. "As horrible as that day was for both of us, it was a turning point. It gave me faith that there's more to our existence than just this world and its chaos. And I'm grateful for that. It really helps, I think, to have faith."

Dr. Patel clasped her hands together. "Fascinating. I've read about near-death experiences, but hearing a firsthand account is powerful. Thank you, Mika."

Most of the group murmured their agreement, except for Marcus who sucked his cheeks.

It felt cathartic to finally share her story, and Mika's negative feelings, even toward Marcus, waned. *Maybe these people are Naomi's found family*, she thought, *and so what if they are? Is that so bad?*

Then Naomi cocked her head at an odd angle. "Remember those aluminum squares? They were called *swim mirrors*. The NCAA coaches placed them on the pool's floor, at the end of each lane, so swimmers could check their form when approaching the wall. After practice, they were lined up poolside and hosed off, but sometimes one or two were left in the water by mistake. Mika, I think you saw your reflection at the bottom of that pool, not your body."

Surprisingly, Mika's defenses did not rise. She took in what her sister said and accepted it could be possible. *And that's okay*, she thought, pleased with how she digested the information, how she could study it, as if from afar, without reacting in a knee-jerk fashion. Maybe there had been a mirror at the bottom of the pool. But even if she wasn't out of her body, a mirror could not explain why she no longer needed to breathe. The unmistakable presence she felt and heard.

"I'm not trying to be a jerk," Naomi said. "I just want you to know the truth about that day and everything else you've been through."

"I understand. We can talk more about it when we're not, you know, tripping. But for the record, I'm still right and you're wrong." Mika stuck her tongue out and Naomi laughed. Everyone did, relieved the loaded conversation ended on a good note.

Everyone except dreary Marcus. "People can be dead for months before they're found."

"Would you like to share, Marcus?" Dr. Patel asked.

Marcus had grown so pale his complexion nearly blended with his shock of white hair. "Their bodies aren't discovered if no one's around to miss them. Especially if the deceased has their expenses paid by direct debit. They sometimes stay undiscovered for years if their bank account is large enough. When these bodies are eventually located, they're placed in a drawer at the morgue while investigators like me look for any next of kin. The same relatives who neglected them are the first to line up with their hands out, hoping to collect whatever equity remains in their accounts and property." Marcus trailed his mournful eyes over each of them. "I did that job for thirty-two years."

"Explains a lot," Ron said, and Grace chewed on her lip.

Naomi and Dr. Patel thanked Marcus, and no one asked any follow up questions. The group quickly moved on to other topics, but Marcus's words infected the mood, dissolving the sense of shared reverie. The sunset dragged on, and events began to transpire for Mika as if broadcast on a wonky screen that morphed everyone into clownish versions of themselves.

Ron's wife showed up. She loomed over them with her hands on her hips, frowning with disdain at the Christmas quilt. Fiercely blonde and tan, Janice wore multiple diamond rings on her fingers, and despite her petite frame, she exuded herculean strength. Her eyes grew razor sharp as Grace and Dr. Patel attempted to parrot Ron's claims the group was a "walking club" that had accidentally overdosed on endurance-building nootropics. Like six-year-olds unable to keep a straight face, Mika, Naomi, and Adrian giggled whenever they looked at each other. Marcus sat hunched and scowling.

"What are you doing with these idiots?" Janice asked her saucer-eyed husband. She snapped her fingers, demanding Ron's hand, her glittery nail polish shooting sparks into the air. The chains around her neck shone like rivers of gold before disappearing into her sun-weathered décolleté.

Janice glared at Mika. "What are you staring at?"

"It's nice to meet you," Mika said, intimidated as hell.

Ron took his wife's hand, and his bones creaked and popped as he got to his feet. "Thank God you came. Get me out of here."

"You're gonna break my fingers." Janice craned her head back to look at her husband. "What the fuck were you thinking? I don't like the look of these people."

"They're not bad, hon," Ron said. "They're a little messed up, that's all."

Mika watched the scene unfold, her brain starting to sizzle like eggs in a frying pan, more specifically the eggs in the *This is your brain on drugs!* commercial from her childhood.

"Maybe it's time, Ron," Naomi said, her expression oddly bright. "Time to tell Janice everything."

Naomi's in the frying pan, too.

Grace clapped her hands, applauding the idea. "Tell her the truth, Ronnie!"

Dr. Patel implored the group to let Ron and his wife leave peacefully, desperate to keep the situation under control.

Janice pulled on Ron's arm. "Tell me at home. Let's go."

Ron said he wasn't sure he could walk, that his feet hurt.

"So much for your walking club," Janice said. "Take tiny steps."

Ron tiny-stepped several yards away from the quilt on the wet grass before asking his wife if he was going to die.

"Not until you sober up and I kill you."

The group watched Janice lead Ron slowly toward the ballfields.

"You're going to be fine, Ronald!" Dr. Patel called out, as if trying to convince herself. Her stick-straight posture bowed, her smile drooped, her pupils bulged. "He's going to sue me. My life is over."

Janice shot a few death glares at the hypnotist before she and Ron melted into the distance.

"He won't be the only one suing you," Marcus said. He poked at one of the colorful ornaments stitched into the fabric of the quilt, delighted by something only he could see.

"I'll make sure Ronny doesn't sue," Grace said.

Dr. Patel swiveled toward her. "Really? You'll do that?"

"He'd do anything for me. I'm like a daughter to him."

Dr. Patel moved closer to Grace, and the two women began whispering to one another.

Mika's attention landed on the section of quilt Ron no longer unoccupied, then she jumped to her feet, pointing. "The eagles!"

At the end of the quilt lay two majestic bald eagles, their white heads and brown bodies dwarfed by their massive, outstretched wings. Even in death they were stunning, talons joined in a final embrace. Mika's brain sizzled and popped.

"Mika, look at me," Dr. Patel said. "That's Ron's blazer on the blanket. He was sitting on it and forgot to take it home. Sit down. You are hallucinating."

Mika turned to Naomi. "Can't you see them?" Her sister's gaze followed Mika's finger, then Naomi's face twisted in horror. Mika turned back to the eagles, and she knew she now saw them as Naomi had: no longer majestic but with twisted, broken legs and shorn-off beaks parted in a soundless cry. Mika backed away from the quilt, away from Naomi and the birds.

Mika felt her sister's dark burdens, an invasive dread rising up from Naomi to smother her too. Panic gripped her, and she ran toward the fading sun.

15

—

Mika ran for what seemed like long time. The ugliness on the quilt began to feel like a lifetime ago, and she basked in the lush beauty of the park. She could hug a tree, she thought, as she trotted along. *I could be one of those people.*

Then the wet grass beneath her sandals turned to dirt. She'd outrun the trees, and now the naked sky became a sudden terror of red. A cacophony of voices erupted around her, and the low sun blinded her. She ran into something solid and warm; leather brushed her cheek before she lost her balance and fell to one knee. A globular shape rolled toward her. The stitches on the ball looked like scars on flesh. She stood and kicked the ball away. It rolled briefly before coming to a stop and leering at her, both dead and alive.

A man's voice rang out. "Time out!" She followed the voice and found the man, pot-bellied, bearded and holding Naomi's softball bat in his hands, ALL-STAR CHAMPS printed in green and gold along the barrel. No, the bat was silver and metal and not painted at all.

Two men wearing baseball gloves approached Mika and asked if she was okay, their clownish faces pinched with concern. She ran from them, leaving the dirt field behind, finding a path that led her through a cluster of tall trees. This new escape reenergized her. Laughing now, she sailed past a stream of people and dogs then slipped through an opening in a short mesh fence and hustled down a muddy hillside, stopping on a footbridge to catch her breath.

Should I go back? Naomi will worry. She balked at the thought of the cursed quilt and decided to find somewhere safe to wait out the worst of the LSD. Mika patted the back pocket of her cotton pants. She had her phone. She could call Naomi and explain she needed a little space.

Mika peered over the side of the footbridge, searching for a place of refuge. She spotted a muddy path that led down an embankment to a delightful wooden gazebo on the edge of an emerald green lawn enclosed by a crescent of trees.

Infused with drug-fueled wonder, she gaped at the ethereal scene. She'd run from Naomi and the monstrosity on the quilt. But now she yearned for Naomi to join her, and to bring Adrian along. The three of them could hang out on the tucked-away gazebo until it was time to catch the bus.

She made her way down the sloping path to the gazebo. Could the grass be that green in drug-free reality? She'd take a picture of it with her phone, Mika decided, and look at it later.

Raising her phone, she stepped from the gazebo's planked floor and off the edge of the world. She heard herself yelp before she was completely submerged in water that shot painfully up her nose. She flailed back to the surface, retching, and stood in the slimy water, shock penetrating her drug haze. The water settled at the base of her shoulder blades, and her circumstances were clear: rather than stepping onto an emerald lawn, Mika had fallen into a pond coated in green algae.

Gasping, she stepped backward and instantly lost both her sandals. The mucky bottom sucked hungrily at her bare feet, and above her, a kaleidoscope of slanted light trails traced the path of the setting sun. She braced for a panic that did not come. The temperature of the pond and air felt exactly the same on her skin, which added to the sense of weightlessness the water provided. She felt pleasantly light, refreshed even, despite the pond's faint gasoline smell. *I'm okay. I'm not hurt.*

Without the full force of gravity to ground her, Mika's place in time and space grew malleable as the hallucinogenic effects of the LSD peaked. Was she even in New York City, she wondered, or was she back in her cottage? She *could* be home, it seemed, back in her bed amid a fever dream, a wall of pitch pines outside her window. She could almost feel the pillow under her head, could sort of see Callum next to her, hear his growling snores. No, she was moving, she felt sure of it, not lying down. Was that soft sugar sand beneath her feet instead of pond muck? Was she walking through the pines, calling her dad's name?

Rolling, rolling, rolling, rawhide!

Eventually—she had no idea how much time had passed—the sound of children's voices reoriented her to her surroundings. Two clown children ran down the path toward the gazebo, coming to a stop when they saw Mika gawking at them from the water. They screamed and hightailed it back up the embankment, melting and gleaming in impossible ways. An unseen woman screeched at them to slow down.

Mika attempted to pull herself onto the gazebo, but her muscles felt rubbery and numb. She hung limply to the edge, exhausted, and rested her cheek against the slimy wood, which really wasn't so bad. She imagined the bus she and Naomi would later board, polished to a shine: a jewel in the belly of Port Authority, waiting for them like an old friend. A friend that *cared*. This pond mishap, the LSD, they were blips, for sure, but she shouldn't overact.

She could sense God's presence in the water, in her body, and throughout the vast cosmos. Everything would be okay, she knew. There was a plan for her, for every soul, and all would turn out as it should. She'd share that message when she got out of this mess. *Stop beating yourself up*, she'd tell people. *You're neither lost nor alone. God is with us all.* She imagined herself conveying this message with convincing eloquence to New Yorkers on the street, their shoulders dropping from their ears as their hearts opened.

Mika reached into the pocket of her cotton pants, retrieved her dripping phone, and placed it on the platform. Tapping the screen with one finger, she could hardly believe it when it glowed to life. Despite the sky's encroaching darkness, this victory thrilled her. Miracles were everywhere.

Mika tried Naomi, but her call went to voicemail. Then the sun began its final descent, and her exuberance waned. Panic poked around her borders, searching for a way in. She considered her options, battling to stay calm. If she managed to pull herself from the water, she couldn't walk through Central Park soaking wet and covered in muck. Even in a city where minding one's business was the law of the land, her condition would attract attention. What would happen if someone called the cops about the weird lady covered in algae and mud? Surely an involuntary escort to a hospital.

The face of Ari the taxi driver popped into her mind. *You need a ride, you can call me and I'll pick you up.* What was his 800 number again, something like RIDENYC? She tapped a couple of possible combos into her phone before getting a connection. It rang twice.

"This is Ari."

"Hi, it's Mika! I need a ride. You said to call if I did. Remember me from a few days ago? The woman with the large eyes? I said they were all the better to see you with. You pegged me for a tourist because of my white shoes? Listen, I know this sounds strange, but I'm in a pond next to a wooden gazebo, sort of hidden under a footbridge in Central Park. I tried to get out, but I'm stuck. I think there's quicksand in here. Quicksand is still a thing; can you believe it?" She laughed shrilly. "Can you come and get me, take me to my sister's place on the east side?"

"I do remember you. You got out of the wrong side of the cab. It's your lucky day because I got some time, and I think I know where you are. My friend got married there on the sly. At the bottom of that dirt path, right?"

"That's it! The tip I'm going to give you, Ari, we're talking three digits."

Ari agreed to come right away, and all she had to do now was wait for him. This simple goal soothed Mika, and she again rested her cheek against the mossy wood, grateful now for the city's trapped heat. The LSD still cartwheeled through her brain, but its intensity had waned. *Please God, let me get out of this mess. Let me bring Naomi home and sleep for five to seven hours and I'll never ask you for anything again.* She formed a plan to clean herself up at Naomi's apartment, then call her sister and demand she meet her at Port Authority.

Soon, the only light came from the glow of distant lampposts, and Mika grew shivery. Wasn't it strange how the cicadas went silent? Their numbers were fewer there than in the barrens, but as the night deepened, the cicadas' hiss had acquired a certain dominance before abruptly stopping. Paranoia sliced through her fading LSD pall, and she ducked her chin below the waterline, attempting to camouflage herself. *Something's watching me.*

Ron's face sprung to mind, and she recalled his description of a UFO sailing silently through the air above his beloved corner. *Right before it came, all the barking stopped. Not a peep.*

A light assaulted her dilated pupils without mercy. Mika had a painful impression of the pond lit up like it was high noon, the spaces between the trees illuminated, before she slapped a hand over her eyes. Then her feet squelched free from the pond's bottom, and her body rose from the water. The tips of her toes brushed against dry wood as she lifted higher into open air.

She flailed her free hand, desperate to find something to hold onto. Her elbow cracked into something hard. She felt wood under her back and dropped her hand from her eyes. Mika was lying on the floor of the gazebo, not floating upward as her addled mind had convinced her moments ago.

"Lady, what are you on?" Ari loomed over her holding a flashlight, pond water slicking his arms and the front of his shirt.

Ari helped her to her feet, and Mika sputtered thanks at him for agreeing to drive her home. Ari said he was happy to do it, but he'd have to get his car and clothes cleaned, and that would cost her extra. Mika squeezed as much pond water as she could from her own clothes, and they made their way back to Fifth Avenue without attracting much attention. She climbed into the backseat of Ari's double-parked sedan, wet and grateful.

The car smelled clean, like the Piney Mart after a mopping, and the two of them settled into a comfortable silence, crossing Park Avenue and heading east toward Naomi's less ritzy neighborhood. Ari glanced at Mika in the rear view mirror a few times, a sweet smile on his face. Mika smiled back. *I could drive with him forever. Is this what love feels like?* Stop it, she told herself. *You're not in love, you're on drugs.*

After saying goodbye to Ari, Mika entered her sister's building and gave a silent prayer of thanks the doorman was on break. She used her key to let herself into Naomi's dark and empty apartment, plugged her now-dead cell phone into its charger, and entered the bathroom. Naomi's shower was cramped, but it had excellent water pressure. To Mika's relief, the effects of LSD continued to diminish as she scrubbed pond water from her skin and hair.

Wrapped in a towel, she went to the fridge and cracked open a Master Blaster. She brought the can into the guestroom, intending to call Naomi, but her phone remained lifeless even after charging it for ten minutes.

With her American Tourister roller bag already packed next to the closet, Mika got in bed and picked up her phone, willing it to reanimate, then opened the silicon wallet stuck to its back. Her debit card was still tucked inside, coated in pond water. Had she paid Ari? She must have. *It's all fuzzy.*

Surely, Naomi would try to call her, and when Mika didn't answer, her sister would return home to look for her. Since Mika's phone wouldn't charge, her only option was to sit and wait. Despite the Master Blaster she sipped, her body and mind fought for sleep. The last thing she registered before dozing off was the sound of her breath, deep and foreign, and the tang of caffeine and carbonation tickling her throat.

Seven hours later, an electronic trill jerked her awake. Mika sat up, still wrapped in a towel, her hair damp and cold on her neck. She shivered in the air conditioning, and the sunlight blotting the sooty window triggered a rush of anxiety.

Paige is going to kill me.

She followed the sound of the ringing phone into Naomi's bedroom and found her sister asleep in bed, sprawled on her stomach and drooling on a pillow. Naomi's cell phone trilled on the side table next to her mattress. Mika snatched it up, livid with both of them for missing the bus, and checked the screen. Naomi had missed a series of calls and texts from Adrian.

Did you find Mika?
Are you okay?
I'm getting worried
Call me back or I'm coming over there
I'm coming over

The full scope of Mika's failure became clear. Her family had likely waited all night for their arrival, their anticipation turning to worry and alarm when they never heard from her. Loathing herself, she imagined her dad growing wild-eyed with paranoia as midnight came and went, shining his flashlight through the windows looking for feds. Her face hot, Mika used Naomi's cell to call the landline at the main house.

Paige picked up. "Where have you been? I've been calling you for hours!" Paige's ragged sobs filled the air between them. "Dad died early this morning."

Mika's wails bolted Naomi out of bed.

16

—

Mika slumped on Naomi's couch, the skin of her bare shoulders sticking to the faux-leather. Naomi and someone from her management company were engaged in a tense phone conversation about her request for time off. Mika followed her sister's side of the conversation without attaching any meaning to it. Her thoughts and emotions floated just of reach.

Adrian arrived and shifted into caretaker mode after learning of Art Crane's passing. He took one look at Mika, said she was in shock, and got her a glass of water. "I'm driving you to New Jersey," he said. Naomi ended her call and brought Mika, still wrapped in an oversized bath towel, into the guestroom to get dressed.

Minutes later, Mika numbly dragged her roller bag down the building's front steps. Declining the doorman's offer to help, she heaved it into the trunk of Adrian's burnt-orange hatchback, and the bag's wheels left a smear of city grit on her jean shorts. Naomi offered Mika shotgun, but she climbed in the backseat instead.

Adrian steered them through midtown gridlock. Horns blared and exhaust fumes sullied Mika's airways as they approached the Lincoln Tunnel. Staring at the back of Naomi and Adrian's heads, resentment bloomed inside her. Naomi had tricked her into delaying her trip home, and because of that deceit, they weren't at their father's side when he passed.

With the city behind them, the sky opened up into a sunless gray goliath. Naomi kept turning around in the passenger seat to ask if Mika needed anything. Naomi's face was an unwelcome reminder that Mika had failed to grant their father's last wish, one of the only things he'd ever asked of her.

Naomi and Adrian rested their hands on the console between them, their pinkies touching. Outside, factories belched toxins into the air. A fat drop of rain hit the windshield, then another, and the sky unloaded its wet burden. Lightning flashed and thunder cracked, dislodging a deluge of grief in Mika that filled her with unbearable pain. She leaned forward, gasping.

Adrian pulled into a rest stop, and Naomi exited the hatchback to buy them drinks. Mika watched rivulets of rain slide down the car windows and listened to the sound of Adrian's gentle voice, not quite following his words. She thought about dying in the pool, existing as a ghost in the chlorinated depths before the lifeguard pulled her body from the water.

Dad is a spirit now, liberated from his mortal coil. He's free, but not gone. I'll talk to him again.

She held onto that buoy of hope, and stayed afloat in a dark and roiling sea.

Paige welcomed Naomi home in a shaky voice after opening the front door of the main house. She wore her pearl earrings and had her dark hair piled artfully atop her head.

Paige ushered the three of them into the living room, and Mika immediately spotted the outline of her dad's body etched into the cushioning of his recliner. The room started to wobble and she willed it back into balance.

Naomi and Paige embraced, and Mika saw her oldest sister struggling not to bawl. Paige could only meet Naomi's eyes for brief intervals, vulnerable now, as if her usual defenses, her grudges against Naomi and the world, were dismantled by their father's death.

"Sorry this reunion had to be under such sad circumstances," Naomi said. She introduced Paige to Adrian.

Adrian, shifting his weight from one foot to the other, inquired about a bathroom, and Paige directed him down the hall.

"Mom's at the store," Paige said to Naomi. "Did you stop in to say hello?"

Naomi shook her head, looking like the child she used to be at the mention of their mother.

"Mika, go tell Mom Naomi is home," Paige said.

Mika left the main house and crossed the gravel to the paved parking lot of the Piney Mart. On her way inside, she flipped the sign on the glass door to "*We'll be back in a few minutes!*" Tessie stood behind the register. She'd lost weight.

"Naomi is home," Mika said.

Tessie moved toward her with surprising speed and enveloped Mika in her strong arms. Mika thought about her mother swinging the bat at Chapman and squeezed her eyes shut till the images dissipated.

Tessie held Mika's face. "He was a good man, your dad. The best. He loved and was loved in return. Not a bad life, you know?"

"He lived a good life. Go say hello to your daughter. I'll lock up."

Tessie Crane smoothed her pleated shorts and said, "I look a mess." But she collected her purse, dog eared a page in her crossword puzzle book, and left. The woman had guts.

Mika noted a new camera secured high on the back wall and immediately knew Paige had purchased it with the cash Mika left her. It struck Mika how insecure Paige must feel, threatened by other women to the point of obsession. A thought popped uninvited into her mind. *What else is she threatened by?*

She counted the cash in the register, flipping the dollar bills face down. She found the back of the bill strangely soothing, even spiritual: Latin words floating above an eagle's wings. *E Pluribus Unum. Out of many, one.* She left three hundred dollars in the register and put the excess cash inside the vinyl envelope underneath the change drawer. The bank deposits would be Mika's job now, a daily task her father had completed for many years. She thought of the toolbox in the shed and its hidden bounty. *He didn't make all of those deposits, did he?*

Returning to the main house, Mika set a goal to escape to her cottage as soon as possible.

Despite the warm weather, she found the three Crane women and Adrian drinking mugs of hot tea and joined them at the kitchen table. Naomi asked Paige how business at the Piney Mart was going. Paige launched into a diatribe about the tourists, whose bathing suits continued to get smaller while their entitlement grew by leaps and bounds. Tessie kept patting her hair and glancing at Naomi. The skin under Adrian's right eye twitched rhythmically. *Poor thing.*

Paige reached out and squeezed Naomi's hand on the table. "You look just the same. Doesn't she, Mom?"

Tessie nodded, her eyes shiny.

"I wish I could have spoken to him before…Mika did everything she could to get me here." Naomi's voice sounded small and pubescent.

"You're home now, that's all that matters," Tessie said.

Naomi hung her head, overcome with emotion. Mika considered comforting her sister but instead went to use the upstairs bathroom. Her father's shaving kit sat open on the porcelain sink, the tail of his blue Gillette razor poking out. *The best a man can get.* Returning to the kitchen, Mika excused herself and left for her cottage, leaving Paige and her mom to cluck around Naomi like hens while Adrian twitched.

At home, she went online and searched Expedia for travel deals. She may have found Naomi, but she didn't feel whole because she'd lost the man who never left in the first place. The man who'd felt his tether to life unraveling, even if his family didn't want to believe it, and offered her some final advice: *You always wanted to travel and see the world. Don't let your dreams pass you by, now.*

17

—

To ensure Naomi could attend, the family held Art's memorial service the day after his cremation. Mika spent the prior forty-eight hours arranging the details of both events with Paige, and to their credit, they'd done so with minimal friction.

A silver urn containing Art's ashes sat on a round table in the funeral home's chapel, flanked by bouquets of local wildflowers and backdropped by a cream-colored curtain. Mika made sure to display a picture of her dad wearing his church pants and favorite Budweiser t-shirt. Paige set a thirty-year-old photo of him dressed in a suit right next to it. Their father would hate the picture Paige chose—suits were for the government agents that brought him nothing but misery—but Mika kept that to herself.

Mika spoke briefly with her niece, Chloe, who flew in for the service. Paige's daughter was empathetic and polite, but Mika could tell the young woman looked at her differently now that she'd left Solstice Funds and worked at the Piney Mart, as if Mika now embodied the girl's worst fear. Naomi and Adrian stayed close to Mika for most of the service, then ventured off to speak quietly with Paige and Bill. *Holding hands*, Mika noted.

Corralled by Bill after finishing off the wine, Art's buddies from the firehouse shuffled by Mika on their way out of the service, wearing ancient wide-lapelled suits and sharing anecdotes about Art that made her smile. Then Callum stood before her, on duty and in uniform.

"Art was a great man." His voice was thick with emotion.

"He thought highly of you, too."

"I've missed you," he said. "You look good."

"Must be the city air."

Callum nodded, not getting the joke. She was grateful he came, that it wasn't just the guys from the firehouse and a handful of regulars from the store.

Paige helped Mika unzip the back of her dress at the cottage. She eyed the clothes strewn around Mika's bedroom without comment, eager to talk about Naomi.

"It's adorable. Naomi sleeps on the fold out couch and Adrian sleeps next to her on the recliner," Paige said. "He's a real gentleman, isn't he, and don't the two of them look good together?"

Mika pitied her oldest sister. *She's in the honeymoon phase. Wait till she hears about the aliens.* Mika had decided not to burden Paige and her mom with those details so soon after the funeral.

"Don't get deodorant on that dress. You only wore it once. No shame in taking it back. Speaking of togetherness, I saw you and Callum talking at the service. Any chance you two might rekindle things?"

Mika offered a noncommittal shrug. "Maybe we can be friends. When are you leaving for the airport?"

"Half an hour or so. It's just like Chloe to book a red eye. Would it kill her to stay another night? You look jumpy, Mika. Are you hitting the coffee too hard?"

"I'm fine." Mika slipped into her softest shorts and tank top, but the fabrics still scratched at her skin. "Can you stick around for a few minutes for a family meeting? Mom's on her way over."

"Might as well. Mom's coming with us to the airport. That's the only way she can get any time with Chloe, when the kid's trapped in a car. If we can keep the headphones out of her ears, that is."

Mika had bought a case of Master Blasters at ShopRite, and she'd ripped through three cans before the service. She'd slept for all of two hours since arriving home, her insomnia pills untouched in her medicine cabinet. She couldn't afford to feel woozy from medication with all the planning she and Paige were tasked with. And if mega doses of caffeine blunted her emotional pain while she checked items off her to-do list, wasn't that a bonus?

Over the last few days, her eyes had closed for periods of time in a series of unrefreshing, long blinks, a kind of sleep simulation, but the chattering of her mind continued unabated. Master Blasters kept her functioning at such a high level that she began to question whether sleep was actually a requirement for life. Could she drink Master Blasters in perpetuity and never sleep again? *Have I turned into a vampire, sucking sustenance from tall white cans instead of necks?*

After their mom entered the cottage in her wrinkled black dress, makeup flaking on her drawn face, Mika invited her and Paige to sit on her couch, then she placed the toolbox on the coffee table in front of them.

"What's this?" Paige asked.

"Dad's secret savings. He kept it on a shelf in Grandpop's shed." Mika opened the toolbox with dramatic flair, revealing the plastic-wrapped cash inside. *Ta-da.* "I found it right before I left for the city."

Tessie and Paige hugged each other and wiped their eyes, only stopping the celebration when Mika said she had another announcement.

"I'll be traveling overseas in the morning," Mika said. "Going on an adventure in honor of Dad. I don't need any of the cash. It's for you two."

Mika had placed an automated order to sell the remaining stocks in her 401k as soon as the exchange opened in the morning.

"Mika, don't be rash," her mother said. "We insist you take your share."

"We do," Paige parroted.

"I'll put my share toward the second mortgage, how's that?" Mika looked at Paige. "You mentioned it's a burden for you."

Paige blushed. "I was horrible to Mom and you when Dad told us he'd found Naomi. I don't know why I'm so darn difficult sometimes. I guess I thought Naomi would hurt us again, but that's not what happened."

Paige and Tessie beamed at Mika. As much as she wanted to bask in their approval, she couldn't embrace the moment because Naomi had not come home in time.

Naomi's delusions were another reason. *I'll tell them about the alien stuff when I'm back from my trip. We'll all be stronger then, and we can get some professional advice, sit Naomi down, and have a tough conversation.* Mika's avoided thinking about how Naomi might react to such an intervention.

Eyes once again glassy with self-recrimination, Paige said, "I lashed out at Mom, brought up the whole mess with Chapman, all because she wanted to see her daughter. I hate myself for that. I really do." She sniffed and wiped her nose with her sleeve. "Darn it. I can't take this dress back now. Who am I kidding, you know I will."

Tessie consoled Paige, telling her she'd been stressed and exhausted after Art injured himself, and they all understood what that could do to a person.

Mika thought about the stories Naomi shared in Central Park about her mom and oldest sister's violent pasts—pasts she knew next to nothing about because they'd been hidden from her. Were the stories true? Had Mika been on the outside all these years?

For a moment, the image of her mom and Paige on the couch grew fuzzy at the edges. Mika blinked until her field of vision stabilized. Was that blip a residual effect of LSD or just a symptom of too little sleep? Probably both, she reasoned. *I'll sleep on the plane. I'll sleep on the beach.*

"I can take a look at that mortgage when I get home," Mika said to Paige. "If you let me."

Paige said she would and apologized for refusing to do so previously. "We better get on the road. I bet Chloe's already in the car, rolling her eyes out of her head. But first, I'm dying to know where you're off to on your trip, and when you'll be back."

"Tahiti. I'll keep you updated."

Paige's smile dipped, but their mother clapped her hands together. "The South Pacific! Oh, good lord. How exciting. When are you leaving?"

"In the morning."

"Don't forget to say goodbye to Naomi before you leave," her mom said. "She and Adrian are crashed out in the living room like two bugs in a rug." Her mom sighed. "Wouldn't that be something if Naomi came home for good and stayed in Chloe's old room? Maybe after spending time with us, Adrian will decide he wants to live in the barrens. Maybe he'll find a job at the county hospital. They're always looking for nurses."

Mika smiled. "That's a lot of maybes."

Preparing to leave Mika's cottage, Paige could no longer behave herself. "As far as Callum goes, he's not perfect, but no one is," she said. "He came today, didn't he? He showed up, even though you two called things off. That shows character." Paige exchanged a knowing look with their mother. "And let's be serious, he's leagues ahead of your past boyfriends."

Mika escorted them to the door, realizing aspects of her life had been covertly discussed among her family, probably for years. Mika, who couldn't make a relationship work. Mika, who chose poorly (with the possible exception of Callum).

She inhaled pine-scented air and shouted her goodbyes to Chloe before retreating to her kitchen and extracting a Master Blaster from the fridge. She supposed she shouldn't be surprised her family noted the obvious about her relationship track record. But they were wrong about Callum. He wasn't much different from other men in her past. They'd all careened through life like untied balloons, making unpleasant sounds as air escaped them, always searching for someone to blow them back up.

It occurred to Mika, as she sat on her couch taking satisfying gulps from the tall can, that perhaps she'd picked men like that for a reason. She knew how to please them, how to keep them afloat with reminders of their good looks and accomplishments. She would tell them what they wanted to hear, and then, for a while at least, she could pretend she was just like everyone else, cloaked in the respectable veneer of coupledom.

Another epiphany surfaced after several more gulps. She'd played the Let's Blame Naomi game for years, laying her inability to make a relationship work at her sister's feet. But what if her sister's cruel goodbye and long absence had nothing to do with Mika's relationship failures? After all, Mika had encountered the greatest love of all at the bottom of a pool at thirteen. Didn't it make sense her later relationships were seeded with undercurrents of disappointment and melancholy?

And it wasn't just her romantic relationships that lacked depth. She loved her family, no doubt about that, but in all honesty, she often felt detached from them too. *Of course you do, and it's nothing to feel bad about. Mortals can't compete with the heavyweight champ of the universe.*

Mika tried to watch TV, hoping the muscles in her neck would unwind. She promised herself the Master Blaster in her hand would be the last of the night. Tomorrow, she'd go back on her insomnia meds. She'd pop two pills on the way to the airport and sleep like a baby on her Air Tahiti flight.

And when Callum knocked on her cottage door, she let him in, because even if he wasn't much different from the men in her past, he'd stuck around the longest, circling the air around her after she grew restless and released him. No longer in uniform, his eyes were puffy and he smelled like alcohol.

"Me and the old guys were giving toasts to Art at the firehouse." He held out his hand. "You look like you could use a dance."

"You shouldn't be driving."

"I wouldn't blow a breath test."

She allowed him to twirl her, spinning once under his arm. He spotted her roller bag lying open on the living room floor, crammed with clothes, and dropped her hand.

"Still unpacking?"

"Packing," she said. "I'm going away for a while to clear my head."

"Yeah, for how long?"

"That remains to be seen."

He crossed his arms. "You were going to leave without saying goodbye?"

She laughed. "Don't look so mad. We broke up, remember?"

"Have we not been communicating?"

"I mean, a couple of texts."

"You don't think you led me on, sending me pictures of your tits?"

"That was a joke. You really couldn't tell? And I was clothed."

His frown deepened. "I'm a joke now?"

He wants to fight. "Maybe this is a bad idea."

"You don't look right, you know. Your color is off and you've lost weight."

"My father died."

"I know. I'm sorry." His chest deflated.

Mika didn't want to hurt him. He'd been there for all of them, more than once, when they needed him. That counted for something. "There are phones, you know. The internet. I'll reach out to you at some point."

"If you say so." He picked up her hand. "Let's finish our dance."

They swayed together as Callum hummed *She's Always a Woman to Me*. He stepped on her foot, and she punched him playfully in the arm.

"Assaulting an officer. I'm going to have to take you in for that." He moved fast. A mischievous spark in his bloodshot eyes, he guided her down onto the couch and secured her wrists over her head in a cop move, tickling her armpits with his free hand. Mika twisted her body, feeling heat rise to her face and the indignity of confronting her own body odor.

"I hate it when you tickle me," Mika said, but a reflexive laugh followed.

"I'll stop if you ask nicely and quit giggling. Bet you can't do either, can you?"

"You're such a child." She twisted one arm free, but he easily pinned it back down, and she could only lay there, stuck and red-faced, sputtering yelps of involuntary laughter despite an overwhelming urge to free herself.

Callum could not have known the intense anger coming to a rapid boil inside her—she turned her head to keep from spitting in his face. *Something's happening. Something's wrong.* She thought of Naomi's fingers tangled in her hair as she choked on chlorinated water. Mika was so fucking *sick* of people holding her down.

Her eyes moved to the window. The darkness outside glared back and her anger turned to fear. *Get away. Get away.* Terror clamped down on her like the metal teeth of an animal trap. The sizzling in her brain returned, popping and cracking like fat on flame, and something twitched deep in the gray meat of her brain, unscrewing itself. A secret door becoming unhinged.

Callum spoke from somewhere far away, asking her what was wrong. His voice faded away, and the darkness surged through the windows and swallowed her living room. Then came the radiant light of a lovely sunny day almost two decades ago.

And she remembered.

Cattails and orchids swayed in the balmy wind. Pine and cypress perfumed the air. After wading in the creek, young Mika and Naomi dried off under a bone-white sun. They were munching happily on PB&Js when a herd of deer entered the clearing.

Naomi held a finger to her lips, signaling they should stay quiet lest they scare the skittish creatures away. Several deer approached the creek and drank the iron-rich water, air blowing from their noses in rapid *chuffs*. She and Naomi watched in wonder, struck by the knowledge it was a magical day and they were experiencing something special. But then the deer and all that surrounded them cracked like a windshield hit by a brick.

The mirage exploded like glass, reflecting its shattered illusion in the slivers hurtling through the air. Sounds, too, emanated from the broken pieces: air puffing from snouts, the blunt noshing of herbivores chewing on young leaves.

The last shards whipped out of Mika's psyche, taking with them the false memory she'd carried for most of her life, and the reality of that day in the clearing escaped a caged recess in her mind. Despite its treachery, she soon longed for the lie to return and shield her from the devastating truth.

When she first saw the beings moving toward the clearing, Mika thought they were beach balls blowing through the pines, or maybe strange kites. She put her sandwich aside and peered into the forest, then the spindly ash-blue creatures snapped into focus. Their heads were wide and bulbous, tapering sharply to pointy chins and held up by long, skinny necks.

Suddenly, Mika understood that monsters not only existed but had her squarely in their sights.

She tried to turn toward Naomi, who reclined behind her in the sun, but her body refused all commands to move. She was trapped, paralyzed in place. She could not see Naomi, nor could she escape.

The creatures drew closer, and Mika caught fuller glimpses of them in between the trees. They appeared both naked and sexless, advancing steadily as if unconcerned with thorny vines and sticker bushes. The monsters entered the clearing on spindly legs, and panic tore through her like a cyclone.

They had elongated craniums, black eyes that covered a third of their faces, and arms like etching branches. Slits for mouths and two small holes where their noses should be. Webbed fingers pudgy at the tips.

One of them, taller than the rest, approached Mika, and her lungs swelled and collapsed like hurricane glass. The Tall One bent over, peering down at her with giant, praying-mantis eyes. The inky pools of its bug-eyes wrapped around the side of its earless head, plumbing her depths but reflecting nothing back, not even her own slackened face.

Mika would have given anything in that moment, even her own life, to turn away, but she could only stare back at it, feeling it catalog every part of her, even the parts she hid from herself. A thought lurched into her psyche. *This isn't the first time. It's done this to me before.* She couldn't feel her heart, only a shrieking emptiness, and wondered if she'd died and gone to hell. Then her heart crashed back into her chest as if falling from a great height, and a ragged scream detonated in her head. Hatred, unfamiliar in its ferocity, took her. If her hands and fingers worked, if her teeth could bite and tear, she would have attacked it with everything she had. *Get away. Get away.*

The Tall One straightened up and moved outside her limited range of vision, as if sensing her revulsion. But not seeing it brought little comfort. Mika had been pushed around before by bigger kids, bullies at school, but always had the option of fighting back or walking away. The degradation of forced paralysis, of feeling like a fly caught in a web as the spider readied its venom, marked the end of her innocence, her childhood.

She assumed it was the last day of her short life. Perhaps she didn't want this life anyway, with its monsters and the pungent smell of urine in her nostrils. But a primal instinct to survive, to battle for freedom, overpowered that sentiment. If only such an instinct could thaw her frozen body.

The clearing teemed with monsters. She couldn't see all of them, but she *felt* them in staggering numbers, too many to keep track of. They swarmed around her like fire ants on a warpath, streaming from their crushed anthill to exact vicious revenge.

The warm wind buffeted Mika's back, and she knew Naomi was no longer behind her. What were the monsters doing to Naomi, and how long could her own heart keep beating so fast?

She fixated on a shady area in the woods: a shallow cave low to the ground, under the exposed roots of a dead oak. Desperate, she propelled her consciousness toward the cave and squirmed inside its crooked mouth. Grasping in the darkness, Mika found something heavy and cylindrical.

Then a monster found her, grabbing one of her ankles. Emboldened by animal rage, she kicked free of its grasp and burst back out into the light, a light now yellow and unnatural, and swung her weapon as hard as she could.

A wrenching pain in her elbow and a wet crunching sound brought Mika back to the present moment in her living room. The weight in her hands dropped away, and Naomi's All-Star bat fell to the floor, the painted barrel splotched with red. It rolled back under the couch where she'd hidden it before travelling to New York.

Callum lay sprawled on the floor next to the coffee table, his nose a bloody ruin, his body limp, a purple welt swelling his forehead. Mika comprehended the violence she'd inflicted. And she knew now why all the Cranes were broken.

18

—

Mika screamed Callum's name until he moaned in response. *He's alive, thank God.* She searched her pockets for her phone then remembered it had stopped working after she called Ari from the pond. A low gurgling came from Callum's throat. Afraid the blood from his broken nose might suffocate him, she placed a throw pillow under his head. Kneeling beside him, she patted him down, looking for his cell phone. Her hand grazed something hard under his shirt: his holstered service pistol. His eyes opened, and he grabbed her wrist and bent it backward. She yelped in pain.

Callum spit blood on the floor then shoved her into the coffee table. By the time she scrambled to her feet, he'd retrieved his gun and pointed it at her from his reclined position. Her bowels clenched precariously, and she backed away from him, stumbling over the raised edge of an area rug.

"What did you hit me with?" Blood bubbled from his mouth. He tried to hoist himself up into a sitting position, grunted, then collapsed onto his elbows. He held his gun with both hands, the grip pressed awkwardly into his belly.

"Try not to move. I'm so sorry. It was an accident, a terrible accident."

"You stupid crazy bitch." His nose had shifted on his face and now pointed toward his right cheek.

"I know you're angry, but I have to call for help." She scoured the floor with her eyes and spotted his phone a few feet behind him on the floor. She stepped toward him, and the gun rose.

Callum aimed for her face. "One more step and I'll put a bullet in you. Don't think I won't."

The force of his hatred sucked air from her lungs. *I can't get to his phone. He won't let me near him and for good reason.* She showed him her palms and took a step back toward the front door. *He might not make it if I don't get help.* His entire head swelled, taking on a crimson cast. Each backward step she took felt like her last; death peeked through the windows, tapping its scythe on the glass.

"I'm going to my parents' to call an ambulance. Don't shoot me, Callum."

"Get on the ground and put your hands behind your head. Do it!" Blood sprayed from his mouth.

Mika shook her head. "I can't let you die." She reached behind her, her stretched fingers grasping then turning the brass doorknob. There was no click of a trigger, no death roar from the gun. Not yet. She swung the door open and sprinted across the gravel in the near-darkness, expecting the back of her head to blow off at any moment. Right before she reached her parent's kitchen door, Naomi came barreling out of it, and Mika crashed into her at full speed. The blow almost knocked Mika over. Her back, bruised by her sharp-cornered coffee table, howled in protest.

"What's going on?" Naomi asked. "I heard yelling."

"I hit Callum with a bat. He needs an ambulance. It was an accident."

"Jesus. Did he hurt you?"

She straightened up and gripped Naomi's t-shirt with both hands. "I remembered what happened to us in the clearing. I didn't mean to hurt Callum. I thought he was one of *them*."

Naomi put her hands over Mika's and tried to loosen her hold. "Calm down. We'll figure this out."

Mika pushed past her, went through the kitchen into the living room, and used the landline to call 911. "There's an injured cop in my living room," she told the dispatcher. "I don't think he can walk, but I'm not sure. He's in the small cottage facing the tree line, not the larger house, okay? His name's Callum Dunbar. Officer Callum Dunbar. He's my ex-boyfriend, and I hit him in the head with a bat. It was an accident. No one else is hurt. He has a head injury and a gun, so please hurry." She repeated the address of her cottage twice and hung up.

Adrian sat up on the recliner. "You beat up your cop ex-boyfriend?" He stood from the couch and snapped a lamp on. "And he's at your place with a gun?"

Naomi had followed Mika inside. "It's okay, the cops will be here soon," she said to Adrian.

"It's far from okay," he said.

Naomi turned to Mika. "You need to go, get out of here, now."

"I can't *leave*. I have to make sure Callum's okay. And the both of you, too."

"In about three minutes there will be cops crawling all over this property," Naomi said. "You can't talk to cops without a lawyer. I can get you a good one, but I need a little time. Does the express bus still stop at the Lighthouse Diner?"

Mika nodded. "Once an hour."

"Cut through the woods and take that bus. Get off at Secaucus, the last stop before the city. You'll see the Skyline Motel right across the street. Check in. Pay cash."

Mika's thoughts whirled. "I can take my car."

Naomi shook her head. "If you leave on foot, they'll assume you're still local."

"It was an accident," Mika said. "Won't it look bad if I leave before the cops get here?"

Naomi pried the landline handset from Mika's fingers and tossed it onto the couch. "We need time to figure out a plan. Time you won't have if you don't get out of here."

"She's right." Adrian's said, slipping his shoes on. "The cops will be eager to nail you for hurting one of their own. They won't care about your side of things."

Mika exhaled. "Okay, I'll go." She addressed Naomi. "Call Paige. She and Mom will be home from the airport soon and should know what they're walking into."

Naomi fished something from her overnight bag then followed Mika out the back door into the night. They ran toward the blackened barrens, stopping at the edge of the pines, both of them breathing hard.

"This is my extra phone." Naomi pressed a cell phone into Mika's hand. "No one has the number except for a couple long-time tenants. If it rings, you know it's me." The wail of an ambulance kicked up in the distance. "It's registered to my management office. They issued us new phones years ago and never asked for it back. Don't forget. The Skyline Motel in Secaucus. Get a room, pay cash, and use a fake name. They don't ask for ID. We used that motel as a temporary safe house."

"We?"

"Free Species."

An approaching ambulance wailed in the distance.

"Stay in your motel room. I'll text or call you from a burner as soon as I can." Naomi pushed her toward the trees.

Another siren with a higher-pitched wail approached. *Cops.* Mika darted into the pines with only the dim light of the cloud-covered moon to guide her. Thorns tore at her hands and shins. She winced from the pain. *I deserve it.*

She reached a sugar sand road that led to a paved backroad, then followed the backroad from inside the treeline to a highway intersection. The Lighthouse Diner glowed bright on the far corner. *Sometimes it's better to hide in plain sight,* Mika thought. And she knew just where to do it.

After her mom's sentencing, she and Callum used to hang out at the Lighthouse Diner before their night shifts. They got to know each other over black coffee and French fries, lip-synching the Motown songs they played on one of the mini-jukeboxes adorning every booth.

Seated inside the diner, Mika played *Just My Imagination* so the waitress didn't feel obliged to make small talk, then ordered oatmeal she didn't eat and coffee she threw back like a shot of whiskey. The booth she'd requested was tucked in a corner and obscured by a mirrored column. It was Callum's favorite booth to sneak an on-duty meal with her, blocked from the view of fellow officers driving by on patrol.

Moving oatmeal around her plate with a spoon, her mind played a highlight reel of the last hour: Callum spitting blood, a Glock pointed at her face, aliens surrounding her in the clearing, degradation and paralysis, the Tall One prying into her mind with its ghastly bug eyes. She felt a sob coming on and pretended to cough. The waitress came over and Mika ordered another coffee, watching for any signs of the express bus outside.

The minutes ticked by and Mika questioned whether hiding in plain sight was a good idea. She'd hoped the relative comfort and safety of the familiar booth would keep her from spiraling, but paranoia began to chip away at her already fragile grasp on reality.

Had the remnants of LSD in her system actually released a hidden memory, or had she somehow created the alien-memory, a result of the one-two punch of suggestion and the lingering effects of hallucinogens? She thought about the Satanic Panic in the '80s, when the country was whipped into collective hysteria resulting in over ten thousand unsubstan-tiated cases of satanic ritual abuse. Authorities had interrogated suspects and potential victims, often children, for interminably long sessions, and many suspects "confessed" out of desperation. People came to believe they were victims of satanic abuse based on "recovered memories" later determined to be coerced by overzealous therapists.

Had a similar phenomenon unfolded after Mika attended two alien-focused gatherings, the latter of which on LSD? The aliens she remembered encountering in the clearing resembled the gray-skinned, bug-eyed aliens familiar to most people, the standard extraterrestrials portrayed in conspiracy documentaries and on Nevada highway billboards. *STOP AT THE FLYING SAUSAGE DINER ON THE WAY TO AREA 51!* What if she'd simply conjured the modern boogeyman in the cultural unconscious?

With trembling hands, she dropped the cell phone Naomi gave her on the table. She wanted to call Callum. A medic or another cop might answer her call, then she could ask about his condition. She picked up the cell and displayed the keypad, but the only numbers she knew by heart were her own and the landline at the main house. She imagined showing up at the hospital and entering Callum's room. Furious screams erupting from his battered face. No, she would stick to Naomi's plan for now. *Get to the motel and check on Callum from there.* But one thing was certain: she was too frazzled to face a bus full of strangers.

She sat a little taller realizing she could remember one more phone number, or close enough. Ari the taxi driver's. Was it 1-800-RIDENYC or NYCRIDE? She tapped on the keypad and figured it out on the second try. Ari picked up, his voice groggy with sleep and irritation.

"Ari, it's Mika. Remember me? You picked me up in Central Park. How could you forget, right? I'm in South Jersey, about eighty miles south of the city, and I have another favor to ask. I need a ride to a motel in Secaucus called The Skyline."

Ari took his time responding. "South Jersey? That's way too far. I can't do it."

He sounded strange. Cold. *What if he hangs up?* "I'll give you a thousand in cash."

"I'm not getting out of bed and driving all the way to the Jersey Shore because some lady *might* be there and *might* have that kind of money on her."

Ari sounded fully awake now. His words and aggrieved tone stung Mika. She thought they'd developed, if not a friendship, at least a warm acquaintance. But she was apparently just *some lady* to him?

"Fifteen hundred, Ari. Fifteen hundred if you leave now and pick me up at the Lighthouse Diner off Route 9. Zip code 08742. You got that? I'll text it to you, too. Can I count on you?"

She could hear him scribbling on paper.

"For fifteen hundred, it's a deal. And I got your cell number if you're messing with me. But I don't think you are. I got a good sense for people's character."

Mika stopped gripping the phone quite as hard. He seemed more like his affable self. "When can you leave?"

"Five minutes. I'll text you when I'm close."

She drank two more cups of coffee before leaving her last twenty on the table and slipping out of the diner to use the ATM outside. She drained the generous overdraft on her checking account, aware of the camera recording her, and slunk into the parking lot to wait for Ari.

Swaddled in a shadow at the rear of the lot, Mika sat on the curb and breathed into her hands. Her back ached, coffee sloshed in her stomach, and her mind raced with thoughts of aliens, whose existence she now questioned, and how she would live with herself after brutalizing Callum. A theory presented itself. What if her family's "idiosyncrasies" weren't caused by insomnia, or aliens? What if the Cranes lived with another genetic condition, a psychiatric one?

It's still no excuse for what you did.

Ari arrived seventy minutes later. He pulled into the parking lot in a flourish of headlights and techno music. He looked relieved when she slid into the back seat of his car but remained somewhat reserved. She let him be, figuring it was better for them not to talk. The less he knew, the better.

Back on the turnpike headed north, Mika watched for the lights of the city, longing to be back among the masses, anonymous once more. Ari pulled off the turnpike and under a graffiti-pocked series of overpasses. A pitted road brought them to a squat two-level building, rife with peeling paint and low expectations. The exterior was bathed in the light of a neon sign mounted on the roof. *The Skyline Motel.* The sign included a rendering of the New York skyline that included the Twin Towers.

Ari parked and counted out the hundreds Mika handed him, holding them up to the interior light. When he finished, she muttered a goodbye and got out of the car, wounded by his remoteness.

He called to her through his open window as she walked toward the motel office. "Hey, lady. You need another ride, you call me. I'll give you a discount."

Annoyed, she spun toward him. "My name is Mika."

A light switched on in his eyes, and he pointed at her. "I know you! You left your bag in the trunk of my car. You got out the wrong side of the car, into traffic. Yeah, I remember you. But I never picked you up in Central Park like you said." He put his car into gear and began to slowly roll toward the exit. "I don't go walking around the park for a fare, you know what I'm saying? I'm a nice guy, but I stay in my car. Nobody's that nice."

Ari peeled away with a friendly honk, leaving Mika stupefied in the parking lot. Her mind raced back to the fuzzy memory of Ari arriving at the gazebo and pulling her from the pond. Somehow his small flashlight had lit up the entirety of the pond's perimeter before he lifted her from the water in her soaking wet clothes. Lifted her with such ease, it felt like she'd floated out of the pond and into the air, the tips of her toes brushing against the gazebo floor.

A mushroom cloud of insight detonated inside her, rattling Mika so hard the parking lot swung like a seesaw. Her knees drew together like magnets, stopping her legs from buckling.

Ari hadn't pulled her from the water. Her memory of Ari in Central Park was bullshit. It never happened, much like her memory of a herd of deer joining her and Naomi for some water and a snack.

They tricked me again.

19

—

Mika sat in an upholstered chair, drinking coffee and watching the sky lighten between a gap in the stiff and pleated motel curtains. The chair, curtains, and bedspread were patterned with the multi-colored, stain-camouflaging swirls of a casino carpet. A bloated television from another era rested on the dresser opposite the bed. She'd tried to watch it but couldn't acclimate to the way the bulbous screen warped the picture.

The motel room, surprisingly clean but lacking wi-fi, offered little distraction. The resulting solitude allowed her to decompress enough to come to a few conclusions while she waited for Naomi's call. She no longer doubted Naomi's abduction and her own immobilization in the clearing were real events, that the aliens paralyzed her to keep her out of the way, tortured Naomi on their ship, then used their advanced technology to implant false memories in the minds of both sisters.

Her head thudded despite the coffee, and she shivered in the clammy air, recalling how the Tall One probed her with its mantis-eyes. *It knew me.* It wasn't her first encounter with the Tall One, she was certain. Mika yanked the curtains closed, shutting out an incomprehensible world. The aliens had likely abducted or otherwise messed with every member of her family. As Dr. Patel explained in Central Park, these encounters, involuntary and stripped from conscious memory, had left behind hidden trauma that went unprocessed by the Cranes.

Realizing her family's insomnia was not the result of their DNA provided no solace. She thought of the exhaustion they'd long endured, their quiet despair and crippling brain fog. The lives they were supposed to lead, the people they could've been, had been stolen from them. Mika pulled her bare feet onto the chair and pressed her forehead against her knees, searching for a reason to feel hopeful.

She couldn't take back what she did to Callum, but at least she knew the truth now. Information is power. If she discovered more about the aliens and their agenda, it could improve her odds of successfully fighting back the next time they came for her. And if she did resist them, as Naomi had managed to do, the aliens might reconsider their view of her family as easy targets to be flung about and tinkered with at will.

Mika's fingers curled, her nails digging into the soft meat of her palm. She understood Naomi's desire to rip back the agency the aliens stole from her. A sudden rash of violent thoughts triggered memories of Callum's battered face, and she turned from them, shaky and repulsed.

Naomi's cell phone vibrated on the side table next to her. She snatched up the phone, but it wasn't Naomi calling with an update on Callum. A text had arrived from one Marcus Kitterman.

WHERE ARE YOU? TEXT ME BACK ASAP

This pest of a man. She got up, swallowed the last gulp of cold coffee from a paper cup and tried to massage the aching knots out of her neck and shoulders. A few minutes later the cell phone rang, displaying an unknown number. It had to be Naomi this time, calling from a burner phone like she said she would. Mika accepted the call, staying silent to be cautious.

"It's me," Naomi said. "You get there okay?"

"I did. How's Callum?"

"Stable and in the hospital with a broken nose, a fractured eye socket, and a concussion. Lost a couple teeth, too."

Waves of coffee crested in her stomach, threatening to rise in a dark tide. *What have I done?* "Is his eyesight affected?"

"Adrian's been calling the nurse's desk for updates. The fracture isn't severe and they don't think the eye itself was damaged, but there's a lot of swelling so they can't say for sure."

"Is Adrian there? Can I talk to him?"

"He's home in the city."

"Can you conference him in?"

"He's either asleep or at work, and…I don't want to bother him."

Mika suspected Naomi wanted to protect Adrian from any further involvement with her fugitive sister, and she didn't blame her.

"What teeth were knocked out?" Mika asked. Callum had worked so hard on his teeth. All the whitening and Invisalign. She prayed his front teeth were okay.

"I don't know."

"Can you tell him I didn't mean to hurt him, that I was somewhere else in my head?"

"Let's leave it to the lawyers to draft a statement. I know you want to apologize to him and you will, but this has to play out a certain way."

"Does Mom know what happened? Does Paige?"

"Yes, but I didn't tell them I know where you are. It's better they know as little as possible in case they're questioned again. The cops were here when they got back from the airport."

"Are Paige and Mom okay?"

"They're worried about you, and Callum. Paige and Bill are at the hospital hoping to visit him."

"And Mom?"

"She's at the store. I've been keeping her company."

The list of Callum's ailments rampaged through Mika's head. A sour taste occupied her mouth, like she'd vomited and didn't brush her teeth. She shut her eyes, craving the onslaught of caffeine and clarity a Master Blaster offered. Coffee was useless sludge.

"Are you still there?" Naomi asked.

"Yeah. Sorry." Mika's eyes popped open. She forgot she was on the phone. *Rolling, rolling, rolling, brain fog!* She stood and paced the carpet in front of the bulbous TV, the patterned carpet rough under her bare feet.

"Callum will recover," Naomi said. "Adrian said a

doctor at the hospital told him she doubts he'll have any lasting damage. Except for the teeth, of course."

Mika wiped moisture from her eyes with the back of her palm. "Thank God."

"I wouldn't go that far. The police are looking for you and they tipped off the media. Also, my Free Species contact is waffling on assigning you a lawyer. They're worried about creating tensions with law enforcement that might backfire and hinder their operations. It's a letdown, I know. But the good news is Ron agreed to represent you. He might be rough around the edges, but he's a damn good lawyer. What room are you in?"

"Thirty-three. So, the press is all over this, I'm guessing? What's the headline, *The Bat Lady Returns*?" Mika allowed herself this bit of levity, encouraged by Adrian's assessment of Callum's injuries.

Naomi chuckled. "*Bat Lady, Next Generation*."

"You're a wanted woman yourself," Mika said. "Marcus is having a conniption because he can't get hold of you. He's texting this phone you gave me."

"Ignore him. He's on a rampage. I had to block him on my main cell phone because he called so many times. I forgot he had the number to the one I gave you. He borrowed it a couple years ago after something happened to his. He's always having phone issues, losing or breaking them, dropping them in the toilet. Don't worry about it. I'll handle Marcus."

Mika walked to the stiff curtains and peered outside. "Naomi, I have to tell you something. I know you think the aliens' focus is on you, and that we, your family, are just collateral damage—"

"Their focus *was* on me. Past tense. I'm positive the last time they took me was that day in the clearing."

"That may be true, but they haven't gone anywhere. They're tracking me, Naomi. They might know I'm here, right now. They took me from Central Park after I lost it and ran off. I fell into a pond, and they somehow floated me out of it and got me back to your apartment."

There was a long silence before Naomi said, "Are you sure about that? You were tripping pretty hard."

"They *took* me. The abductions didn't end with you in the clearing. I'm certain of it. They could still be taking all of us."

"Mika, you don't understand. I would *know* if the aliens were anywhere near me. Physically near me, I mean. I still sense them sometimes, poking around my mind from a distance, and when I do, my body reacts. I get physically ill. I throw up, have migraines. But it's nothing compared to how wrecked I felt in their actual presence, up close and personal. When I could see them and smell their stink. When they fucking touched me."

Why didn't she tell be this before? "Do you ever communicate with them?"

"Communicate?" She spat the word out so hard Mika flinched. "I do everything I can to block them out. But sometimes, when it gets too quiet, I feel them occupying a space in my head like a rotten organ spewing filth into my bloodstream. That's why I moved to the city, why I live next door to a busy bridge. I have to keep the quiet away. But I'm telling you, sensing them from a distance is nothing compared to encountering them in the flesh. So, I would know, Mika. I'd know if they were close.

"Maybe you can sense them too. Maybe that's what happened to you in the park. My advice is to try not to think about them. Don't give them any of your time or energy. Focus on the life you'll have once you get out of the mess you're in now. Hopefully you'll sleep again, now that you know the truth. If you sense them again, do whatever necessary to shut them out. It's not easy, but it's possible."

Mika paced on the carpet. "I can't just ignore them. I have to find out what they want, and what it will take for them leave our family alone, once and for all."

"You can't *communicate* with those things. Don't be an idiot!"

Mika froze mid pace. "Geez."

Naomi exhaled. "None of this is your fault. I'm frustrated with myself, not you. Maybe telling you about the aliens was the wrong thing to do. I thought I could help cure your insomnia, begin to make up for the pain I caused by leaving. It was a dumb move, a selfish one." Her voice dropped. "Like insisting we play that stupid kid's game in the pool. I was trying to show off, impress the other kids."

"What kid's game?"

She felt Naomi close like a heavy door. "It doesn't matter. Sit tight and wait for Ron to get there. He'll arrive in a couple hours."

Mika pressed the phone harder against her cheek. "Is there something you're not telling me about what happened in the pool? If so, you need to say it now."

"Let it go, Mika. You have more important things to worry about. When Ron gets there, you two will come up with a legal strategy, then he'll accompany you to the station to turn yourself in. Ditch the cell phone I gave you. Toss it out the window when you're on the road with Ron. The next time we talk, it'll be in person after you make bail."

Mika murmured her agreement and ended the call, frustrated by Naomi's reticence. Seconds later the phone rang.

"Forget something?" Mika said. Hearing no response, she pulled the phone from her ear and looked at the caller ID. A blocked number. She heard breathing and horns blaring on the line. Horns caterwauled outside her motel, too. Standard city noise.

Mika frowned. "Who is this?"

"Put Naomi on the phone."

She silently cursed at the sound of Marcus's voice. "She's not available. Can I take a message?"

"She'll be fired if she doesn't contact management. The washers and dryers in the basement aren't working after all the rain. The board is apoplectic over her absence, and I can only placate them for so long. Put her on the goddamn phone."

"She's not around at the moment, but I'll let her know you called."

"You damn well better."

"I know you're bored, but why don't you find something else to do besides obsess over Naomi?"

"I certainly don't need to keep myself busy. What are you implying?"

"Just making conversation."

"For your information, this nonsense with Naomi interrupted a fruitful morning of day trading."

"But the stock market doesn't open for another half hour, Marcus. What's your portfolio look like, anyway?"

"My portfolio?"

"Your investment portfolio. What are you trading?"

"It's really none of your concern, but I already told you I dabble in stocks."

"But what sectors are you trading? What companies?"

"What is this, an interrogation?"

"Not at all, but I find it odd you can't name a single stock you're so busy trading before the market even opens. How's the premarket volume this morning, anyway?"

"I own several stocks," he stammered. "There's…the Russel."

"The Russel two thousand? Hello? Marcus, are you still there?"

"I'm here."

"That's a market index, not a stock. So, you're day trading an index fund in the premarket? A little unusual, but okay."

"You listen to me, you obnoxious little bitch. I saw you on the news. I know what you did. Stop your game-playing and tell me where Naomi is."

"It's none of your business," Mika said. "My sister is not your family, not your next of kin. She's nice to you because she is a kind person—and let's face it—because it's her job. She won't be the one holding your hand in the end. You'll probably die alone unless you reconsider your entire personality."

She hung up and blocked Marcus's number, quaking from the nasty exchange, from the cruelty of her words.

20

—

Mika texted Naomi to tell her about her conversation with Marcus, leaving out the worst bits. *Sorry I picked up*, she wrote. Seeking to distract herself, she turned on the antique television and watched a daytime host discuss a celebrity divorce on the distorted screen. She shut off the air conditioning to better hear the TV, and the air grew oppressively muggy. Mika gave up and entered the bathroom, eager to take a shower and brush her teeth, then remembered she didn't have a toothbrush.

Looking in the bathroom mirror, she spotted two flecks of dried blood on her cheek. *Callum's blood.* She wanted to cry but was too dehydrated—the dregs of the room's plastic coffee pot would probably spurt from her eyes instead of tears. She turned from the mirror, knowing if she continued to inspect her face, or finger-combed her hair, she'd likely discover more of the burgundy shame.

The grout on the bathroom floor had cracked between the dull tiles, but the bathtub gleamed and exuded the faint aroma of bleach. A limp towel hung from the rack next to the toilet. That towel and a single thin square of paper-wrapped soap would have to suffice.

She stepped into the tub and cursed when the clogged showerhead shot a sideways stream of water out of the tub and onto her formerly dry clothes. *I'll run a bath instead.* Ron wouldn't be there for a half hour, so she had a little time to soak her sore muscles. After bathing, she'd call the front desk and see if they had any toothpaste. A long shot at best. When she'd checked into the motel, the clerk on duty had shoved her keycard through a slit in his bullet-proof, polycarbonate enclosure with a dismissive grunt. Customer service didn't seem like a high priority.

Mika settled in the tub, replaying her conversation with Naomi as water gushed from the faucet. Naomi said Mika might sense if the aliens were close, but Mika wasn't sure. She didn't recall sensing them in Central Park, but she'd also been inundated with sensory data at the time, thanks to the LSD. *Who's to say I won't sense them while sober, now that I know they exist?* If so, she could at least secure a weapon. But what good would a weapon do if they paralyzed her again?

I'd prepare myself mentally, steel my mind to resist their prying and control.

If she *could* feel them coming, what else might be possible? They had accessed her mind; could she access theirs too? What if she hadn't been overwhelmed by shock and terror during her encounter with the Tall One in the clearing? Could she have searched for its weak spots when it invaded her consciousness? Perhaps scaring her was the whole point. What if, by terrorizing their victims, the aliens overrode any possible defense against their telepathy? *So, if I can stay calm, maybe…*

No. She flicked bath water with her index fingers, frustrated. That explanation seemed too pat, too easy. Surely, she wouldn't defeat the aliens with some sci-fi movie of the week resolution she came up with off the cuff. Yet, it was all she had. It was a start.

She thought of her father's last weeks, the pain he endured from his facial wound. Her face grew hot with anger, but she once again rejected it. The warm water rose in the tub, and Mika brought her hands together in prayer. She reached out to God seeking guidance and courage.

When finished, she spoke out loud to her father's spirit. "If you're there, Dad, I hope you're at peace and know that Naomi accepts your apology. She doesn't blame you for anything. We all love and miss you so much."

She refocused on her phone call with Naomi, the muscles in her shoulders uncoiling in the hot water. Naomi implied that something they did in the pool, some *stupid kid's game*, had triggered her abduction flashback. *What games did we play?* She thought back to her childhood while the water swelled to her chest. Marco Freaking Polo? She sank deeper in the liquid heat and concentrated on those three words. *Stupid kid's game.*

When the tub grew close to overflow, she flipped the drain lever with her toes and watched the waterline recede on the porcelain, her thoughts drifting. If only she could nap, her brain might find the answers she needed while she slept. Wouldn't it be lovely, she thought, to float away while her unconscious did the work?

A bolt of clarity energized her heated limbs.

The stupidest kid's game in the world was surely Dead Man Floating. She sat up in the tub, sloshing water on the floor.

Of course, Dead Man Floating. How could I forget? As morbid as it sounded, the game once amused them. They took turns holding their breath and floating face down in the pool while the other counted the seconds aloud. When the counter got to thirty seconds, they tapped on the floater, and then the two players switched positions. After each round, the amount of time underwater increased by five seconds until the floater held their breath for a full minute or gave up. If they both reached the minute mark, whoever held their breath the longest won the game.

Naomi, face down in the pool and holding her breath, must have waited for Mika to tap her out. But Mika had been distracted, acting as a wanna-be coach in the shallow end with one of the younger kids. Mika had forgotten about the game, about counting the seconds. She'd forgotten about Naomi until she'd noticed her thrashing in the water.

Mika knew what Naomi was doing before the horror of her abduction returned to her. *Holding her breath.* No doubt her sister grew impatient and uncomfortable waiting for Mika to tap her out. But Naomi, young and confident, did not give up. She held her breath for as long as she could. *Just like I did before I drowned.*

Mika's muscles tightened up again, and gooseflesh chilled her skin. What if she and Naomi connected with the same presence in that pool but in profoundly different ways? Mika thought of her encounter with the

Tall One in the clearing, the feeling she had, through her terror, that they'd met before. Did she not feel similarly about the celestial presence she encountered in the pool, that glorious *yet somehow familiar* being?

What if she didn't connect with God the day she drowned? What if she, like Naomi, connected with an alien presence and not a spiritual one, a connection that triggered Naomi's fateful abduction memory? Mika shook her head; she didn't want to believe it. Surely, she knew the difference between gods and monsters, between evil and all-encompassing love.

There's only one way to find out.

She kicked the drain lever back up with her toes then took a gulp of air and dipped her head below the water, her eyes squeezed shut against the soapy sting. Her hands clenched the sides of the tub to keep herself submerged. The water rushed into her ears, and when it found equilibrium, all was quiet save her thumping heart.

Like Naomi, she could hold her breath for a long time. However, doing so under pressure made it more difficult. Attempting to quell her excitement and dread, Mika recalled happy memories of swimming in the wild ocean and cold quarry, Naomi by her side. How their skin never grew pruny, no matter how long they swam.

Mika's lungs burned but she didn't resurface, maintaining her hold on the tub, persisting even when the pressure in her chest increased tenfold, far exceeding the known limits of her endurance. Her body convulsed in frantic attempts to suck air from its oxygen-barren cavities, yet she held the downward push of her grip. *I have to know.*

Then a muffled *thwok* reverberated beneath her sternum, and something strange and fleshy twitched shut at the base of her throat, like a drawbridge closing. She expected to choke, but instead the burning in her lungs receded to a dull throb, and she wondered how she could feel such relief without inhaling any air.

A swirling sensation dizzied her and she braced for the panic sure to follow. Instead, she felt herself gliding in long slow circles as if attached to the spoke of a giant wheel, all while perfectly aware she lay in a bathtub of soapy water with her eyes squeezed shut. Mika became aware of a burgeoning joy, a presence welcoming her, but she knew now not to trust it. Even so, the aches in her body, her pain and exhaustion, dissipated like rising steam.

"Are you there?" Mika asked the question with her mind, and a familiar voice spoke to her for the first time in almost twenty years.

I am always with you

"Who are you?"

I spoke to you in the clearing
tried to comfort you
but you were afraid and could not hear me

Mika turned to ice in the warm water. The Tall One was communicating with her, the alien with bottomless black eyes who'd peered into her soul as she sat paralyzed. "What are you?"

I can show you more
but you must choose to see

209

A righteous anger rose. "You want to show me things, to torture and brainwash me like you did Naomi?"

We made a mistake with Naomi
overwhelming her
We will not do the same with you
We do not torture
We do not kill
Violence is not in our nature
We failed Naomi
and will not take her again
But we are always with her
and also with you

She simmered, thinking about Callum's injuries, her family's heartache, and the nerve of this thing to call itself nonviolent. "If you're always with us, how can you not know about the violence you caused, violence that was a direct result of the harm you did to my family?"

The violence was human-inflicted
We do not feel rage
We do not hate
We do not have strong negative emotions like humans

The Tall One's words grew faint, and Mika's mind strained to hear them.

We exist not as individuals
but together as one hive
like many species on Earth

To separate from the hive
to speak to you like this
causes great discomfort
I do it for you

"What do you want from my family? Why did you show Naomi the terrible things people do? Are you trying to teach us some kind of lesson? Do you think we can change our world? If so, you targeted the wrong family. The Cranes have no power. We can't even sleep."

We regret that our endeavors
overstimulate the human central nervous system

"How magnanimous of you."

We showed Naomi—

"*Forced* her to watch."

So she could understand
how one species can strip another of its sentience
keep it traumatized and in pain
and then say, look at our prey
they are stupid and cumbersome
They are not like us
They do not attach to their children
or suffer as we do
They are so unintelligent
so devoid of an internal world
that their distress is of little consequence

BAM BAM BAM

She felt the bathtub shake.

BAM BAM BAM

Mika's head rose from the water and she opened her eyes. Her communication with the Tall One terminated.

BAM BAM BAM

Someone pounded on the door of her motel room. She jumped from the tub, sure the door would break if she didn't reach it quickly.

"I'm coming! One minute!" She cursed Ron and his mammoth hands.

"Secaucus Police! Open up!"

The police?

"Hold on! I need to get dressed!" She threw her clothes on so fast she slipped on the wet tiles and almost fell back into the tub.

A string of barked, muffled orders was followed by even louder bashing. Mika exited the bathroom room just in time to see a crack zig zag down the center of the bulging door. The door flew inward off its hinges and slammed against the wall, the inside doorknob punching a crater in the plaster. Three cops, one broad-shouldered woman and two stocky men, entered the motel room with their guns drawn. They barreled toward her, and a moment later, Mika's cheek hit the rough carpet, and one of the male officers knelt on her back. He handcuffed Mika's wrists behind her and recited a list of her legal rights.

The cops dragged her outside onto the second-story landing then down the steps to street-level. The same surly clerk Mika had dealt with the night before stood on the curb outside the motel office. The clerk shook his fists at the cops, demanding they pay for the damages, veins bulging on his forehead like angry blue worms.

The cops led Mika into the parking lot, and she spotted a pale blur in her peripheral vision. Someone skulked between two parked cars, crouched and white-haired. Marcus stood from behind a dinged-up Subaru, wearing sun glasses.

A cop pushed her head down, thumping it against the top of the car door before shoving her into the backseat of a police cruiser. Mika's scalp screamed and her wrists howled from the too-tight handcuffs. Through the back window, she saw Marcus emerge onto the open pavement, growing smaller as the cops pulled away. She thought back to her conversation with Naomi in the motel room. Naomi said Marcus had borrowed her cell phone in the past, the same phone Naomi gave to Mika.

That stalker put tracking software on it.

21

—

At the police station, a female officer with callused palms fingerprinted Mika then escorted her down a hallway to a cramped holding cell. Mika caught a glimpse of herself in a glass panel on the entry door. Her hair, drenched with soapy water, had air-dried into an assortment of greasy-looking cowlicks.

Snapping on a fresh pair of powdered gloves, the officer said she needed to inspect Mika for contraband. "Trust me, I don't like this any more than you do," the officer said, pulling down a privacy shade on the door.

After the awkward strip search, Mika received permission to make a phone call. A large square speaker bolted to the wall of the holding cell, equipped with a dial pad, served as the phone. She called the landline at the main house, hoping Naomi would answer, and almost cried in relief when she did.

"I'm at the Secaucus police station. They're about to transfer me to the jail."

"I know. Ron called me from the motel. The manager told him you were arrested. He's on his way to see you now. How are you doing?"

Oh, just peachy. Mika's migraine raged. Every cell in her body craved the rush of a Master Blaster, that sharp fizzy burn in her mouth. She scratched at her thighs and the side of her ribcage, wondering if a squadron of bed bugs had made a meal of her at the motel.

"How's Callum?" Mika asked.

"No updates."

She asked about their family and Adrian, and Naomi said everyone was thankful Mika had a lawyer on the way. Naomi's management company had granted her emergency leave. Adrian was still in the city but would be back to visit on his day off. "Don't worry about us," Naomi said. "You have enough to focus on."

"Marcus did this," Mika blurted. "He gave the police my location. I saw him at the motel, lurking in the parking lot during my arrest."

"*Marcus* was at the Skyline?"

"I think he installed tracking software on the phone you gave me. He probably installed it on your regular cell, too. I bet that's how he always knows where you are."

Naomi cursed, but her anger gave way to concern when Mika broke into a coughing fit. "Mika, are you okay?"

Mika continued, determined to tell her sister what she'd discovered. "I'm fine. There's something else you should know. That day in the pool, we were both underwater. I think it's easier for the aliens to infiltrate our minds, to fully connect to us, when we're deprived of oxygen.

"I tested the theory at the motel. I held my breath to near unconsciousness and spontaneously connected to one of them. It spoke to me, Naomi, and I recognized it. I heard that same voice when I was drowning. I remember now. We were playing Dead Man Floating, and I didn't tap you out. I forgot about the game. You kept holding your breath, and then you felt them, didn't you? I connected with them in the pool, too, but I interpreted it differently. I thought I'd drowned, that I'd died and heard…" She couldn't say the words. *The voice of God.* She'd been such a fool.

"You spoke to one of them at the motel?" Naomi hissed the question.

"Telepathically. It said they don't want to hurt us, and they regret what they put you through."

"And you believe it? They're pure evil, Mika. I told you not to engage them. I told you to block them out!"

Mika didn't want to argue, but she wasn't going to let her sister steamroll her. "How far has doing it your way gotten us?"

A loaded silence followed.

"I'm not trying to hurt you, Naomi, but I need you to hear me out. Connecting with the aliens is not a one-way street. That's a good thing. The more I communicate with them, the more I can learn about them, pry into their minds like they do to us, dig around for vulnerabilities and anything we can use against them." Another coughing fit assailed her sore chest and throat.

"You sound really sick, Mika."

"I feel like hell."

"Are you eating? You have to keep your strength up. I'll put money on your commissary when they move you to jail."

"My what?"

"It's a bank account for prisoners. They'll give you access to it once you're processed. Ask the guards for your account number. You can buy snacks and drinks. There won't be a lot you can eat at mealtimes. You'll need the extra calories."

Oh, yeah. Mom had one of those accounts when she did time.

A male police officer with withered skin and wet, rheumy eyes appeared at her side. "Crane, you got a visitor."

"Ron must be here. I'll call you back." Mika suddenly felt eager for legal advice, the words *processed* and *jail* ringing in her ears.

"I'll be here. But please Mika, do *not* try to communicate with them again, at least until we can talk in person."

"Did you ever hear one them speak to you in your head? Telepathically?"

"Never." Naomi's voice hitched, and Mika sensed her fear and regret. "I'm worried about you."

"No matter what happens I'm glad I know the truth. Thanks for that and for Ron...and thanks for coming home."

"Thank me by blocking them out."

The officer re-handcuffed Mika then led her down another hallway. Sunlight from a series of skylights stamped bright squares of morning sun on the scuffed floor. He guided her to a windowless room larger than the holding cell and furnished with a metal table and two chairs, all bolted to the floor.

Mika expected to see Ron but instead found Callum leaning against the wall, his right eye sealed shut in a bulbous mass. Her heart flailed against her breastbone like a moth hitting a lightbulb. Callum's protruding forehead met the flesh around his right eye in a gruesome plateau, and dried blood crusted a section of his hairline. She glanced at her police escort, but the cop averted his gaze.

"I appreciate this, Jim," Callum said to the cop. He spoke with a slight lisp, two black holes where his front teeth used to be. The officer shook his hand and slunk out of the room, shutting the door behind him. Alone with Callum, Mika felt vulnerable with her hands cuffed behind her back. She stepped back toward the closed door, afraid he might charge her. Or shoot her. When he didn't react, she lifted her eyes to his swollen face. "I hate myself for doing that to you." The words fell to the cement floor, wholly inadequate.

Callum sniffed derisively and gestured to one of the chairs. "They can't record us in here."

Mika sat, eager to explain herself. "I didn't mean to hurt you. I had a flashback, and it completely consumed me to the point I didn't know you were there. I felt like I was literally somewhere else in time. Your face, I'm so sorry. And your teeth. You can get dental implants. I'll pay for them, of course." She tried to adjust the strange chirpiness in her voice. "I'll do anything—"

He shushed her. "They suspended me without pay, pending an investigation into how and when the bat was removed from the station house."

Her heart fell. "They recognized the bat?"

"Of course they did. That paint job, the lettering? People remember it from the Bat Lady video. The fucking thing's famous. They checked the evidence log. They know it wasn't signed out or destroyed after Tessie's case closed. I'll lose my job, my pension too, if they convict me of stealing evidence. I'll do time. Cops don't do well in prison. Some perp will finish the job you started. That should make you happy."

"I won't let that happen."

His good eye glistened. "I tried to help you and your fucked-up family. And this is what I get? *This?*" His voice cracked. "Why, Mika? Tell me why?"

Without thinking, she scooted forward in her seat to get closer to him. Callum balked and leaned back, away from her.

He's traumatized. All those years on the force, and it was her who almost killed him. Even now she couldn't give him what he wanted. Couldn't tell him the whole truth. But there was one thing she could do for him. "Did the union get you a lawyer?"

He nodded.

"Tell your lawyer you saw me and that I confessed to stealing the bat. I'll write a statement swearing to it. Just give me the details." She lowered her voice to a whisper. "Remind me how you did it, so I know what to say. There's a blind spot, right? The station cameras don't pick up the side entrance to the evidence closet."

He sniffed loudly then winced in pain, but his demeanor changed. A faint hope dawned on his swollen face. "You could say you took the locker key from my keyring and replaced it after you took the bat, so I didn't notice. That you entered through the side door when Sergeant Mendez went on break to eat his meal. I'd talked about him, so you knew he was a neat freak who couldn't stand crumbs on his desk, and he went to the kitchen every night like clockwork at two a.m. And you knew me and Jenkins were on patrol, that no one else was at the station."

Mika nodded her head vigorously. "I'll say exactly that. I'll swear to it."

"You'll do extra time."

"I don't care."

"You say that now, but when—"

"I'll do it today. I'll confess right now."

A commotion erupted outside the interrogation room. Ron exploded into the room, his hair gelled, face shaven, wearing another one of his trademark linen suits. He smelled like Old Spice and bravado. His soaring form froze when he spotted Callum.

"You're the ex-boyfriend, aren't you? The cop. You're supposed to be in the hospital." Ron shook his head. "Bad move coming here. Really dumb." He turned to confront the rheumy-eyed officer who stood flustered outside the doorway. "This man isn't on the visitor's list. But you knew that, didn't you?" Ron spun again, surprisingly agile, and jabbed a finger at Callum. "I should thank you. This could blow the state's whole case, you showing up here."

"I called him," Mika lied, "and asked him to come."

"Not another word," Ron said to Mika, his eyes never leaving Callum. "What are you still doing here? Get out."

"Ron, don't speak to him like that," Mika said.

When Callum didn't move, Ron snarled at the officer cowering in the hallway. "You wanna go down for a colleague who intimidates witnesses? Guess you don't have a family to feed."

The officer glanced at Callum and gestured to the door. "Time's up."

Callum tried to muster some dignity, holding up his battered head as he exited the room, his good eye boring into Mika.

"I want to write a statement." Mika spoke loudly for Callum's benefit. "For the record, I stole the bat I used to attack Callum from police evidence." She heard how absurd she sounded: a bad actor in a network procedural. *Oh well, I'm sticking to the script.*

Ron shut the door so just the two of them remained in the windowless room.

"Hello to you too, Mika. I'm your lawyer, so let me do the talking on your behalf from now on, okay? Don't speak to anyone other than me about your case, especially not the yahoo you worked over with a bat."

"I'm sorry Naomi dragged you into this," she said.

Ron's face softened. He took off his jacket, sat across from her, and folded his hands together on the table. His gold wedding band gleamed. "You shouldn't have talked to your ex, but him coming here? That's a clear attempt at manipulation, and it will benefit us. He should know better. Don't be a sucker and buy into any sob story he's giving you." He smiled grimly. "We have the upper hand now."

"I attacked him, Ron, with the bat I stole from his station house. I want to confess."

"That's the scam he wants you to run, huh? Look, the bat's his problem. You have enough of your own. I get it, you feel bad about bashing the guy. Not such a nice dude though, in my opinion. Shows up at your place, uninvited and drunk—they ran his blood at the hospital. Maybe he's bitter about getting dumped. Maybe gets rough with you on the night of your father's service. Think about that. What kind of man hassles his ex on the night of her father's funeral? An obsessive type, that's who. A man who thinks women owe him something. He sees you packing up to leave and snaps. Of course you protected yourself."

Mika shook her head. "I remembered an alien encounter from childhood. Dr. Patel said we might have spontaneous recall after getting dosed, remember? Well, I did. That's why I attacked Callum, I thought I was attacking *an alien*."

He studied her, rubbing his wedding ring with the fingers of his opposite hand. "That's not helpful. Not helpful at all. Bringing up the contactee group, that quack hypnotist, or anything about aliens will not bode well for us."

Mika stood. "Ron, I'm grateful you came, and I know you want to help, but a public defender might be a better choice for me. You're too close to all this." She wanted out of the stuffy room. It stank of Old Spice and bad decisions.

The creases on Ron's face etched deeper. "Hold your horses. Don't say something you'll regret. You're upset after seeing your ex banged up. I get it. You and me? We can take it one step at a time. We'll talk again before your arraign-ment. If I came off a little hot headed, then I apologize. Don't make any rash decisions, okay? I'm going to see Naomi and meet your family now. I'd hate to bring them more bad news."

"Give me your number," Mika said, eager to get rid of him. "I'll call you and let you know what I want to do. Listen, I really do appreciate—" Her words fell victim to another coughing fit.

Ron asked her if she wanted a glass of water, but she couldn't respond. Nails were stuck in her throat and rough concrete filled her chest cavity. Every cough dealt another scraping blow. When the worst of it passed, she took her hand from her mouth and saw bright red on her palm.

"Sweet Jesus." Ron got up, yanked open door, and yelled into the hallway that she needed medical attention.

Blood, metallic and salty, coated her gums. She recalled her dad's slashed jaw, Callum's brutalized face, and her own face flecked with blood in the motel mirror. The recent events of her life played through her mind in jerking vignettes splattered in crimson. She thought of the Tall One's virtue-signaling, how it heralded its kind as *non-violent* despite the trauma they inflicted. Mika spit blood on the floor. Naomi wanted her to block out the aliens instead of fighting back, but she was all grown up and didn't take orders from Naomi anymore.

<hr />

Five hours later in the county jail's infirmary, Mika sat on a cot with her tongue sticking out. On either side of her, cots leaned against a pale wall like they were posing for a police lineup.

The young, gum-chewing nurse leaning over Mika spotted the tissue damage in her throat using a penlight. She ushered Mika to a desk in the corner of the airless room, sat down behind a computer monitor, and instructed Mika to sit on the immovable stool across from her.

The nurse typed on a battered keyboard. "The irritation looks recent, and there's a lot of it. You'll need a scope. That's a tube with a tiny camera on the end. A doctor will slide it down your throat and figure out what's making you sick. We can't do it here. You'll have to go to the hospital." She clicked her computer mouse a few times. "You're in luck. There's a van scheduled for the morning. I'll try to get you on the roster, but if I can't, you'll have to wait a week. In the meantime, I'll give you a strong anti-acid."

Mika put her hand on her chest. "Are you sure it's not my heart? Heart problems run in my family."

The nurse chewed her gum thoughtfully. "It's possible, but I think it's your upper digestive track, honey. My guess is the muscles in your esophagus are dysfunctional, either lax or spasming. Bottom line, those muscles aren't doing their jobs properly, and the enzymes in your stomach are shooting up into your throat, maybe as high as your mouth. Instead of digesting your food, they're digesting you."

"I'm eating myself alive?"

The nurse grinned. "A few nibbles, yeah. That's my guess. A doctor at the hospital will say for sure." Her fingers hovered expectantly over the keyboard. "How many alcoholic drinks do you consume a day?"

Mika shrugged. "Maybe three or four a month."

"Caffeinated drinks?"

"Could caffeine cause this?"

The nurse chuckled, and Mika caught a whiff of her spearmint gum and the garlic it couldn't quite mask. "Maybe if you drank enough to kill a buffalo. What? Don't look so scared. This is most likely a treatable condition. Going forward, try not to irritate your stomach. Eat bland foods like potatoes and oatmeal. Gravity is your best friend in this situation. Remain partially upright even while sleeping. No lying flat, okay? Good luck." She pushed a buzzer on her desk and indicated Mika should exit her office. A guard appeared outside the caged window of the infirmary door.

Mika stood. "Wait, there's something else. I need Slumbutrol for my insomnia."

The nurse tapped on her keyboard and squinted at her computer screen. "We don't have it on your meds list."

"I have a prescription."

The pleasant smile abandoned the woman's face. "Well, we don't have a record of it." She hit the buzzer again and tapped the window with her clipboard. A guard brought in another inmate and escorted Mika out.

22

—

A correction officer buzzed Mika into the Women's Pod, a two-story, pie-shaped unit with a blue metal staircase standing in contrast to the white walls. The inmates' voices ricocheted off the cement with nothing porous to absorb them, a shrieking cacophony that hushed when Mika entered the pod. While the inmates sized her up, she gripped her provided bedroll and followed a guard to the stairs, wearing navy prison scrubs.

A half-dozen inmates leaned over the second-floor railing and recited the repetitive *Batman* theme at Mika, interspersed with riotous cackling. *Da na na na na na na na*. The choir grew as she ascended the stairs and more inmates recognized her. She wore a neutral expression and ignored the taunts. *Don't show weakness or you'll be an even bigger target.* She'd watched enough television to know that.

The pain in her throat, chest, and bruised back flared with every step she ascended. A nagging itch, difficult to pinpoint and impossible to ignore, crawled over her body.

The guard led Mika to the open door of a two-person cell then abandoned her. She placed her bedroll on the empty top bunk and tried to appear casual when greeting her cellmate Jessica, a petite redhead with barely-there eyebrows and an array of homemade tattoos on her arms.

"Don't look so nervous," Jessica said after shaking Mika's hand like they were meeting for a business lunch. "And don't worry about the girls giving you shit. They're just having a little fun. We watch the local news, so everyone knows who you are." She grinned. Her teeth had an orange hue. "I'm happy you're my cellie. And don't worry about the stench. You won't notice it in a day or two." The jail smelled of mildew and chemicals.

Jessica had an old friend, it turned out, who did time with Mika's mom. Tessie Crane taught Jessica's friend how to curl her hair by rolling it in toilet paper, Jessica said, and her friend liked it so much, she kept curling it that way after getting out. As far as Jessica was concerned, she assured Mika, the Cranes were good stock, her kind of people, and everyone knew Tessie got a raw deal. Jessica went on to reveal she had a stash of e-cigarettes, snacks, and soda stuffed in two pillow cases under her cot.

Jessica pulled the pillow cases out and gestured for Mika to have a look. "Take your pick. You can owe me for it."

Mika selected two bottles of Mountain Dew. She had zero chance of napping, anyway, with all the yelling and clanging and bright lights she couldn't shut off. She opened one of the bottles, setting a goal to consume only enough to keep her headache shy of excruciating.

A buzzer went off, and Jessica ushered her downstairs to line up behind other inmates waiting to receive their meds. Mika swallowed the antacid a guard handed her then returned to her cell with Jessica. Several inmates followed them inside, spitting out the pills they'd hidden in their cheeks and passing them to Jessica.

Mika watched, both fascinated and skeeved, as Jessica crushed the variety of pills with a dog-eared romance paperback and funneled the damp powder into a de-labeled soda bottle half-filled with an orange goo. This goo, Mika came to learn, was a mixture of dissolved lozenges and water the inmates called Joint Juice.

Jessica shook the bottle with the pizazz of a seasoned mixologist then invited Mika to take a swig. Mika politely abstained, sipping her Mountain Dew, which dulled the sharp edge of her headache even as it burned her throat and set off tiny detonations in her belly.

After all interested parties fairly consumed the Joint Juice, the visiting inmates dispersed and Jessica quickly fell asleep. Mika sat stiff and upright in her bunk, her back against the wall. She drained the rest of her soda, opened the second bottle, and wondered what was next for her. An indictment? Formal charges? She'd been eager to get away from Ron, but he was her best resource for information on her case. She needed to call him, regardless, to find out how to get Slumbutrol on her meds list. But Mika also had a statement to write. For someone with nowhere to go, her to-do list loomed large.

Mika ventured downstairs to the main rec room and spotted several inmates with computer tablets. One of them, sixty-ish and petite, picked up on Mika's interest and nodded at Mika's half empty bottle of Mountain Dew. After a quick negotiation, Mika reluctantly exchanged her soda bottle for fifteen minutes of tablet time, telling herself she'd soon access her commissary and buy another bottle.

Sitting at an empty table away from the other inmates, she wrote Callum a detailed email confessing to stealing the softball bat from his station house. Sure, the confession might seem ludicrous to anyone who read it. An obvious lie. *Can they prove it, though?* She didn't think so. She sent the email and the digital *swish* released some of the pressure compressing her head. She'd done what she could for Callum. *I can let him go now.* She imagined a cord connecting the two of them, thin and tattered. It snapped in two and disintegrated.

Mika felt a modicum of peace. She breathed deeply through her physical pains, the unthinkable things she'd witnessed and done, and the still-lingering shock of her father's death. Her thoughts shifted to her family and their future. By accepting whatever plea the state offered, she would spare them the spectacle of another trial. Her family would miss her, mourn her incarceration, but they'd get through it. *They have Naomi now.*

Mika felt a strange flatness when considering her family. Had her mom felt similarly while serving time? Perhaps this flatness was a self-defense mechanism, one that lessened the stress of homesickness while incarcerated.

Other inmates were gathered around tables, playing card games and chatting. Mika heard snippets of their boisterous conversations about their kids, love interests, and friends on the outside. The inmates were survivors making the best of their time in jail, so why did their desire to wring support from one another seem so frenzied and desperate?

The inmates were no different than anyone on the outside. Mika chuckled to herself. *I've been in jail one day, and I'm already calling it the "outside."* But it was true, people generally wanted the same things: a family, a partner, close friends, a pet, something to get them through the nights until there were no more nights to get through. They were all sinking ships signaling to each other across a vast, uncaring sea.

Whoa. Such bleakness surprised her, yet the sentiment chimed through her without a false note. *Something's shifting inside me*, she thought. *Changing how I see the world.* Was she a nihilist now, a misanthrope questioning the very fundamentals of life, the call to find a tribe and reproduce? *Nah.* She'd just picked up a raging case of jailhouse blues. *I need a pick-me-up.* She scratched at her arms and thought about scoring another Mountain Dew, but she had other, more pressing tasks on her checklist.

She waited in line for a phone to open up, then made a collect call to the number on Ron's business card.

"It's good you called, Mika. We have a pre-indictment conference set up for the day after tomorrow. There could be some wiggle room on your charges if you go on record about Callum stealing that bat. I know all about its illustrious history now, but that's beside the point. It changes the whole game, that bat. A prosecutor can't paint Callum as an innocent victim if he's a crooked cop out there poaching evidence. If he's not a credible witness, that makes it easier for a jury to believe you acted in self-defense."

"Ron, I want you to know something before you say anything else." She steeled herself, expecting his volume to increase. "I emailed Callum a statement confessing to stealing the bat from his station house. I'm sure his lawyer has it already."

Ron surprised her by taking it in stride. "First off, no one's going to believe any malarkey about you rummaging through a police station undetected. And it doesn't matter what Callum *manipulated* you into confessing during his ill-advised visit." He shifted gears. "Are you getting hassled in there? If so, I can get you moved to protective custody. Say the word, and I'll have you classified as a public figure."

Mika stayed on track. "Whether they believe my confession or not, I won't stop repeating it. Knowing that, do you think you can still represent me? If so, we need to get on the same page about something: Callum's the victim here. He can't lose his career and face charges while he's recovering from the injuries I gave him. Who will hire him then? How will he pay his medical bills?"

Ron cleared his throat. "It's noble wanting to throw yourself on the sword for your ex, but no one is going to believe you. I sure as hell don't. And Naomi would never forgive me if I let you self-destruct. Look, the D.A. doesn't want another Crane trial making headlines. Plenty of people still consider your mother a vigilante hero. People were pissed the Chapman kid got a slap on the wrist, and the D.A. knows damn well one of them could end up on your jury. I think we have a solid shot at a plea that gets you out of prison in a year.

"Plus, there are mitigating circumstances here, aside from the actions of your drunk, aggressive ex. Your sister said you were only home for a couple days, and she found twelve empty energy drinks scattered around your place. Five hundred milligrams of caffeine a pop. You're lucky you're alive."

Mika made a face. "Twelve? I don't think I drank twelve." Then she recalled her overstuffed recycling bin, and how she'd resorted to leaving empty Master Blasters on various surfaces in the kitchen and living room, white cans with red rocket ships greeting her at every turn.

Ron pressed on. "Naomi told me you were throwing those drinks back like water in the city, too. I looked into it and guess what? When a person ingests that much caffeine, they can experience episodes of acute psychosis. There you were in New York, under stress and face to face with Naomi after all those years. You're mainlining caffeine because you left your insomnia medicine at home. And not just any insomnia med, but *Slumbutrol.* The pharmaceutical company that manufactures Slumbutrol is facing a class-action suit as we speak. Turns out, those pills hijack the dopamine receptors in your brain, render them inoperable, so the only way to stop feeling like dogshit is to take more. And get this, Slumbutrol withdrawal is now thought to cause delirium, paranoia, dissociation, a whole grab bag of ailments. You can't stop that drug cold turkey, Mika. You have to taper!

"So, there you were, jacked to the rafters on caffeine and going through withdrawals. And in the middle of that shit show, your pop passes away, may he rest in peace." He cleared his throat, uncomfortable. "We won't mention the LSD episode in the park. That would bring up a lot of questions we don't want to answer. But I've got a lot of great stuff to work with. I don't want to get your hopes up, but if the stars align and you do the right thing, there's a chance you won't get any prison time."

He paused then spoke somberly. "Janice and I talked a lot the last few days. I told her the truth about what the guys and I saw on our corner in South Philly. She believes I saw a UFO but said the abduction stuff, the memory wipes and all that, is a bunch of bull, and I think she could be right. I can't speak for anyone else in the group, of course—and, I want to be clear, I love Naomi like a daughter. But she is a natural leader, the kind of woman people believe in and want to follow. Your sister Paige, she said you always looked up to Naomi, that you followed her everywhere she went. Look, I'm not pointing fingers here, Mika. I bought into the whole thing, too."

Mika drummed her fingers on top of the phone casing. "It's great you and Janice are working things out. Really, good for you two. But if we're going to move forward together, then—"

"For now, the only thing we need to agree on is how we're gonna tell your story. I'll go over it again. You have a sleep disorder and were put on an addictive prescription drug with serious and undisclosed withdrawal symptoms. To cope with your withdrawal and fatigue, you ingested a near-deadly amount of caffeine and didn't sleep for days. Then your gun-toting drunk ex-boyfriend subjected you to an unwanted visit—on the day of your father's funeral, no less. You felt threatened and defended yourself. It's as simple as that. I *do* want to move forward with you, Mika. First we get you out on bail, then out of this mess altogether. After that, sky's the limit. We'll sue the shit out the cops, the energy drink folks, the Slumbutrol folks. All of them."

"I'm sticking by my confession, and what I did to Callum was not self-defense as you explained it," Mika said. "I need you to understand that. And you can think what you want about Naomi and aliens. I know my truth."

But did she? Her heart fluttered. Caffeine and Slumbutrol withdrawal caused a ton of brutal side effects. *Including paranoia and delirium.* She gritted her teeth. *No, I won't let him rattle me.* Lawyers manipulated people for a living.

"Don't be stubborn," Ron said. "I hear the doubt in your voice. Tell the truth about Callum and the infamous bat. Your family doesn't want you sitting in jail. They need you. Play this wrong and you could go away for a long time. And not to some country club like you're in now. To prison, where every time you take a shit it will be in front of an audience. You'll be locked up with murderers, women who'll peg you as an easy mark the second they see you. Lifers with nothing to look forward to except making you miserable. Let's strategize again right before the conference. I'll see you in person then. In the meantime, call your family. Talk to them."

"You're a good friend to Naomi," Mika said, and she meant it. Emotion hoarsened her voice. "She's lucky to have you, and so is Janice. I'm sorry, Ron, but you're fired. I want a public defender. Thank you again for everything."

———

She returned to her cell, to her awkward sitting position on the top bunk. An hour ticked by with Jessica still passed out on the bunk below her. Mika yearned for something more than caffeine, Slumbutrol, or even sleep. The yearning had built inside her since her arrest at the motel, a want too awful to acknowledge. But after twitching so long with wretched wakefulness and pain, Mika had no energy left to lie to herself. She wanted to connect with the Tall One. Not to try to suss out its alien agenda—she couldn't even focus long enough to get through a paragraph of Jessica's romance novel—but to relieve her emotional and physical pain. She'd taken steps to mitigate the damage done to Callum. Didn't she deserve a brief reward?

Mika closed her eyes and pressed her hands over her nose and mouth, preparing to hold her breath for as long as possible, but those efforts proved unnecessary. After only a few seconds of oxygen deprivation, she felt a movement in her throat, a fleshy drawbridge closing among the irritated tissue.

Something twitched in her gray matter, and she found herself gliding in long circles again, as she had in the motel bathtub. In her mind's eye, she saw herself swirling through inky liquid on the outskirts of a great and looping current. *I'm in the Wheel*, she thought. *That's what I'll call it.* The soothing energy of the Wheel eased her pain and invigorated her spirit. She sensed the Tall One, but they did not speak. After several minutes, she opened her eyes and broke the connection. *Just a little taste*, she thought, *to get me through the night.*

She pressed her back against the hard wall, and guilt pointed a finger at her. Had she forgotten her family were still targets? Did she not want to free them from their alien puppeteers? She should have tried to infiltrate the Tall One's mind, search for a weakness to exploit. *I won't connect again until I have a plan.*

23

—

At eight in the morning, a voice crackled through the pod's loudspeaker:

"Murphy, Rickles, and Crane, report to the guard desk."

What now? Mika dropped from her bunk to the cement floor. Her body howled in protest, cramped after sitting up all night, but the burn in her throat simmered on a lower heat. Keeping her upper body vertical had helped, as the nurse recommended.

Jessica finally woke up, and on the wrong side of a hangover, from the looks of it. She scowled at Mika from the bottom bunk, dried orange goo crusting the corners of her mouth. "Where's my goods?"

Mika titled her head. "What goods?"

The redhead's gray eyes shrank into her face. "You owe me for the Dews."

"Oh! Yeah, I didn't forget. I'm ordering commissary today."

"Five for two. I give you two items, you owe me five. Due last night. That was our deal."

Mika bristled. *Quite the shakedown.* "The guard's calling me. Let me check in down there, and then I'll order you five items. What are you looking for, snacks or soda?"

"Anything you order won't come for two days. You missed the cutoff."

This was bad news for Mika's migraine. "Is there any way you can front me another two Dews until then?"

Jessica stood, squaring up on Mika until their faces were inches apart. "Do I look stupid, Crane?"

"No, of course not." Confused, Mika stepped back from her cellmate's sour breath, from the malice she exuded. *Geez.* What happened to the fun-loving Jessica of yesterday? *Imagine sleeping for twelve hours and waking up with a chip on your shoulder.*

The buzzer went off again. "Murphy, Rickles, Crane. Guard desk. Now."

"I have to go." Mika escaped downstairs and milled around the guard desk with the other two summoned inmates. Rickles, lanky and youthful-looking despite a thick head of gray hair, looked slightly more approachable than raven-haired Murphy, who strutted around with the dodge and sway of a boxer-turned-pickpocket.

Mika asked Rickles if she knew what the guards wanted, and Rickles grunted something about going to the hospital. *Oh yeah.* Mika had forgotten about her impending doctor's visit. *I can ask for a Slumbutrol script and pain meds.*

Jessica descended the metal stairs. Her steely gaze landed briefly on Mika before she beckoned Rickles and Murphy to her side for a private conversation. Mika grew uneasy watching the three of them huddle, realizing she'd made a crucial mistake with Jessica. If commissary items were currency, as good as money, then she'd inadvertently stolen from her cellmate, insulted her, too. *I'll make it up to her.* She had to. *I need more Dews.*

Two guards handcuffed Mika, Rickles, and Murphy, then shackled them at their ankles and shuffled them, single file, through a labyrinth of buzzing doors into the warm sunshine and onto a waiting transport van. Mika found herself in the unenviable middle seat in the back of the van. After they pulled onto the highway, Mika's attempts at small talk with her fellow inmates went nowhere, yet the two women chatted to each other as if she didn't exist. *Real mature.*

The van stuttered and jerked through morning rush hour traffic, the weak air conditioning failing to reach the inmates. After lurching along for forty minutes, Rickles and Murphy started jockeying for extra room. They widened their knees as far as their bound ankles would allow, invading Mika's limited space. They were looking for a reaction and she didn't give them one, even as her discomfort reached claustrophobic heights.

Rickles elbowed Mika in the ribs and pushed her into Murphy, who pushed back.

Mika tried to reason with them. "I'm going to do right by Jessica as soon as we get back. Forget five for two. I'll double that."

"I think you should triple it," Rickles said. "And throw some items our way too." Murphy cackled, nodding in agreement.

A guard piped in from the passenger seat. "Keep it down, ladies." He didn't bother to turn around.

The van darted forward in quick bursts, then jolted to stops that knocked bones against metal. Mika suspected the guard's awful driving was purposeful, a way to work off his frustration at being stuck in traffic. She didn't suppress her ugly thoughts about him. The nausea twisting her belly was exasperated by every thump of the brake, every breath of the stuffy air.

Mika leaned forward to address the guard in the passenger seat. "We need some air. Can you roll a window down back here?"

"They don't go down, idiot," Murphy said, before leaning over Mika to talk to Rickles. "She doesn't know much, does she? Some people gotta learn the hard way." The two inmates exchanged quick, knowing glances, then both reached for Mika, straining against their handcuffs to deliver shallow punches. On instinct, Mika dropped her head between her legs, protecting her face. The van came to an especially abrupt stop, and the back door opened.

"Playtime's over," the guard said. "You're here."

The guards ushered the women from the van and led them into the hospital's prison wing, where their ankle shackles were removed. Rickles and Murphy waved goodbye with their middle fingers as one of the guards brought Mika into a private room that smelled like rubbing alcohol. A male guard instructed her to lie on the exam table then secured her arms and legs to attached restraints. Mika did a mental scan of her body, searching for new injuries, more pains to add to her collection. Rickles and Murphy had left her shaken and scratched, but unhurt.

Wait till the adrenaline dies down, then you'll feel it.

"I'm not supposed to lie flat," she told the guard.

He shrugged. "You should have thought about that before getting physical in the van. You could be here for a while, but a doc will show eventually. Get comfy and don't cause any more trouble unless you want me to write you up for fighting. That would put you on restriction: no tablet time, no phone time, and no commissary."

The guard left and Mika could do nothing but stare at the ceiling. She noted how pristine and shiny the large, white ceiling tiles were. So pristine the discolored edges on one tile stuck out, a tile sitting slightly askew. Time inched forward, and she could feel the sour flow of enzymes creeping up from her stomach and puddling at the bottom of her throat.

Before this moment, Mika had assumed her rock-bottom moment would always be her performance at the Marriot Marquis, but surely she'd reached a new low now, lying there chained to an exam table as her confused body tried to consume itself. *Don't be an idiot,* she thought. *Your rock bottom moment was attacking Callum.* She fell into a bleak malaise, her litany of pains flaring. *And this is just the beginning. How will I survive being locked up year after year?*

She closed her eyes and prayed to God for help and guidance. Then she remembered that for most of her life, and at that very moment, she'd prayed to a monster and not a god. Yet she continued her pleas, and once again, she barely had to hold her breath before serenity filled her empty places. Her missing pieces.

She knew it was wrong, knew the comfort provided was likely a manipulation, the guise of a destructive alien agenda. Still, she granted herself another guilt-free reprieve and glided in the Wheel's dark current. Soon after, the Tall One spoke to her.

The doctor and nurse will arrive soon
They cannot look inside you
We will have to intervene
No one will be hurt

Mika spoke quietly, though she knew she didn't need to speak at all. Verbalizing afforded her the illusion of distance and a semblance of control. "Why can't they look in my throat?"

They will see that you are different
Do not be concerned
They may appear distressed when we take them
but they will not feel pain.
They will return believing they performed an endoscopy
The doctor will tell you the procedure showed sores
behind your voice box
consistent with laryngopharyngeal reflux

Dread polluted her newfound comfort like an oil spill. She understood all too well the violation about to be inflicted on the medical staff.

"You took my father, didn't you, from the forest and then later from his hospital room?" she asked. "Did you take me, too, when I visited him?"

We took your father from his hospital room
to remove a device from his body
We were concerned he would harm himself further
You were sedated on that occasion

"You put a device in his face to track his movements?"

And monitor his bodily systems and emotional states

Mika recoiled, angered by this violation. "You put one inside me, too, didn't you? I felt it move in my throat."

You and Naomi are always with us
There is no need for a device

"Then what are you trying to hide from the medical staff?"

A muscle not part of human anatomy.
It prevents water from entering the lungs
when underwater for extended periods

"What are you saying?" Repulsed, she pulled further from the Wheel's serenity. Existing in two places at once, she felt the length of the exam table beneath her while continuing to drift in the outskirts of a cylindrical current. Her fingers moved to her throat. "Did you implant an alien muscle in my fucking throat?"

No implantation was necessary
You and Naomi are hybrids

part human and part hive
The stimulation of this muscle triggers your transformation

Her laughter rang shrill. "I was created the old-fashioned way, and I have the birth certificate and baby pictures to prove it."

You are your parent's child
but also ours
It is ironic that human DNA is compatible with the hive
given that humans are the most violent species on their
planet
and we are non-violent
We have created hybrids for a long time
but it is rare to have them connect willingly to the hive
You are a great achievement
You belong with us
You know this Mika
We feel what you feel
We are always with you

She was about to open her eyes and escape the Tall One's trickery, but she held back. *What if I'm the one lying? Lying to myself.* She couldn't deny her deep connection to the Tall One, the presence she first heard under chlorinated water on a chilly June morning, but had felt her entire life. Perhaps her missing pieces were finally clicking into place. *Be careful what you wish for.*

Her thoughts returned to the approaching doctor and nurse, innocents about to be subjected to a trauma they wouldn't recall. Trauma that would likely impact the rest of their lives and send them spiraling into lesser versions of themselves.

"If you feel what I feel, then you know I want you to leave the staff here alone."

It will be over soon

"Then what? If you take them this once, you'll never do it again?"

If you are called upon again for a similar exam
we will do what is needed

"This could go on and on, involving more and more people?"

That is possible

"There has to be another way."

You don't belong here
in a cage or on this planet
If you stay here
we will always be with you
but there is another option
We can take you from this place and bring you home

"As a fugitive? I can't go back to the barrens."

Your home is with us
You belong with the hive

"So, I'm some lab rat you want to keep as a pet?" She swallowed a bitter laugh, afraid of how it might sound in her ears. "Why did you create me and Naomi, anyway? Just to experiment on us, ruin our lives, then give us the option of being stuck in some creepy zoo for your kind to gawk at?"

We believe
you can be happy here
and whole
It is also our hope
you will choose to help us

The Tall One's voice began to warble and fade.

Invaders enslaved our ancestors
who continue to suffer on our home planet
Our ancestors call to us
They cry out for mercy
We process their pain inside the core of the Wheel
as you call it
We are always with the ancestors
but cannot ease their anguish
It is not in our nature
You can choose to end their pain
You are one of us
but also human
and therefore capable of both great passion and violence
We evolved out of those behaviors
hundreds of thousands of years ago
That is both our strength and weakness

We created you and Naomi to free the ancestors
There were many failures before you
which we regret

Mika opened her mouth, a barrage of questions on her tongue. The Tall One spoke first as if sensing this.

There is much for you to learn
But I grow weary
apart from the hive
Do not fear
Let us all join together

The Tall One's voice faded, and Mika sensed the dark waters she swam in expand to an unfathomably distant horizon. And for the first time, she saw countless pinpoints of lights moving in a much swifter current below her. She observed this light show, far beneath her weightless legs, feeling like the sole audience in a planetarium watching a time-lapse of the Milky Way. She understood that if she entered those deeper waters, joined those swirling lights, she'd be plugging into a new transmission, one with a bandwidth far beyond her connection with the Tall One.

A part of her revolted, remembering how smothered she felt seeing those wretched birds on the Christmas quilt—the moment Naomi's mind had invaded her own. *What will become of me if I plug in?* Would she disappear, overwhelmed and absorbed by an alien consciousness?

Mika recalled her bus ride into New York, on her way to look for Naomi. She'd been determined to get the answers she needed, to move on from her failures and find her place in the world. And now, here she was, on the brink of uncovering a great truth. A truth she must confront.

Mika communicated her consent wordlessly and dove deeper into the Wheel, aware of the shuddering of her body still bound to a hospital bed. Swept into a new and rapid current, her mind naturally adjusted to the mammoth superhighway replacing the gentle path of connection she experienced with the Tall One. Caught in the expansive breadth of this new channel, she felt invigorated. Fulfilled. *No drink, no drug, could ever feel this good.* The hive spoke.

You are with us

Her lips tingled pleasantly, as if she'd voiced the words herself, and at long last. She thought of a question. *What is the Wheel?* And the answer came instantly, not in words but in an awakening of knowledge she already possessed, like the sudden recall of a dream. Mika did not speak with the hive but rather communed with them, as one would with nature.

24

—

The Wheel Mika drifted through was a telepathic simulation of the liquid-filled chamber occupying the lower level of the hive's spacefaring ship, a chamber built to mimic the sea of their home planet. When not performing necessary tasks, members of the hive retreated to this lower level to process the emotional signals of the hive. The oldest hive members, elders revered for their wisdom and experience, entered the innermost core of this vast swirling current, where the distress signals of their ancestors were processed.

Millions of years before the hive existed, the ancestors lived peacefully on the home planet. Amphibian in nature and highly attuned to other members of their species, the ancestors excelled at avoiding predators both on land and in the sea. Over time, they honed their collective consciousness, employing herd maneuvers so evasive their predators went extinct or adapted to other diets. It was then, the hive believed, the Creators took special notice.

The Creators, a highly advanced species of unknown origin, visited the home planet and infused their DNA into a subset of ancestors before leaving, never to return. The hive emerged from this genetic engineering as a different, but not separate, species. Hive members had several new adaptations, including a significantly larger and more complex neocortex, that increased their lifespan, dexterity, and intelligence, all of which far surpassed those of their ancestors.

For eons, the hive lived in harmony with their ancestors on the home planet. The hive evolved, developing technologies and advancing to the point they detected an anomaly in the outer orbit of their star system. The anomaly, they came to understand, had been left behind by the Creators for the hive to one day discover and utilize for interstellar travel. Capable of emitting two separate energy waves, it could propel the hive's ships through space, as if on existing tracks, to and from another star system at many times lightspeed.

When they traveled to their first star system, the hive detected similar energy waves in the outer orbit of its sole life-bearing planet, which allowed them to travel to yet another star system. This second star system, too, contained a life-bearing planet with an entry and exit point in its outer orbit.

The life-bearing planet in each of these star systems housed a sentient species of remarkable intelligence, which the hive concluded, after studying the genetics of such species, had also been seeded by the Creators. These sentient species, like the hive, were all obligate bipedals with similar adaptations to their DNA affording them maximum dexterity and intelligence.

The Creators had left behind a network of gateways through the galaxy to introduce the hive and its siblings to one another. Many of the siblings were not yet spacefaring, while others had begun exploring their star systems but remained mired in their warmonger nature, such as the Homo sapiens of Earth.

The hive observed their siblings, studied them, but otherwise did not interfere with their evolution. Although the hive had evolved into a spacefaring species, they remained entangled with their ancestors, sharing a collective consciousness. When traveling in between star systems, the hive became temporarily cut off from the consciousness of their ancestors. This break in connection did not concern the hive, as their ancestors had lived with sustainable resources and without predators for hundreds of thousands of years.

But after one journey, hopping from star system to star system, the hive was inundated by distress signals from the ancestors. They immediately returned to their home planet, but due to the time dilation of superluminal travel, several thousand years had passed on the planet by the time they arrived. The ancestors had been enslaved and farmed, caged in the deepest waters of their planet's sea. Unknown invaders had long since abandoned the planet, but they left behind an impenetrable infrastructure that trapped the ancestors in an automated cycle of forced feeding and breeding. Destroying these machines, which were powered by the light of the planet's star, would kill many of the ancestors, making such efforts impossible. The hive could not harm the ancestors—it was not in their nature. And so the ancestors suffered, blind now after millennia in the dark.

Having no other option, the hive sought to become Creators themselves and design a new kind of hive member, one who lacked their genetic moral restrictions—one who could end the suffering of the ancestors. The hive developed a means to transport matter through physical barriers. This technology was unable to penetrate the invader's infrastructure, but it could move Mika through the walls of her cage, should she choose to escape her imprisonment.

As all of this knowledge awakened in Mika, she felt the Tall One reach out to her from inside the Wheel's glowing core.

We cannot kill
And thus we made you

Mika rode the spiraling current down to the inner layers of the Wheel, assimilating what the hive now offered her. She could remain incarcerated and seek out their comfort whenever she needed it, or she could join them on their home ship. She understood this while aware that, in another world, her limbs were bound.

She drew closer to where the elders endured the ancestor's pain. The Wheel's radiant core, once a pinpoint of copper light, was now a red and molten sun. Curiosity spurred her descent, despite the hive's growing hesitance. She was still partly human, after all, headstrong and rebellious.

Soon, she connected to the chaotic frequency of the ancestors, a maelstrom of pleas like the wails of a million infants. Mika bore witness to their pain, their cries for mercy and shrieks of agony. This frequency clarified and focused her mind, triggering a new and powerful instinct inside her. She drew nearer to the core, driven by a desire to act, to take on her fair share of the burden. She wanted to shoot into the core like an arrow, but the hive warned her off. It was not safe, they insisted, even if the core was only a simulacrum.

Circling the red-hued current directly above the core, a want rippled out of her and washed through the Wheel: she would to do whatever it took to stop the ancestor's pain. The joy of the hive rippled through her in response.

Mika understood what Naomi had not. The hive wanted Naomi to comprehend the ancestor's suffering, so they'd tried to contextualize it in earthly suffering, showing her humanity's carnage as a precursor to revealing the ancestor's plight. An approach that failed woefully. Mika needed no such misguided comparison. Her connection with the hive was much stronger than Naomi's. Mika understood who and what she was, understood her true purpose for the first time. Even so, she found herself thinking like an inmate, always on the take. The hive wanted something from her, so she could ask something from them in return. Negotiate her terms.

Her eyes fluttered open, and the ceiling tiles of the exam room came into focus. She felt the synthetic chill of air-conditioning and squinted against the harsh fluorescent light. Then, another light, a brilliant blue glow, materialized in front of the closed exam room door.

The glow expanded until it blotted out everything else in Mika's vision, affording her what looked like an unobstructed view of a clear, blue sky. She saw what she always did when staring at a cloudless sky for any length of time: the pale squiggles of her white blood cells flitting around inside her eye, each cell exhibiting a life of its own while remaining part of the larger organism known as Mika Crane. *Fascinating*, she thought. *Beautiful.*

Her time inside the Wheel, her reunification, had eased her pain and cravings. She barely flinched when a low rumble shook the room and she lifted from the exam table, free of her restraints.

Don't be afraid, the Tall One said. *Sleep.*

She was not. And she did.

25

—

Night had come to the barrens. Mika stood on sandy soil just inside the tree line outside her cottage, one hand pressed against the peeling trunk of an oak tree. The shock of her location change felt like stepping into a cold shower, and she gasped for breath, shivering despite the warm air. When the icy grip on her lungs faded, she registered an unusually pleasant sensation. Her muscles and joints felt supple and nimble, her mind alert and fully present. Gone was the stifling weight of fatigue, her near-constant companion, and caffeine had nothing to do with it.

Feels like I slept for hours.

Mika walked out of the forest and skirted the edges of the shrub-filled plot of land. She avoided the light spilling from her cottage, cloaking herself in shadow outside her living room window. Through slatted blinds, she observed three figures seated at the round table adjacent to her kitchen: Paige, Naomi, and her mom sharing a meal.

Excitement underpinned this solemn moment. Mika planned to deceive her family, but in doing so, she'd set them free. Muted signals from the hive rippled through her. They were with her, always with her, but stepping back to allow her this time.

Naomi held court at the table, saying something that made Paige and Tessie Crane giggle. Naomi nibbled corn on the cob, her hair tousled and hanging in her face, resembling the teenager she once was. Mika watched her mother and sisters, curious whether the sight of her family would cause her to second-guess her plans. But instead of doubt, grief surfaced— different grief than the kind she'd felt over her father's passing. This grief grew from the roots of nostalgia rather than loss. Seeing her family through the window, she experienced the same flatness she'd felt toward them in jail. This was why she grieved.

Mika waited for Naomi to venture into the kitchen alone. Finally, she did, clearing the dishes from the table and carrying them to the sink. Naomi rinsed plates under the faucet, her back to the window. Mika tapped on the glass, trying to be discreet, but Naomi didn't hear her over the running water. About to tap harder, she noticed her reflection in the glass and yanked her hand back, startled. Mika's reflection had an eerily smooth, unfamiliar quality, like an A.I. portrait of a fictional character. Naomi shut the water off and stepped toward the living room.

Naomi, I'm outside. Meet me on the weedy side of the cottage. Come alone. Mika projected the words with her mind. It happened naturally. Instinctually.

Naomi froze in mid stride and turned to the window, tracking Mika's signal. Their large eyes met, and Mika gestured for Naomi to join her. Naomi dipped her head in acknowledgment, then she collected the trash bag from the can under the sink. Tying the bag closed, she stepped into the living room to tell Tessie and Paige she was taking the garbage out. Mika retreated to the patches of sweet fern on the side of the cottage, and Naomi met her there moments later.

Naomi's questions came in hissed whispers. "What are you doing here? Did Ron get you out?" She blanched at Mika's prison scrubs. "Why are you still wearing those?" She scrutinized Mika's face and scowled.

"What are you looking at?" Mika asked.

"You look different." Naomi wrinkled her nose. "And you smell like a litter box. How did you get out?"

"The hive freed me."

"The *what*?"

"I was taken."

Shock deepened the hollows of Naomi's face, aging her a decade. She swung around and scanned the blackened forest at their backs, her head dipping into her shoulders like a fighter ready to swing. She turned back to Mika. "They took you from *jail*?"

"A hospital."

Wind rustled the surrounding pine needles into a gentle roar, yet Naomi flinched as if ducking a blow. "Where are they? Are they here?"

"Don't worry," Mika said, smiling. "They'll never come near you again."

Naomi titled her head. "Did they hurt you?"

"I feel better than I have in years. Maybe ever. I'm sad though. I'll miss seeing you in person."

"Am I going somewhere?"

"I'm the one leaving, and I need your help. I need you to tell Paige and Mom you saw me, that I got you alone and asked you to relay a message. Tell them I love them, but I know I'm not cut out for prison and wouldn't survive it. Say I escaped but refused tell you how. That I'm heading overseas to start over. I have the funds to get established with a new identity, and if they don't hear from me, it's only because it's safer that way for all of us."

Naomi peered at her. "Where are you really going?"

"With them."

Her eyes bulged. "You can't be serious."

"You hate the aliens, I get it. You moved next to a noisy bridge just to block them out, but it's different for me. I'm supposed to be with them, I know that now. It's jail I find intolerable. I can't live in a cage. You understand, don't you?"

Naomi shook her head, muttering *No no no no.* "I won't let you do this to yourself or our family."

The irony. "You left, didn't you? That was your decision and this is mine. Maybe I'm putting too much on you. Maybe I should go in there and tell Mom and Paige myself."

Naomi shook her head. "It's not a good idea to see them right now. You don't look like yourself."

"Enough of this. Let me see your phone. I want to see what I look like."

"It's in the cottage."

Mika felt her sister's conflicting signals, her stress and panic. The cord between them was still strong, but thinner now, the edges frayed and snapping. It struck Mika that human attachment, human love, was a fickle thing, given and taken away at will. Later with the hive, back inside the Wheel, Mika could let it all out, all the grief she didn't yet feel. If it came at all. The hive would carry her through it, share her burden as their own. The hive accepted her unconditionally. They were always with her.

"Why are you grinning like that?" Naomi's suspicion rippled through Mika, prickly and hot. Then Naomi's features softened in the dim light. "I'm sorry. It's been a shit day, and it keeps getting worse. You were right about Marcus turning you in. I'm afraid of what I'll do to him if I see him again. I can't work at the building anymore."

"He admitted to turning me in?" Mika asked. Weirdly, she didn't loathe Marcus anymore.

"No. This tech guy Ron knows found spyware on my cell phone. I'm sure Marcus also installed it on the one I gave you, like you said. There's no way to prove it until your property is released. Not sure that will happen now, since you're on the run." They locked eyes, and for a moment all that existed was the two of them and the chorus of croaking tree frogs. Then Naomi's expression soured.

"You should've blocked them out. But instead you let them in, let them change you. No matter what they promised, they'll hurt you like they hurt me."

"Naomi, you misinterpret their intentions, which is understandable after what they showed you, all that violence and horror. What they did to you was wrong and awful. It was stupid and hurt you deeply. They know they made a mistake, an unforgivable one, and they regret it. But they had their reasons, and it wasn't to torture—"

Naomi put her hands up. "I won't listen to you defend them. I'll walk the fuck away."

To hate the hive was to hate herself, and for that Mika pitied her. "I'm sorry. Let's change the subject. Will you stay here then, if you quit your job?"

Naomi exhaled. "I've missed the peace here, missed Mom. Adrian likes the area, and it's not too far from his family in Connecticut. We've discussed possibly relocating, getting out of the city."

Mika grinned. "I thought you'd written off humanity."

"Not like you have."

Mika's smile drooped. "You and Adrian can live in the cottage."

Naomi's jaw flexed. "For a little while, maybe, until your new friends pay a visit."

Despite the contempt in Naomi's voice, Mika felt her heart swell. "You don't need to worry about moving or keeping anyone safe," she said. "You'll never feel or see the aliens again. They let you go, Naomi. Can't you sense it? You're free and so is our family. Going forward, none of you will be taken or interfered with in any way. That's a promise."

Naomi searched Mika's face, probing her signals. Then her gaze grew unfocused, and Mika felt her sister's search turn inward.

Naomi's mouth fell open in shock. "They're gone."

"Yes."

"You did this?"

Mika nodded, beaming warmth at her sister. She sensed Naomi's joyous urge to embrace her and welcomed it. But Naomi hesitated. Naomi was ashamed of her joy, Mika sensed, because her freedom had come at a price.

"You don't have to go, Mika. If those things put you back in jail before anyone notices, you can fight your charges in court."

"It's too late for that."

"Ron said he could argue self-defense and diminished capacity. You won't get a long sentence."

Mika pitied her sister. Naomi didn't want to lose her, but a part of her understood she already had. Naomi wanted Mika to stay but also celebrated the liberty her departure brought. Mika could read her sister well, always had. They were two peas in a pod. And Naomi had suffered long enough.

"I'm not going back to jail," Mika said. "I know where I belong."

Naomi dropped her head. Her voice choked with emotion. "This is the last thing I wanted for you."

Mika sent her consoling signals. "You wanted me to know the truth, and I'm so glad I do. So tired of pretending I belong here."

Naomi's eyes glistened in the near-darkness. "How am I supposed to say goodbye?"

"You don't have to. I'll visit when I can. All by my lonesome, I promise."

Naomi's foot tapped the sandy soil. "What should we say then?"

Mika considered it. "I forgive you. Do you forgive me?"

Naomi's mouth slid toward a slanted grin, not quite making it. "I do."

The back door of the cottage banged open, and their mother's voice rang out in the night. "Naomi, where on Earth did you disappear to?"

Mika slid along the siding and peeked around the corner to take a last look at her mom. Tessie stood under an overhead light, her curls on point, hands on her hips, looking cozy and formidable in crisp jeans and a flowered t-shirt.

The sound of a phone ringing wafted through the open door. Moments later, the ringing stopped, and Mika heard Paige's muffled yelling. Tessie retreated inside, and seconds later, two heavy cars pulled into the driveway, rumbling over the gravel. Ribbons of blue and red light danced around the side of the cottage where Mika and Naomi stood.

They locked eyes, knowing news of Mika's escape had broken.

"What about Adrian," Naomi said quickly. "Will he be left alone too?"

"Whatever plagues him, it's not us."

Perhaps it was Mika's use of the term *us* that made Naomi turn away first. Mika slipped back into the pines and prepared to go home.

26

—

From the archives of www.thesandpiper.com
The Sand Piper (Southern New Jersey's Daily Digest):
A Year Ago Today: The Latest Updates on the Crane Escape
By Min Leong / September 1, 2025
9:38 p.m.

In recognition of the one-year anniversary of South Jersey native Mika Crane's mysterious escape from a guarded hospital room, we present this up-to-the-minute recap of the latest updates on the case. Known as "Bat Lady: Next Generation," this epic story continues to enthrall people around the world.

At a press conference on Monday, Crane family attorney Ron Andino announced the filing of a lawsuit against the federal government, accusing the FBI of unlawfully harassing the Cranes for the last twenty years. Tuesday evening, an FBI spokesperson denied their agents had ever interviewed the Crane family, and Andino responded by releasing clips of security footage from as far back as 2002 showing well-coiffed men and women in dark suits entering the Crane's convenience store and flashing FBI identification. Cell phone video, also released by Andino, revealed unknown intruders skulking around the woods behind the Crane property as recently as last month. Yesterday, an anonymous Twitter account, purportedly representing a group of retired federal employees, identified one of the intruders as an FBI agent working for a mysterious "black ops" government office. The online community known as #BL2 immediately announced they were investigating these claims. The FBI has yet to comment on the release of the videos.

This suit against the government is the latest in a string of cases filed by Andino. Earlier this year, he sued Gilt Pharmaceuticals, the manufacturer of insomnia drug Slumbutrol, as well as FOMO Foods, maker of the energy drink Master Blaster, claiming both products were dangerous, highly addictive, and had severe side effects undisclosed to the FDA.

A much-beloved character in the #BL2 universe, Andino first made headlines shortly after Crane's escape by suing Secaucus County Jail for the "cruel and unusual" treatment Crane allegedly received during and after her transport to Hudson Hospital, where correction officers left her restrained in an exam room for five hours.

At Monday's press conference, Andino displayed medical records from the jail's nurse practitioner detailing Crane's diagnosis of suspected reflux disease, as well as the nurse's recommendation that Crane keep her torso elevated to prevent stomach acid from rising into her upper digestive tract. The medical records, Andino said, supported his theory that Crane experienced intense and prolonged discomfort that resulted in her desperate escape.

Meanwhile, reports that Crane did not sleep during her stint in jail were corroborated by her cellmate Jessica Carroll this week. In a series of tweets, Carroll stated Crane was "scary skinny," talked to herself continuously throughout the night, and refused to eat. Carroll speculated, as others have, that Crane's weight loss allowed her to slip out of her restraints before escaping. Jail officials continue to insist Crane was properly restrained.

Under public pressure to provide an update before the anniversary of Crane's escape, the New Jersey union for correction officers, Local 105, released a statement last night admitting Crane had "scuffled" with other inmates on the way to the hospital, and officers failed to include the incident in a report. Citing the omission as a coverup, #BL2 immediately cast doubt on all official statements regarding the viability of Crane's restraints.

Hudson Hospital continues to be deluged with negative PR and conspiracy theories. As readers may remember, last fall a maintenance worker claimed the brand-new ceiling tiles in Crane's hospital room showed signs of damage after her escape. At the time, a hospital spokesperson admitted the new tiles had been installed over the original, damaged tiles to save costs. The original tiles, the spokesperson stated, were moldy from flood damage and had unforeseen "corrosive effects" on the new tiles.

This morning, the exasperated hospital spokesperson reiterated on CNN that the "extremely minor" damage to the new ceiling tiles was not caused by Mika Crane. They denied Crane could have entered the hospital's duct system through the ceiling of her hospital room then found her way out of the building (a popular #BL2 theory), claiming security footage covering all possible exits was reviewed with no sign of the inmate. Hordes of social media posters insist Crane's body is stuck in the hospital ventilation system, and that she likely starved to death.

Mika Crane's escape has prompted a renewed critical look at the prison sentence handed down to Contessa "Tessie" Crane, the vigilante store clerk and original "Bat Lady," whose attack on would-be robber Edward Chapman went viral in 2022. Ongoing social media discourse suggests public sympathies toward Tessie Crane continue to be divided. No word yet from Andino on any pending lawsuits involving her sentence.

Callum Dunbar remains an Ocean County police officer after being cleared of allegations he stole the infamous bat that Crane used to assault him from his headquarters. Despite reports from women who publicized evidence showing Dunbar pursued them on dating sites while in a relationship with Crane, he's garnered support from fans on social media. This afternoon, Dunbar announced on Instagram that he's set to moonlight as the "reformed f-boy" host of *Catch Them in the App*, an upcoming reality show on The CW Plus documenting public confrontations between participants and their cheating partners.

As for Mika Crane, unconfirmed sightings of the escapee continue to roll in from around the globe, most recently in the Philippines. The Los Angeles-based TikTok star known as Ahmed the Great spoke out today on behalf of the #BL2 community, noting Crane's unfulfilled desire to "explore the far corners of the earth." Their greatest hope, said Ahmed, is that Crane is now "traveling further than she ever imagined."

~Epilogue~

Mika wouldn't have recognized Naomi if not for her sister's signals, shriveled and stooped as she now appeared. Naomi's large eyes had grown so hooded her eyelids likely impeded her vision. By Mika's count, she'd seen Naomi only three days ago. But during that time, the hive had spent several hours traversing the star map, and a half century had passed on Earth.

The home ship hovered, cloaked in the stratosphere, eleven miles above the Crane compound but close enough for targeted audio and visual surveillance. Mika, of course, needed no technology to connect with Naomi, but she enjoyed watching her and Adrian on the transformed Crane Compound. A solar-powered, electric-car charging station now stood in place of the Piney Mart, and a sign in front of the immaculately preserved main house welcomed visitors to the *Historic Pine Country Inn.*

Inside Mika's renovated cottage, Naomi and Adrian sat in separate chairs playing a holographic board game projected into the air of the living room. Their white hair glowed in the sunlight spilling through the windows.

greetings Earthling

Mika expected Naomi's shock, and perhaps her ire, for cracking a joke without first explaining her long absence. But she did not expect her sister's immediate and powerful hatred. The hive sensed Mika's hurt feelings and consoled her. She sent them back her warmest gratitude, so thankful to no longer be flailing through life alone and panicked.

Naomi staggered to her feet and used her cane to lurch toward the bathroom, retching bile on the floor before she made it.

Adrian rushed to her side. "What happened? What's wrong?"

"Something went down the wrong tube." Naomi wiped her mouth with the back of her liver-spotted hand.

Adrian helped her back to her chair. "Stay put," he said and filled a glass with water. "Drink some of this, and do it slowly."

"Don't fuss. I'm fine," Naomi said.

Mika could tell Naomi worried about Adrian, about keeping him safe.

Don't be afraid
It's just me
like I promised

Naomi swung her cane in the air, battling an invisible enemy. A soft voice emanated from the cane. "Emergency services has been contacted. Say 'help' or tap twice on any hard surface to connect to an elder care representative. Say 'cancel' or—"

"Cancel!" Adrian yelled, and took the cane from her hand. "Are you having another stroke or trying to give me one?"

Naomi shook her head. "Some ugly-looking bug flying around. I took a swing at it."

Adrian stood over her with his hands on his hips. "The kids are coming back soon. Do you want them to never leave us alone with our great grandchild again?"

Naomi settled down, and Adrian returned to his seat. The couple continued their game. After several minutes, Mika wondered if Naomi could still detect her signals.

I read you loud and clear, Naomi communicated. *But you don't feel like Mika anymore. Not much of her left, is there?*

I am here
and I am whole

Bullshit. I want you to leave now and never come back. Do you understand? Stay the fuck away from us.

Her sister's tough-guy act made Mika cringe. Embarrassed for her, Mika turned her focus to the playpen tucked in the corner of the living room. The purest sound she'd ever heard emerged from the small body inside it: the excited babbles of a baby girl.

The baby's irises, black and bright as the ocean under moonlight, blended seamlessly with the pupils of her large eyes. A black-eyed child was rare indeed, and joy rippled through the hive. The baby reacted to this joy by heaving herself up to a sitting position with an adorable grunt.

Naomi gaped at the child, and her wrinkled hands curled into fists.

"Go. It's your turn," Adrian told her, but Naomi didn't seem to hear him.

Naomi communicated a string of threats and violent obscenities to Mika, which Mika found untoward and unfair. *Naomi can be rather feral at times,* Mika thought. Especially now with spit frothing at the corners of her thin mouth.

Although the hive had no tether to Naomi, they felt Mika's disdain toward her sister and encouraged Mika to find tolerance and understanding. As agreed, Naomi and the rest of the Crane family had been cast adrift from the hive. But newer Crane generations were not part of the deal. Mika didn't bother trying to explain this to Naomi, sensing she wouldn't be receptive to logic.

The baby threw her chubby arms in the air with glorious enthusiasm, using her back and core muscles in ways she might never have before, given the way Adrian gasped.

The hive marveled at the baby's strength, and they were proud. A great celebration spread throughout the home ship, from the depths of the Wheel to the observation room Mika occupied.

On their most recent journeys, the hive had discovered a young, warmonger civilization on the cusp of locating the star map left by the Creators. These siblings were not as brutal as humans but capable of causing much harm. Because of this, the hive needed more than Mika to protect the ancestors who survived the Great Liberation. They needed to build an army.

If you enjoyed In Daylight, please consider leaving a review or rating on your favorite retailer's website. Thank you for reading!

Visit www.CarolineFlarity.com
for more on this author and her books.

Printed in Great Britain
by Amazon